What Reviewers Say About The Authors

Karin Kallmaker

"Kallmaker has a sure sense of the [...] power of eros. The two are combined [...] with pleasure." – *Bay Area Reporter*

"Kallmaker does not disappoint anyone expecting sex on every page. It's there; it's hot; it's imaginative; and the bonus is that it's well-written and well, entertaining." – *Lambda Book Report*

"Kallmaker adds plenty of heart-stopping, toe curling, multi-orgasmic sex to her erotic repertoire." – *Bay Windows*

"Kallmaker's characters are engaging, her sex scenes are intense—she's the lesbian hybrid of Joyce Carol Oates and Danielle Steele." – *Book Marks*

Radcly*f*fe

"*Change of Pace: Erotic Interludes*…is…not only about sex, but also about love, longing, lust, surprises, chance meetings, planned meetings, fulfilling wild fantasies, and trust. Radclyffe is masterful at wrapping subtle plots, inspired settings, and entertaining characters around an incredible variety of hot sex scenes." – *Midwest Book Review*

In *Sweet No More*…"Radclyffe then takes the reader into the darkened corners of a BDSM world and blends male terminology with female anatomy in a disconcerting meld of the boldest and most brutal sexuality." – *Eroticarevealed.com*

"Radclyffe can write…sex scenes, so hot, fresh, and so alive that the scenes radiate off the page." – *Lambda Book Report*

"Another form of transgression can be about the connections we form that defy societal expectations…like the woman headed to a sex club who wants to shed her sweet image in Radclyffe's story." – *Best Lesbian Erotica, 2008*

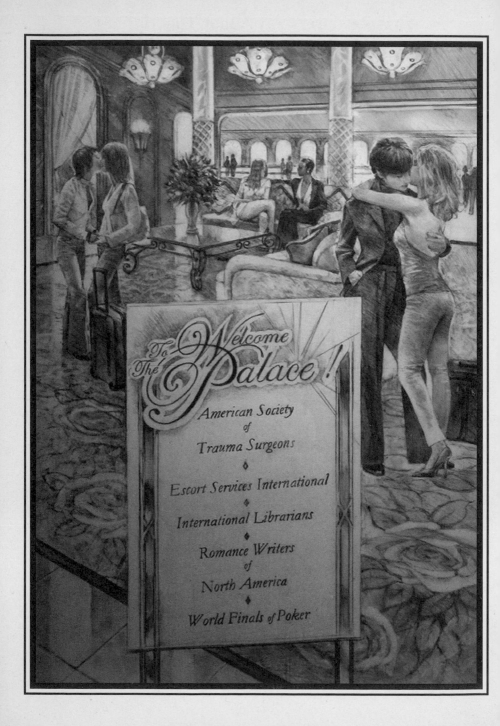

Welcome To The Palace!

American Society
of
Trauma Surgeons

◆

Escort Services International

◆

International Librarians

◆

Romance Writers
of
North America

◆

World Finals of Poker

IN DEEP WATERS 2

Cruising the Strip

by

RADCLY*f*FE &
KARIN KALLMAKER

2008

IN DEEP WATERS 2: *CRUISING THE STRIP*
©2008 RADCLYFFE AND KARIN KALLMAKER. ALL RIGHTS RESERVED.

ISBN10: 1-60282-013-9
ISBN13: 978-1-60282-013-5

THIS TRADE PAPERBACK IS PUBLISHED BY
BOLD STROKES BOOKS, INC.
NEW YORK, USA

FIRST EDITION, MAY 2008

CREDITS
EDITOR: CINDY CRESAP
PRODUCTION DESIGN: J. B. GREYSTONE
FRONTISPIECE: BARB KIWAK (www.kiwak.com)
COVER GRAPHIC: SHERI (graphicartist2020@hotmail.com)

By Radclyffe

Romances

Innocent Hearts

Love's Melody Lost

Love's Tender Warriors

Tomorrow's Promise

Passion's Bright Fury

Love's Masquerade

shadowland

Fated Love

Turn Back Time

Promising Hearts

When Dreams Tremble

The Lonely Hearts Club

The Provincetown Tales

Safe Harbor

Beyond the Breakwater

Distant Shores, Silent Thunder

Storms of Change

Winds of Fortune

Honor Series

Above All, Honor

Honor Bound

Love & Honor

Honor Guards

Honor Reclaimed

Honor Under Siege

Justice Series

A Matter of Trust (prequel)

Shield of Justice

In Pursuit of Justice

Justice in the Shadows

Justice Served

Erotic Interludes: *Change Of Pace*
(A Short Story Collection)

Erotic Interludes 2: *Stolen Moments*
Stacia Seaman and Radclyffe, eds.

Erotic Interludes 3: *Lessons in Love*
Stacia Seaman and Radclyffe, eds.

Erotic Interludes 4: *Extreme Passions*
Stacia Seaman and Radclyffe, eds.

Erotic Interludes 5: *Road Games*
Stacia Seaman and Radclyffe, eds.

By Karin Kallmaker

Radclyffe's Acknowledgments

By the time I finished my first cruise with Karin Kallmaker, I was ready to book a return trip. Everything about *In Deep Waters 1: Cruising the Seas* (Bella Books, 2007) from the first page to the last, was fun, creatively challenging, and satisfying. What more could an author want? Well, I wanted to do it all again—and luckily, so did Karin (which is a very good thing, because we'd already promised our respective publishers one volume each before we'd even set sail the first time). I think we both worried a little bit more on the maiden voyage because what if we didn't get along? What if we couldn't concur on a story order? What if, gasp, we couldn't agree as to who was on top (or not)? As it turned out, we had no trouble either time negotiating a more than satisfying arrangement regarding scenes, accoutrements, and accessories (and who got to play with what when). Vegas is one of my favorite cities and thanks to Karin, it is now one of my favorite literary haunts.

Many thanks to Cindy Cresap for forging a whole from twenty-four selections by two authors with different voices, different rhythms, and different styles. An anthology with multiple authors is far easier to edit because the individual selections are not as intimately related as they were designed to be in this collection. Thank you, Cindy, for making this such a rewarding literary threesome.

Barb Kiwak and Sheri deserve kudos for the outstanding artwork, frontispiece and cover, respectively.

And lastly and most especially, to the readers, thanks for joining us in Vegas, and no matter what your pleasure, I hope you have as much enjoyment in the reading as we did in the writing.

— Radclyffe, January 2008

Karin Kallmaker's Acknowledgments

If you really enjoy something, I recommend doing it at least twice, especially if it involves partnering up with someone whose love of the results matches your own.

Working with Radclyffe is like finding the perfect partner for tennis—one challenging enough to get you out of your own zone, leading to the mutual goal of a fantastic volley based on complementary strengths. For this anthology, she lobbed balls over the net and waited patiently to see if I could return service. When I did, *ooo, baby*, did we have fun!

Having collaborated before on *In Deep Waters 1*, we spent less time making sure we were in sync and more time just plain playing. I hope readers are as amused and excited as I am by the results. Any resemblance of our characters to persons living are purely coincidental. Let's just say that I suspected Radclyffe of having a twisted and inspired sense of humor, and I wasn't wrong.

Speaking of characters, several of mine from previous works make an appearance in this volume. With a librarian's convention in town, "Twenty-One" of course makes Marian and Liddy from *One Degree of Separation* a natural choice. Brandy and Tess of "Lucky 7" first appeared in *All the Wrong Places*. "Lucky 7" continues the storyline from "Cruising Solo" in the first *In Deep Waters*. Author Carolyn and her agent Alison, from *Paperback Romance,* are attending the romance writer's convention, reaping the rewards of fifteen years' pride in "Payout."

Though I want to say that such stories, and the few other affectionate jokes in this volume, are all for the readers, honesty demands that I admit that I love revisiting my old friends. I truly hope that readers enjoy the results as much as I do.

Gambling is often compared to the risks of love and relationships. I'm not sure why, since inherently gambling means someone loses and someone wins, and the odds are always lopsided. So while we play with the metaphor, it is flawed. In practice, writing with Radclyffe about gambling, love, and sex defies the metaphor completely, because everyone comes out a winner.

— Karin, January 2008

CONTENTS

FOLLOWING SUIT

Radclyffe

The instant I stepped inside the Palace Casino, I saw her holding court with a hundred avid readers right in the middle of the grand lobby. Heads were going to roll in publicity as soon as I got to a phone. I only agreed to attend this conference because the VP of Marketing assured me, on his life—and more importantly, his annual bonus—I wouldn't have to breathe the same air as her. And here we were arriving at exactly the same time. Wonderful bit of planning.

"Welcome to the Palace, Ms. Wainwright," a handsome young man looking somewhat ridiculous in his red uniform with gold tasseled epaulets and shiny buttons announced as I quickly composed my face into what I knew was a cover-shot worthy smile. "Let me assist you to reception. The bellman will take your luggage directly to your suite."

"Thank you." I avoided his offered arm while I watched Byrne Ambrose sign autographs and pose for photos and generally charm the pants off her audience. A smiling, gushing, absolutely thrilled group of devoted readers, all of whom just happened to have been *my* readers first. It didn't help that in addition to being charming, Byrne was a walking heart palpitation. Tall, slender, and dark-haired with pale skin and piercing dark eyes. A full, sensuous lower lip and a mouth made for kissing. Not that I was ever one to underestimate my own powers of allure, I nevertheless knew that my blond hair and blue eyes gave me a somewhat girl next door appeal. A critic had once compared our writing to our physical appearances. Her observation that my romances glowed with sweet sensuality while Byrne's simmered with dark eroticism somehow managed to intimate that I was unadventurous in bed while Byrne set the sheets afire. Foolish to think that the surface reflects the depths of anything, and even more foolish of me to be bothered by a stranger's assessment. Probably if she hadn't been comparing me to Byrne…

I heard the click and whir of a camera nearby and realized I was staring at the object of my supreme annoyance. Adjusting my smile, I did the only thing I could. I walked directly across the lobby to Byrne.

"How good to see you again, Byrne," I said, holding out my hand.

Byrne looked up slowly from the book she had been signing, her eyes even darker than I remembered. For an instant I saw a spark of surprise, or perhaps pleasure, before her handsome features settled into a practiced, gracious expression. She took my hand, and in true Byrne Ambrose fashion, raised it to her lips. More cameras flashed and whirred.

"Amelia. Always a pleasure."

"Isn't it just." Her voice, rich and smooth as dark chocolate, rippled through me, and I forced myself not to react to the undeniable wisps of pleasure stirred by the soft glide of her mouth on my skin. I swear some of the women standing nearby almost swooned. Carefully, I withdrew my hand. "I understood you were touring in England. How fortunate you could make it for the conference."

"When I heard you'd be here, how could I not?"

Easily, I thought, trying not to grind my teeth. *You could have stayed in Europe so that for once, we didn't have to share headliner status.* Not only was I ten years older, I'd been writing almost twenty years longer than she had when she burst onto the scene two years earlier with her unique and, unfortunately, very skillful blend of simmering sex combined with soaring romantic passion. She was very good, and I wasn't too small to admit that. Nevertheless, being constantly compared to her as if only one of us was really capable of writing powerful romance wore on my nerves. And worse, every time I saw her, I was more drawn to her.

"You're absolutely right," I said lightly. "What fun would it be without the two of us here?"

"No fun at all."

Though her tone was surprisingly serious, I saw sardonic amusement dance across her damnably handsome face before I moved a few feet away to sign some autographs of my own. Even as I tended to business, I could hear her laughter in the background, and every note shimmered through me as if she were breathing her pleasure into my ear.

After thirty minutes of chatting up the crowd, I pleaded travel fatigue and escaped to my suite. I *was* tired. I'd just finished my latest novel barely on deadline before packing and flying all day to get here for the opening of the National Romance Writers conference in the morning. As soon as I closed the door behind me, I kicked off my heels and stripped out of my traveling ensemble on the way to the bathroom. A long, hot shower eased some of the aches and weariness, and by the time I'd finished, I was hungry. I unpacked my silk robe, because I never cared much for the terrycloth ones provided even in the best of hotels, and went to investigate the welcome tray of hors d'oeuvres sitting in the center of the coffee table in the lounge area of the suite. I don't know how I missed the bottle of champagne in the ice bucket by the sofa when I came in, either. That was certainly a nice amenity. The complementary appetizers included an assortment of fresh fruit, cheese, crackers, and even a generous serving of caviar in an iced crystal goblet. Hmm, a *very* nice welcoming gift. Idly, I lifted the card and for some reason read it, even though I knew the bounty had been left as a courtesy by the hotel.

Of course, I was wrong.

Amelia, I'm so happy you're here. I hope we have a moment to compare notes on romance. Byrne

I hated the little skip in my heart when I saw her name. She had beautiful handwriting too, very much like her. Bold and dashing. Oh, it was so hard not to like her. I even liked her books, damn her. With a sigh, I removed the gold foil from around the mouth of the champagne bottle. Before I had a chance to remove the wire basket securing the cork, the doorbell rang. I set the champagne on the coffee table and went to answer. Expecting housekeeping, I peered through the security lens. Wrong again.

"Byrne?" I released the latch and opened the door before I remembered I was barefoot and braless and wearing a short silk robe. Since Byrne's eyebrows rose infinitesimally as her glance swept over me, I knew it was already too late. She'd taken in the whole of me, which meant she also noticed my unabashedly erect nipples.

"I'm sorry to disturb you," Byrne said in that bedroom voice, "but these conferences are always so hectic and we so very rarely have a chance to talk." She smiled somewhat apologetically. "But I see this is a bad time. Perhaps we could—"

"No," I said quickly, opening the door wider and surprising us both. "Come in. Please. I was just about to break out the lovely champagne you sent. Won't you join me?"

"How can I refuse?" Byrne sat beside me on the pale green damask sofa and reached for the champagne. "Shall I finish opening it?"

"Yes, please." I turned slightly to face her and curled my legs beneath me, very aware that I was nearly naked next to a very sexy woman. Whom I loathed. Byrne had changed into slacks and an open collar dark blue linen shirt, and she looked carelessly delicious. "Crackers?"

"I'm sorry?" Byrne handed me a flute of champagne.

"Are you hungry?" I asked, flustered for no reason that I could imagine.

Byrne glanced at the very eye-catching tray, then back at me. "Does craving your company count?"

"That's an excellent line," I said, hoping to hide my ridiculous thrill of pleasure. Clearly, she had some agenda that would soon become clear.

"It's the truth." Byrne sipped her champagne and allowed me to look into her eyes, eyes that were completely devoid of any subterfuge. "I've always been a huge fan of your work, and I've never had a chance to tell you that."

I made a demurring noise and chided myself for being flattered.

"No, I'm serious. I've been coming to your readings and panel sessions for years, but of course, you never noticed me. Why would you, with so many readers clamoring for your attention?"

Oh, I would have noticed you in the audience. There aren't very many women who stop my heart just at the sight of them.

"And then," Byrne went on, "when my books came out, everything happened so fast, I've never had a chance to really talk to you."

"That happens when you're an overnight sensation." I discovered my champagne glass was empty and put it down.

Byrne finished hers and set her glass aside. She leaned closer, her voice dropping lower. "No one will ever write about love and passion the way you do. Your work always excites me."

I felt myself flush and was helpless to stop it. "One of us should get pen and paper and write this down before we lose a perfectly good seduction scene."

"Is that what this is?"

Embarrassed that I had revealed the attraction I had been denying for months, I tried to laugh it off. "Tell me you haven't noticed this setting is perfect for…"

Byrne leaned close. "This?"

And she kissed me.

Somewhere in the recesses of my mind I registered that the kiss was not in the least bit diffident or uncertain, but neither was it arrogant. It was simply a kiss, a wonderful kiss, bestowed by a woman who clearly wanted to kiss me, if the deep murmur of pleasure accompanying the glide of her warm mouth over mine was any indication. Byrne Ambrose, my hated rival…well, of course, not hated…more like *annoying* rival, *wanted* to kiss me? And God, could she kiss. She cupped my face in her soft, warm palm and thoroughly explored my mouth with a gentle but insistent tongue. I could feel her body hovering just millimeters away from mine, but she didn't push for more contact. Instead, she allowed my breasts, suddenly tense with the surge of arousal rushing through me, to lift and brush against her chest. That whisper of contact sent a sliver of excitement piercing through the core of me.

"Oh my God, you can definitely practice what you preach," I gasped, pulling back, trying to get my bearings. What was she doing? For one horrifying second I contemplated this could be some kind of publicity stunt, but unless a winged photographer was hovering twenty stories above ground like a giant Tinker Bell, there was no way anyone could see us. "What…"

"Do you know," Byrne said breathlessly. *Breathlessly?* "I really love your love scenes."

As she spoke, she skimmed her fingers up and down my arms, inside the silk robe. My skin flamed as if I'd been out in the sun for hours, and to my amazement, I found myself unbuttoning her shirt, my fingers flying with a will of their own. "I don't care if you hate my books," I whispered, "if you kiss me like that again."

And she did. Only this time, she eased me back on the sofa and pulled the sash on my robe, exposing me. She leaned halfway against me, her hip turned sideways between my legs, her upper body supported with one arm along the back of the sofa. She kissed me until my head was spinning, even though I was lying down. I pushed inside her shirt and discovered skin, only skin. Smooth, slightly damp, hot skin. She groaned as I held her small breasts in my hands, rolling her firm nipples under the pads of my thumbs. I thought of the love scenes *she* had written, committing them to memory while telling myself I simply needed to know what the competition was offering. But her words revealed her passion so bravely for all to see, I couldn't forget the images she created. Her words had taught me what she needed, what she sought, what she hoped for from a moment like this, and I gently pushed her away. When she drew back, uncertain, I softened my apparent rejection with a brief caress to her cheek.

"Come to bed, Byrne."

She nodded, her eyes glimmering, her pale pale skin

RADCLY∫FE & KARIN KALLMAKER

flushed with desire. I pushed the shirt down her shoulders and she left it behind on the sofa. As we crossed into the bedroom, she unbuckled her belt and unzipped her slacks, shedding them by the bedside while I dropped my robe on a chair. When we came together beneath the cool, pristine sheets, we were both naked. When she would have moved above me, I shook my head and pressed my palms to her shoulders.

"Lie back," I murmured as I knelt between her thighs. For a second I thought she might refuse, because I could tell it wasn't what she expected. I caressed her thighs and kissed the base of her stomach. "Please. I know you want this. So do I."

With a quiet groan, she relaxed beneath me. "I think about you...sometimes...when I'm writing."

"Think about me now. How much I want you."

I gently touched my tongue to her clitoris. She was hard. Her legs clenched and she pulsed against my lips. I love the taste of a woman, sultry and rich. A pleasure so poignant, yet so fleeting, I always want to linger. As I took her slowly, learning all her tender places, she writhed beneath me, her breath growing shorter and more labored. She didn't ask for what she so clearly needed, and I adored her for her unselfishness. Only a woman would sacrifice her own pleasure for that of another. I kissed her where her heart beat beneath my lips and pulled her into the heat of my mouth, sucking as she grew to fill me.

"I'm going to come," she whispered, a warning and a question. Her fingers trembled in my hair.

I reached up and placed my palm over her heart where it pounded beneath her sleek body. I felt her orgasm tremble through her limbs, hammering inside her chest, beating inside my mouth. She was beauty, she was grace, she was every perfect word I had ever hoped to write.

She cried out softly as she came, and when her cries had died away, I kissed her one last time before stretching out beside her. Her eyes were soft, her smile satisfied. Wordlessly, she dipped her head and took my breast into her mouth. I wasn't as unselfish as she. I urged her to hurry, to take me, to make me come. She wrote her desire for me on my body, with the bold strokes of her hands and her lips and her tongue. When she slid her fingers inside me, I closed around her with the fierceness of possession, wanting to own the passion she exposed so freely in the pages of her books. I had always known her power, now I felt it. Her knuckles, round and strong, stretched me, opened me, and I welcomed her.

"More," I asked, uncertain my words had enough strength to reach her. But she heard. I didn't feel her turn her hand, I didn't feel her mold her flesh to my flesh, but I felt her in the core of me, strong and hot and reverent. She held still and let me move around her, rocking infinitesimally on her smooth, hot fist. I reached blindly for her other hand and when I found it, pressed her fingers to my clitoris.

When she caressed me, the swell of heat wrenched a cry from my throat and she murmured soothingly as I came around her, over her, for her.

"Oh my God." I opened my eyes to find her watching me, although I hadn't felt her leave me. Her expression was slightly worried and I smiled. "I'm fine. Wonderful. Beyond wonderful."

Her stark beauty dissolved into a youthful tenderness, and the pleasure she didn't bother to hide stirred me anew. "Again," I whispered, and she stroked me until I came in her arms.

The room had grown dark, but I could see her features by the light filtered through the gauzy drapes as she lay on her back, looking contemplative and content.

"What are you thinking?"

She turned her head and smiled at me. "Of a love scene I want to write."

"Do I know the characters?"

"In a way." She kissed me. "It's a story about how love inspires us. Allows us to do more, be more, than we ever thought we could." She propped herself up on her elbow and regarded me seriously. "You are responsible for whatever success I have."

"Well, now, that's a hell of a thing to say," I complained. "How am I supposed to be jealous of you now?"

Byrne glided on top of me, her slick, hot thigh meeting my slick, hot center. "You have no reason to be jealous. You're beautiful, accomplished, and sexy as hell. Me, I'll be happy to follow wherever you lead."

"Even when I'm in the mood to follow you?"

"Especially then."

Byrne slid into me again, and true to my word, I followed suit.

FULL HOUSE

....

Radcly*f*fe

*D*on't touch me, I mean it. I think I'm going to explode." Liz Ramsey dropped the suitcase she had insisted on carrying, despite her lover's protests, just inside the door of their suite. "My God, what is it out there? A hundred and thirty degrees in the shade?" She kicked off her sandals, one of which flew across the room and landed on the coffee table, and pushed damp strands of coppery-brown hair out of her face. "Oh, pardon me. I forgot. There *is* no shade in this entire state." She rounded on Reilly. "Whose idea was this?"

"I'm sure it was mine," Reilly Danvers said instantly. "And it was really stupid of me. Absolutely dumb idea."

"Don't be nice when I'm being unreasonable. It pisses me off." Liz glared at her lover of only a few months. Here *she* was a rumpled mess, and Reilly looked comfortable and cool in a light blue T-shirt, faded denim jeans, and loafers without socks. Her dark hair was windblown, her gray eyes worried, and she still managed to look sexy. *I love you. God, I love you. And I hope I haven't made the biggest mistake of my life.*

Reilly piled the rest of the luggage on the floor. "Why don't you lie down for a few minutes, and I'll get you something cold to drink. How about iced tea?"

"I don't want to lie down. I don't want iced tea. I want..." Liz looked down at herself and realized she couldn't see the tops of her navy linen shorts because her pregnant abdomen was in the way. It was bad enough that her breasts were larger than they'd ever been, but now she had a bowling ball where her waist used to be. "This is supposed to be our honeymoon, and I'm hot and my feet are swollen, and you don't even want to have sex with me."

"Excuse me?" Reilly's voice climbed an octave and her eyebrows followed. "Of course I want to have sex with you. I always want to have sex with you. I love having sex with you. I love you."

"We haven't had sex in a week, and now I'm even bigger than I was before. I don't blame you for not wanting to have sex with me." Liz turned her back. Her voice shook. "I knew this was going to happen. We should have waited until after the baby was born to even try to have a relationship. What was I thinking? Talk about the shortest honeymoon in history."

"Baby." Reilly tiptoed up behind Liz and carefully placed her hands on Liz's shoulders. She kissed the back of her neck. "I couldn't have waited one more day, one more *minute*, to be with you. There's no way I could've waited six months." She guided Liz around to face her. "I think you're the most beautiful, sexiest woman in the world."

"Then why don't we have sex anymore?"

"I think it's been five days," Reilly said cautiously, running her hands up and down Liz's arms. "And two of those nights I was on call and last night we took the red-eye."

Liz brushed impatiently at the moisture on her cheeks. "What about the other two nights?"

Reilly grinned. "We were watching Frodo destroy Saruman and save Middle Earth."

"We're not watching epic movies ever again," Liz said. "At least not until after we have sex."

"Absolutely." Reilly swept her arm around Liz's waist and guided her toward the bed. "Why don't you take a nap and later we'll order room service and watch…later we'll have screaming monkey sex."

Liz narrowed her eyes. "Are you *sure* you're not having second thoughts about marrying me?"

"I have a million thoughts about it every day. All of them happy." Reilly drew down the covers on the bed and kicked off her loafers. Then she pulled her T-shirt over her head, tossed it on a nearby chair, and unzipped and stepped out of her jeans. Naked, she sat on the side of the bed and held out her arms. "Come here and let me undress you." When Liz shuffled a little closer, Reilly unbuttoned her blouse and then her shorts. Resting one hand on Liz's hip to steady her, she pushed Liz's shorts and panties down. "Step out of these, baby."

"You don't have to pretend you want sex, just because I said—"

"You're tired. You've been working overtime for the last month just to get your caseload free enough for us to take this time off. We've been up half the night." Reilly slipped Liz's blouse off and placed both hands over the perfect mound of Liz's lower abdomen. As she leaned forward to kiss the smooth, pale skin, she whispered, "Take off the rest."

"I love when you touch me like this." Liz stroked Reilly's hair while Reilly, her eyes closed, rubbed her cheek gently against Liz's belly. Liz couldn't believe how much it excited her to watch Reilly do that. It was something she never would have thought erotic, and yet seeing the pleasure on Reilly's face, the contentment, made her quicken with an almost painful rush of heat deep inside. "I love you."

Reilly tilted her face up, her smile enough to banish all Liz's fears. "Even if it was my stupid idea to come to Las Vegas now?"

"*I* was the one who wanted to be here when Bren got her book award," Liz reminded her. "I probably shouldn't have dragged you out here. Especially when I'm fat and bitchy."

"You didn't drag me anywhere. She's your best friend, and I wanted to be here, too." Reilly swung her legs onto the bed and patted the space beside her. "And I was the one who suggested we take some extra time to make the trip a honeymoon. Plus, you're not fat. You're pregnant."

Liz climbed into bed and fussed with the pillows behind her back until she could find a half-comfortable position. "I notice you didn't say I wasn't bitchy."

"I wouldn't call it bitchy."

Liz ran her fingers through Reilly's hair, then cupped the back of her neck and kissed her. "What would you call it?"

"Excitable." Reilly nuzzled Liz's breast before lightly kissing her nipple.

"Mmm. I do seem to be that." She'd never been easily aroused or particularly quick to orgasm, but around Reilly, she was both. It wasn't just the newness of the relationship, either. Reilly made her happier than she'd ever imagined possible. Reilly filled her life with promise, and whenever she thought of her, love and passion and desire were so inextricably bound that her body could barely contain the emotion. She wanted her. Endlessly.

Reilly stroked Liz's belly then claimed her mouth again. Liz murmured deep in her throat, loving Reilly's slow, easy kisses. Those kisses were deceptively simple, so soft and languid that Liz was always lulled by the sheer pleasure of Reilly's tongue playing over the sensitive inner surfaces of her lips and teasing just inside her mouth. Just when she felt herself floating, drifting in a warm, sensual haze, she would realize she was completely aroused and often very close to coming.

"I'm not feeling so bitchy now." Liz dragged her nails unhurriedly up and down Reilly's back. "You're getting me excited."

Reilly drew one leg over Liz's thigh, her breath coming fast. "Really? And we're supposed to be taking a nap."

"I didn't agree to that."

"Sometimes you *do* sleep better after an orgasm." Reilly glided her fingers down the slope of Liz's belly and caressed between her legs. "Ah, God, baby, you're so wet already."

"Your kisses." Liz turned her face to Reilly's neck, desperate for Reilly to touch her, to stroke the spot that always made her come. She wanted to come, but not so fast. Catching Reilly's hand, she lifted it back to her breast. She kissed Reilly's neck, then drew away to look at her. She loved to see the wanting that Reilly never tried to hide. Reilly never hid anything from her. Not her love, not her desire, not her need. "Your kisses always make me ready."

"Remember the first time?" Reilly cupped Liz's breast in her palm, squeezing gently while she rubbed the ball of her thumb over Liz's nipple.

Liz could only nod, her breath too short for her to speak.

"I love when you come while we're kissing. I love the way you steal my breath, the way you make those little sounds against my mouth." Reilly went back to kissing her, and when she did, she slid her tongue into Liz's mouth and her fingers between her legs.

Liz cried out, the sound muffled against Reilly's lips. She

sucked on Reilly's tongue and tried to keep her eyes open as Reilly pressed against the base of her clitoris and then a little lower, feathering through her wetness. Reilly's eyes were dark vortices, swirling with desire and demand. Liz poured herself into those eyes as she spilled over the exquisite fingers carrying her to her climax.

"So," Reilly murmured when Liz cradled her head against her shoulder and made little whimpering sounds of pleasure, "still think I don't want to have sex with you?"

"I know you only did it so I'd be quiet and go to sleep."

Reilly laughed and stretched, satisfied with herself, amazingly content. "Yep. That's the reason. It doesn't have anything to do with the fact that my heart just about stops every time you come because you're so damn beautiful."

"You're really happy?"

"Beyond. What are you worried about?"

Liz traced circles with her fingertips in the middle of Reilly's stomach. "Our relationship is kind of on fast-forward, and I don't want you to feel like you're missing anything."

Reilly turned on her side and propped her head in her hand, studying Liz's face. "What could I be missing?"

"Well, the fact that I was pregnant when we met…" Liz sighed. "I never asked if it bothered you that you weren't there. At the beginning."

"I saw the first ultrasound almost as soon as you had it done," Reilly said. "I'm watching the baby grow inside you every day. I can feel her move when I hold you during the night." Reilly stroked Liz's cheek. "If we'd met after the baby was born, hell, when she was two years old, it wouldn't have made any difference. I would have loved her and you just the same."

Liz caressed the curve of Reilly's flank, then over the rise of her hip and down her muscled thigh. When she couldn't reach the tender, hot delta nestled between her legs, she tried to shift onto her side and was reminded just how much her body had changed. "I feel incredibly lucky that you're okay about having an instant family, but I hate that I can't even make love to you the way I want to."

Reilly frowned. "I'm completely and totally satisfied."

"Well, I'm not," Liz said with some heat. "You might be feeling all king of the jungle, seeing as how you only have to look at me to make me come, but I happen to have a few alpha urges of my own, you know."

"Alpha?" Reilly tried unsuccessfully to smother a smile. "Are you trying to tell me you want to throw me down and fuck my brains out?"

"And if I did?"

"I'd say go for it," Reilly said, her voice suddenly husky. "You want me, you got me. Anyway you want it."

"And that's just the problem," Liz grumped. "I can't lie on my stomach very comfortably any longer."

Reilly's brows drew down and then her grin widened. "Ah, you don't want to fuck my brains out, literally. You want to—" She ran her thumb over Liz's lower lip and shivered when Liz licked it.

"Yes. I want you right here…" Liz circled the end of Reilly's thumb. "On the tip of my tongue."

"Jesus, baby," Reilly groaned. "Kill me, why don't you?"

"That was so not my plan." Liz sighed. "God, I really want you."

"Settle back and get comfortable." Reilly straddled Liz's body, kneeling close to her shoulders. She caressed Liz's face and slipped her thumb into Liz's mouth. Liz's hands roamed over Reilly's thighs as she sucked and nibbled on her thumb. Reilly's vision hazed and the muscles on the inside of her legs fluttered and jumped. "Your mouth is so hot."

Liz released Reilly's thumb and smiled up at her, skimming her fingers between Reilly's legs. Her hand came away wet. "I thought you were completely and totally satisfied."

"That was five minutes ago. That was before I thought about your lips and how good they feel closing around me. How sweet it is when you suck me."

Liz dug her fingers into the hard muscles of Reilly's ass and dragged Reilly down against her mouth. Reilly was hard there, too, and Liz loved knowing she had done this. She had made this woman, her woman, hard for her, wet for her, and soon, she would make her come for her.

Reilly pushed her fingers into Liz's hair and braced her other arm against the wall, supporting herself so she could look down into Liz's eyes while Liz did the things to her that always made her come. The push and pull of Liz's mouth merged with the ebb and flow of the blood in her veins, until pleasure surged and she climbed for the edge.

"I'm coming," Reilly whispered, and Liz relaxed the pressure, letting her slide down from the peak just a little. Reilly took a shaky breath. "You want me to wait?"

"I want you out on the edge."

"I don't know if I can today. Jesus, I almost came just then."

Liz smiled against Reilly's heated flesh. "I know." She moved one hand to Reilly's chest and smoothed her fingers back and forth over Reilly's breasts. "Let's climb again."

Reilly's stomach tightened as Liz's lips closed around her. The ache to let go was overpowering. This time it seemed only seconds before she was almost there. "I'm going to come."

Again, Liz relaxed, and Reilly mumbled an incoherent plea. "Shh, I know. I know you want to come. You're so hard right now. I love the way you feel in my mouth." She stroked Reilly's tense stomach and then her thighs. Everywhere she touched, Reilly quivered. "Okay? Can you hold yourself up?"

Wordlessly, Reilly nodded. "I'm okay. I can go again."

"We'll see." Liz used her teeth this time, and as soon as she sucked, Reilly threw her head back and released a strangled cry. Liz relented just a little, licking the spot she had grazed with her teeth. Reilly jumped and her fingers spasmed in Liz's hair. "Good?"

"I have to come," Reilly gasped.

"Sure? One more time?"

"I'll try."

Liz felt Reilly's orgasm throbbing for release between her lips. She fondled her carefully, circling and stroking, keeping the pressure light, as Reilly rocked against her mouth. She loved taking her almost over the edge, time after time, thrilling to the anticipation of that instant when Reilly finally surrendered to pleasure. Right now, Reilly needed desperately to come and she was holding back for Liz, and Liz loved her for it. She tightened her grip on Reilly's ass and curled her other hand between them, sliding inside her.

"You'll make me come!" Reilly warned, pushing deeper into Liz's mouth.

Liz was already making Reilly come. She felt Reilly's muscles clamp around her fingers, felt her swell between her lips, felt her whole body tense.

"Oh God, oh yeah." Reilly's head fell forward against the wall but she kept her weight off Liz's body. "I'm coming this time."

Liz kissed and stroked and soothed her until Reilly regained enough strength in her legs to push herself over onto the bed. Liz awkwardly turned onto her side and kissed her.

"See what I mean about alpha urges?"

Still gasping for breath, Reilly grinned. "Are you like this when you're not pregnant?"

"I don't know. I never was before, but then," Liz drew a finger along the edge of Reilly's jaw and down the center of her throat, "I wasn't with you before, either."

"Maybe we should just keep you pregnant all the time, just in case," Reilly suggested.

"Honey," Liz said, laughing, "as much as I'm looking forward to our new family, I think one will do me for quite a while." She kissed Reilly. "But if you keep looking at me the way you are right now, you don't have to worry. Because I'm back to that wanting to fuck your brains out thing again."

"Then we're going to be very busy for a long, long time."

WHAT HAPPENS IN VEGAS...

Karin Kallmaker

hy are we here?" Marcie pushed her wild brown hair out of her eyes and squinted in the hot wind that blasted across the hotel parking lot. "What on earth possessed Nirvana and Sunshine to pick Las Vegas as the raffle prize? It's...it's..."

Keri counted the pieces of their luggage as the bags were transferred out of the limousine into the care of the bellhop. "It sold a lot of raffle tickets. You said it was twice last year's sales."

"It did sell a lot of tickets, and I guess I never thought I'd win. But now that I'm here, it's so...so..."

Keri glanced up to watch Marcie's expressive shrug. "It's so unreal?"

"That's a start." Marcie turned her china blue gaze to Keri. "It's all fake, all for show."

"And we get to spend five days and four nights as a part of the show." Keri pulled Marcie along the curved entrance driveway until they reached the blissfully chilled lobby. "Thank you again for inviting me. I know some of your friends might have expected you to ask them, especially the ones who aren't too sure about you dating me to begin with."

Marcie relaxed once they were enveloped by the air conditioning. With a pleasing glint in her evocative eyes, she said, "You're way more fun than they are. Especially late at night."

Keri grinned and ducked her head. "I really try to make that true."

"Will you look at this place? Incredible." Marcie looked up at the massive atrium's ceiling. "It's like the Sistine Chapel."

Opulent didn't even begin to describe the Palace Hotel. Everywhere Keri looked there were rippling fountains or banks of exotic plants, lushly velvet cushions and elegantly dressed women ensconced on them. It felt like an oasis after the dry desert air.

Marcie had her denim jacket—necessary when they had left Syracuse that morning—draped over one shoulder. She gave an approving look to the row of orchids, but the gaze she turned to Keri was troubled. "This is a desert, and people all over the world are dying for water. Did you see those fountains?"

"I saw them." Keri shrugged. After almost forty years of not giving a stale doughnut about other people, she'd gotten sober and realized her every thought and need was not the center of the cosmos. "I saw the endless building projects, and I know there already isn't enough water for the people who live here, let alone the new construction. You know how it goes—somebody really rich is going to have to lose a lot of money before anything changes." Keri tucked Marcie's hair behind her ear and was rewarded with a tiny shiver that zinged through her fingertips. "Meanwhile, this is the first time we've gone away together. So I suggest…"

Marcie smiled into Keri's kiss. "I quite agree."

A smiling woman in hotel livery bore down on them. "Welcome to the Palace, ladies! I'm Harmony, and I'm the VIP coordinator this evening. I've just been informed you're the winners of one of our Getaway Fundraising vacations. Congratulations—you are in for a wonderful stay."

They were invited to "step right this way," and Keri smothered a laugh when Marcie did her best to imitate Harmony's sassy walk. Keri had a decidedly unpolitically correct moment imagining Marcie in the high heels that Harmony was wearing.

There had been a time—before dumping the fleshpots and booze of Manhattan for the ivory towers and sobriety of Syracuse—that Keri wouldn't have been seen with a woman who wasn't a high femme, including stilettos. There'd been a time when unfailingly practical, comfortably beautiful women like Marcie hadn't registered on her radar. She'd liked young and aggressive, but now maturity and self-knowledge were turning her on like nothing ever had before. Sobriety had given her new eyes that saw deeper, and the world around her had blossomed into subtle colors of endless variety. Tech support in a college town paid far less than it did in Manhattan, but the other plusses were as good as money in the bank to her.

She'd already liked the pace of upstate New York when she'd volunteered to work in the collective grocery store. From the moment she'd met Marcie she'd been captivated by the steady, unwavering take-me-as-I-am manner. Marcie knew who she was, knew why she was here, knew why she laughed, why she cried. Keri was no fool—volunteering for several of

Marcie's other causes had led to their dating, which had led them here, to Las Vegas.

Keri didn't want Marcie to change one single thing about her, so her sudden fantasy of Marcie in high heels was confusing. Maybe it was just old habits. After all, on the ride from the airport alone, they had passed dozens of images of buxom, mostly naked, long-legged women-as-eye-candy billboards. She couldn't deny it: part of her had responded with, "Oh, baby."

She couldn't pull that attitude with a woman like Marcie. Marcie was nobody's *baby*. But she surely did know how to move her hips. For a forty-something woman she was dead sexy, stilettos or not, and her sensuality was another thing Keri really liked about her. Used to be a tab of X and tequila shooters had been the only way to get turned on, but now she knew the miracle of a long bubble bath, slow touches, and lots and lots of kissing.

Harmony was showing various points on the map to Marcie. "Your vacation includes a salt massage at our spa for each of you. The spa is located here—" She tapped the map. "Just call to make a reservation. A romantic dinner for two has been planned for this evening, with a reservation already made for eight p.m. at Imperial, which overlooks the lake and fountains from the south."

Marcie was better at remembering details, and Keri let her attention wander to the rest of the grand lobby. She had expected the discordant clanging of slot machines and the stifling stench of cigarettes, but only at the far end could she see the beginnings of a casino. Instead, the lobby seemed designed as an informal, well-lit place to relax and socialize. Three women in sensible shoes hauled heavy book bags off the ground and onto their shoulders as if girding themselves for more walking. Two had water bottles clipped to their belts, prepared for all eventualities. They disappeared in the direction of the conference center.

Several stunningly attired women entered from the casino, waved a greeting to an equally elegant and curvaceous female—in killer pumps—and the four of them turned toward the shopping concourse carrying nothing more than cute little handbags. Keri couldn't help but watch after them.

As her gaze came back to the lobby, she spied a handwritten board welcoming various conventions to the hotel. There were surgeons, writers, poker players, and librarians. But it was "Escort Services International" that caught her eye. The two voluptuous brunettes with gorgeous full hairstyles and flawless makeup who lounged on one of the love seats as they chatted, well, they were not librarians. They might be a baby dyke's wet dream about librarians, but that they were the escorts, and the water bottle carriers the librarians, was far more likely.

If she were a good lesbian, she would attempt to explain to the escorts that their profession was oppressive and they needed to cast off the shackles of the patriarchy, but damn, they looked hotter than hell.

You're in Vegas, Keri reminded herself. You don't have to be a good lesbian here. She glanced over at Marcie, who looked incredibly fuckable, too. Her gaze slid past to the two brunettes. You could be a very *bad* lesbian in Vegas. Trouble is, she told herself, going back to the far more pleasing picture that Marcie made, you're falling for a granola lesbian, and that collection of toys you've got back home is going to go on collecting cobwebs and dust.

Their room key cards clutched in her hand, Marcie led the way to a bank of elevators. The bellhop, summoned by the ever-cheerful Harmony, patiently followed along. They were passed by a much faster moving couple—oo, Keri thought, more dykes—with an equally swift bellhop. Their high-tech suitcases and leather bags were flawlessly matched. The medium-build, shaggy-haired woman was holding hands with a tall, caramel-skinned beauty in thigh-high boots and a short dress cut down the front to heaven. Their quick walk suggested they had an itch and were in a hurry to scratch it.

You're obsessed with sex at the moment, Keri thought. Fancy hotel, Marcie looking adorable—get her into the room and get her naked. You'll both feel better.

The power couple was long gone by the time a glass elevator arrived to whisk them up to the twentieth floor.

"Honey! Look at that pool!" Marcie gazed down at the lush, tropical grounds as they ascended. "Let's grab our suits and go for a swim."

It looked like the perfect setting for a Roman revel. Keri was starting to feel overwhelmed. She'd thought her one goal was to get Marcie into a hotel room, alone, and start their vacation off with a real bang. The pool looked...delicious. There were scantily-clad women lounging on chaises and for shame, for shame, Keri thought, she ought not be responding that way to such rank and obvious objectification. She thought of Marcie in a swimsuit and her composure got even more ragged.

"We have to be ready for dinner by eight."

Marcie glanced at her watch. She sounded just like a little kid when she pointed out, "That's almost two hours."

Keri gave her an indulgent smile. "Okay, honey. We'll go for a swim." Later, Keri thought. Later, we'll have all the time in the world.

❖

"You nearly burned yourself." Keri kissed the outline of Marcie's swimsuit strap across her gleaming shoulder.

Marcie shook her wet hair. "It was such fun. Okay, I swear out a truce with Las Vegas. While we're here, I'll stop complaining about how unnatural it all is, and how wasteful and—"

Keri kissed her soundly on the mouth. "Me, too. What happens in Vegas stays in Vegas, isn't that right? So nobody has to know that we liked the pool and intend to try the other four pools. Or if we decide to have veal for dinner."

"I'm not going that far." Marcie laughed and kissed Keri back. "We won't confess that your tongue was hanging out a *mile* over those women at the pool."

"It wasn't a *mile*," Keri protested.

Marcie leaned back against the counter, still smiling, but her expression more serious. "Is that what you like? All the hair extensions and surgical enhancements? Is that what women were like in the big city?"

"I'm just looking. I do like to look at women." She wasn't going to apologize for that. "But yeah, back in Manhattan, I drifted toward that type. That's all they were to me, too, a *type*." Keri trailed her fingertips lightly down Marcie's tummy. "I wasn't capable of seeing more. I know what I've got, now. And…I'm feeling things I haven't before."

"I'm glad you could come with me," Marcie said softly. "I know we've only been dating a short while, but…I like you. Thank you for caring enough about yourself to get sober."

Keri grinned. "I like being around you, too."

"Good, because I think you're stuck with me."

"I think we're going to be a little bit late to dinner," Keri said, then she gave in to the overwhelming urge to nibble Marcie's lovely, full lips.

They moved together for several minutes, sharing long, deep kisses, but no more words. Keri didn't know why Marcie, as soon as they started fooling around, stopped talking. She knew why she did—she was afraid some of the things she wanted to say would appall Marcie. Marcie was no virgin and no prude, but she was totally vanilla. She'd be shocked and uncomfortable if Keri were to admit that right now she wished in the worst way she were packing so she could push Marcie's legs apart and have her right here on the counter. That right now, looking at the light in Marcie's eyes and feeling the heat of her skin, she didn't want to make love, she wanted to fuck. She wanted to do Marcie until her hair snarled, her eyes glazed, her skin slicked with sweat, and they were both drained beyond coherence.

If she started talking like that, she'd never stop. Marcie lit a bone-deep fire inside her, and she was worth learning some patience. It was also true that since giving up booze she hadn't really been cat-scratch-fever with a woman. Given that seeing the world through clear eyes and keener perceptions was at times overwhelming, she could only imagine how intense hot, wild sex would feel to her. It wasn't something she wanted to experience with just anyone. Marcie was not just anyone, though. She trusted Marcie completely.

She slipped her hand between them, grinning at what she felt on her fingertips. "Are you going to be soaked like this all through dinner?"

"With any luck." Marcie looked almost shy. "We're going to be late if we don't start getting dressed."

Reluctantly, Keri let Marcie go. Her own hair was drip dry, but Marcie took more time because the wild curls were always a challenge to tame. Keri went to get her best clothes out of the suitcase. They only differed from the rest of her clothes because the black jeans were new, sort of, and the shirt was black silk.

She padded over the thick blue carpet, liking the way it felt under her feet. It was soft enough to fuck on, but floors didn't have the appeal to her forty-year old body they once did. She couldn't wait to try the king-sized bed. She went back to the bathroom to find Marcie leaning forward to peer at her face in the mirror. She wore only her bra and panties so far and Keri couldn't help herself. She ran an appreciative hand over the curve of Marcie's ass.

Marcie's responsive shudder took Keri's breath away. Their gazes locked in the mirror and Keri slowly pressed her fingers into the crotch of Marcie's panties.

"I'm not sure you're going to make it through dinner in this condition." Keri hooked her fingers around the fabric and pulled it out of her way. Marcie was steaming hot.

"There's no time," Marcie protested. "You know how long it takes me to—"

"There's time for this, honey." Keri got right behind her, trapping her against the counter. She pushed two fingers inside Marcie's heat, which felt fantastic. "I'll go down on you later, I promise, and you know I don't care how long it takes. I know this isn't your first choice, but it could be faster. Could be what you need right now."

Marcie made a sound Keri hadn't heard before, then she pushed her ass back into Keri's crotch. "God, Keri, why does that feel so good?"

"I don't care why." Keri couldn't help herself. She wrapped an arm tight around Marcie's waist, and used her hips to thrust her hand even more firmly inside. She gritted her teeth so she wouldn't say words like *pussy* and *juicy* and explain, in between her own groans, how hard her own clit was getting from the way Marcie looked, her breasts heaving, her face flushed, her body braced to push back as Keri got even more forceful. "Come, baby, on my hand."

Marcie let out a surprised gasp and did just that.

❖

"Okay, so we've talked about everything else over this wonderful dinner." Marcie licked the spoon free of rum cocoa sponge cake. She lowered her voice. "Everything except what happened in the bathroom."

"What about it?" Keri's pulse had still not recovered. She really enjoyed sex with Marcie, adored going down on her, and appreciated the same in return. Before they'd gone to bed the first time Marcie had explained her belief in the naturalness of the female body and how sex should reflect that. Even before that, their obvious chemistry had prompted both Nirvana and Sunshine to pointedly discuss, in front of Keri, the heterosexism that tainted much of lesbian sexuality these days. It still made her mad that they'd equated her butchness with thinking and wanting to be like a guy. They were Marcie's closest friends, so she hadn't retorted that she was a woman who fucked women who liked to be fucked by women, and anything she did, therefore, was about being a lesbian and not some secret longing to degrade her sex partners to the status of *the little missus*. "I gathered that you, well, enjoyed it."

"It felt, well, like…it was new. I mean…"

"Was it okay?"

"Yes." Marcie's eyes widened in emphasis. "It was, I mean if it was for you."

"Baby, I *loved* it."

"That's new, too—you haven't called me baby before."

Keri felt her cheeks color. She hadn't realized she was doing it. "Sorry. I know you find it infantiliz—"

"Not the way you said it then," Marcie said quickly. "It felt…safe, nurturing."

"Okay." An unexpected glow of pleasure radiated through Keri's chest. She wants to be my baby, she thought.

The rest of dessert was consumed with many shy glances, and Keri wondered what Marcie was thinking about. More fucking? She hoped so, because there was a multi-screen, full on, Marcie-on-her-back-Keri-on-top scene repeating in her head so loudly sometimes she missed what Marcie said.

They left the restaurant arm-in-arm. Catching sight of their reflection in one of the many mirrors, Keri said, "You look so beautiful in that color." The deep Caribbean blue tunic over a long, simple wrap skirt in the same color brought out the delicate, light color of Marcie's eyes.

"Thank you. You look pretty damn good yourself." Marcie turned slightly and Keri wondered if it were her imagination that Marcie's nipples were hard and pressing into her arm through the thin black silk shirt. She wanted to explore Marcie right there, find out if she was right.

Marcie patted her tummy and said, "I could use a little stroll…before…"

Keri finished the sentence in her head with, "Before I fuck you senseless," but she was pretty sure that wouldn't be Marcie's choice of phrasing. All she said was, "Me, too."

Marcie fished in her pocket and withdrew a plastic card that Keri first thought was a room key. "Our bundle of freebies had this gift card to Prada. A hundred bucks probably doesn't go that far."

Keri tucked Marcie's hand under her arm and turned toward the curving escalators that led to the designer shops. "Let's go see."

Marcie's prediction turned out to be correct. For the items that even had price tags the gift card hardly dented the cost. Much as Keri would have liked to have seen Marcie in Prada heels, she knew neither of them could afford that kind of extravagance.

"It was still fun looking around," Marcie said. They exited

the store and stepped out of the way of two leggy, shapely women. Keri recognized them from the lobby—the two slinky brunettes.

"I'm going to get it right now, Kitty," one was saying to the other. "I'll wear it to the poker finals. I won that gift card and I'm going to use it, even if I have to make up the rest."

"Ladies," Keri said. "Would you like another gift card? We can't use ours."

"Oh wow, you're kidding, right?" The taller of the two gave Keri a skeptical look. "Why would you do that?"

"I can't throw it away." She glanced at Marcie, who nodded encouragingly.

"Well, hey, that's really sweet." Perfectly painted lips curved in a smile. "Here, it's not right if I don't give you something back. I've got a gift card to the toy boutique that our convention is having in one of the suites. The last thing I need is more toys."

She pressed the card into Keri's hand and accepted the Prada card in return. "Suite fifteen hundred."

"Women like that are selling toys?" Marcie was genuinely puzzled as Keri led her to the elevators.

The distant ringing of slot machines was a match to the alarms going off in Keri's head. You're going to freak her out, she told herself. If you bring toys up, and she says no, things will never be the same. You're falling for her, and after all the bad times, she's a great time you shouldn't mess up.

"Not those kinds of toys, honey." She had a sudden inspiration. "I think we should go pick out something really outrageous as a gag gift for the Solstice White Elephant." Keri's heart was beating inside her eardrums.

"Oh, you mean…"

"Lube, silicone, leather."

"I'll bet a hundred bucks doesn't buy much in that store

either. I've never actually shopped for that kind of thing before." Marcie was blushing. "When in Vegas…"

Just a few minutes later, Keri was feeling seriously faint as she watched Marcie mull over the choices in dildos. She was very business-like, picking them up to see how much they weighed, and only rolling her eyes at one so large it could have served as a table leg. Keri kept her hands in her pockets as Marcie touched vibrators and even some of the bondage supplies. When she got to the lube samples Keri finally got up the nerve to make it clear she wasn't exactly a novice.

"Try this one," she suggested, squeezing a single drop onto Marcie's fingertip. "I think that stretchy and slightly viscous is the most…natural."

Marcie's eyebrows arched as she rolled the lube between her fingers and thumb. "That's…I didn't think it would feel quite so real." A gorgeous flush crept up her throat.

"I know the older I get the more a little extra moisture helps."

"I hadn't noticed you lacking." Marcie sniffed the lube, but Keri knew it was odorless.

"Nor me you. All I have to do is look at you and…" She winked. "Course, there are high stress days where worrying about being wet enough is almost enough to turn off the libido. Lube is like permission to get ready. If there's a hurry, it's permission to skip foreplay and just—" She broke off, blushing. "Like this afternoon."

"I've never been into fast and…hot and bothered, I mean… the way you make me feel." Marcie kept playing with the slippery stuff on her fingertips as if she couldn't help herself. "I've always wanted the slowness, the time."

"It's almost like a ritual with you. I love the care you take to set the stage, and how it always seems like an occasion,

I really do." But it doesn't always have to be that way, Keri wanted to add.

"Maybe I've been unimaginative for the last twenty or so years. Or maybe it's you bringing out something in me." Marcie moved closer and whispered, "Your fingers felt really good inside me. I really didn't need...time. I needed...you."

"Baby," Keri whispered back, "I could do that to you right now."

Marcie swallowed hard. "Shall we get these things? Um, this one—we could say it was a holistic art work and see who figures out first what it really is."

Keri liked the size and look of the marbled toy. It was a classic non-representational shape, sleek from tip to base. Today was the first time she'd really explored the inside of Marcie, but her guess was the toy would be a good fit. Not that she would suggest they use it. This was a gag gift. Right.

"What about lube? If we give someone a toy, they ought to have lube."

Marcie held up a small bottle of Nirvana brand. "Sunshine will think that's funny."

"Nirvana won't."

"Nirvana doesn't think anything is funny, but that's okay."

The traded gift card just covered the two items and Keri tucked the toy package under her arm as if it were perfectly natural to walk around that way. Marcie opened the lube bottle to smell it as they waited for the elevator to arrive. She tipped a drop onto her index finger and rubbed it around. "A little really goes a long way."

Keri watched Marcie smoothing the lube between her fingers and thumb, and imagined those slick fingers pushing between her legs. Not that lube was necessary at the moment. It would just feel really sexy and good, Marcie playing with her cunt, fingers slipping through all the folds, circling her clit, teasing at her opening—Keri hid a shudder. If she didn't get a grip, she would no doubt scare Marcie with her intensity. "A little goes a long way, especially on a tile floor, but that's not a good thing."

Marcie laughed and closed the flip top when the elevator arrived, hiding it in her skirts again. "This is one occasion that our habit of never using plastic bags is a little embarrassing."

"It's just a short distance."

There was no one on the elevator. Marcie stepped inside and Keri moved right behind her. The doors closed and Keri slid her free hand onto Marcie's waist, shifting forward so they were in the same pose they'd been in the bathroom earlier.

Marcie pushed her ass into Keri's hips as she made a wonderful, half-moaning, yielding sound. Keri felt disoriented, and the tight ache of her breasts was close to painful. When the elevator doors opened it was Marcie who broke their contact. She glanced over her shoulder at Keri, her eyes dilated and breath coming in gasps. Apparently, what she saw in Keri's face was okay, because an anticipatory smile flitted across her lips.

Keri reminded herself that Marcie hadn't agreed to unbox the dildo, and she certainly hadn't said she wanted Keri use it on her. Marcie had seemed to accept that it was a joke. She set the box down on the dresser across from the bed, though, and Marcie set the bottle of Nirvana lube next to it. Besides, the dildo was not necessary given what she wanted to do to Marcie with just her hands.

"Well, this has been quite a night," Marcie said.

"It's not over, baby," Keri said softly. She turned Marcie to face her. "I want to finish what we started."

She wasn't particularly gentle as she untied Marcie's skirt so it could fall to the floor. Marcie gasped as Keri shoved her hands inside her panties, cupping her ass. They kissed, hard, a kiss she only ended to lift Marcie's tunic over her head. It drifted across a nearby chair, and she pulled Marcie aggressively into her arms.

"I really want to make love to you," Keri whispered into Marcie's ear. "Please, baby, just let me take care of you the way I think you need. The way I need to tonight."

Marcie pushed her away. She slid the straps of her bra off her shoulders and slowly peeled down the cups, not quite exposing her nipples. "What happens in Vegas…?"

"Stays in Vegas."

"Nobody back home has to know." Marcie shimmied her bra a little lower. "It's none of their business."

Keri's mouth was watering. "Nobody has to know what?"

Marcie caressed Keri's cheek. "First time I saw you I got the most outrageous thoughts in my head. I scared myself with the things I imagined doing with you."

"Like what?" Keri captured and kissed Marcie's hand.

She swallowed. "I like my friends. I like the way we live. But I don't know how sex got to be…part of the way of life. I mean, does how we have sex really have an impact on global warming? Live simply, that was the T-shirt you were wearing when you came into the store that day. I looked at you, and I thought 'Live simply, but I want her to fuck me hard.'"

Keri's nipples tightened and her fingers curled with the effort not to grab Marcie and throw her on the bed. "But when we went to bed the first time you said—"

"I was scared. I didn't know how to say what I wanted. I could only say what I was used to. You made it fantastic. I realized I wanted more…"

Keri was getting lost in the soft blue of Marcie's eyes. She looked so vulnerable and yet so ready to try something new. "Do you know how to say it now?"

"I'm not sure. But I think if we practice, I'll learn."

Taking a steadying breath, Keri pulled down Marcie's bra and filled her palms with the luscious, full breasts. She meant to be gentler than she was as she caught Marcie's erect nipples between her fingers and thumbs. "Tonight's different, but not every night has to be like tonight. We can do anything we want. It's Vegas."

Marcie shuddered and let out a moan. She put her hands on Keri's, encouraging the attention to her breasts. She threw her head back, a beautiful line of luscious woman.

Words, so hard before, flowed out of Keri. "I love touching you, and kissing you. I like it when we're so close our eyelashes brush. You wrap me up tight and close when we make love. Tonight I don't want to do that."

Marcie's lips had parted as her hands slowly slid along Keri's forearms, eventually to her shoulders. "Tell me what you want."

"I want to dissolve you into the bed, baby. I want to make you come on my hand again, harder this time. I want us both to get so worked up that it feels like we'll never get enough, so we keep doing it." She wrapped an arm around Marcie's waist and pushed her fingers between Marcie's wet thighs.

Marcie's mewl of pleasure was all the encouragement Keri needed. She pushed her roughly back onto the bed. "Let's do it this way for now. I'll keep my clothes on and fuck you, and we'll see how wet you can get me. You're getting taken care of tonight." She couldn't stop the words, she meant them. "I love your cunt, baby, and I want to worship it, fuck it, and fuck you so good that you go on craving me. I love the candles and the long, slow baths, but I want it like this, too."

Marcie arched her pelvis into Keri's jeans. "The first time I saw you, with your shoulders stretching that T-shirt, I wanted you to push me up onto a counter and have me. I'd never felt like that before. I wondered if it was a midlife cri—"

Keri kissed Marcie hard. "So what if it is? So what?" She sank two fingers into Marcie. "Does this feel good?"

"Yes, Keri, please." Marcie's eyes had widened, but they weren't frightened or confused. Keri felt herself tipping over a cliff she hadn't realized was there—she didn't just like Marcie, she loved her.

"That's what I want to hear, baby." She knew her black slacks were getting smeared and it excited her even more. She was sober, Marcie wasn't just another body, and the crystal-clear perceptions of subtle shifts in Marcie's eye color, the mottling of her skin as her abandonment grew—Keri realized she'd never been present when doing this to any other woman. But she was in this room, in love with this woman.

She pushed in four fingers, filling Marcie completely, and gloried in Marcie's, "Don't stop!"

"Oh, I'm not going to stop, baby. You're going to come on my hand, then you're going to come on my face, then I might carry you into the bathroom and fuck you there."

Marcie, usually without words during sex, found her voice. "Is that what you want to do to me? Yes, that's what I want. Fuck me like that tonight. Fuck me, baby, please."

Marcie cried out and Keri smothered the half scream with a gasping kiss. "Anything you want, everything you need."

Keri finally got out of bed to close the drapes. Marcie had really liked looking out at the lights while Keri went down on her, but they were so ever-present the room was too bright to sleep. At least for her. Marcie was sprawled across the bed in total abandon to the night, her hair wild on the pillow. Her little half-snore was breaking Keri's heart in the best possible way.

The unopened box with the toy gleamed in the flickering light just before the drapes whisked closed. What happens in Vegas might stay in Vegas, but Keri had a feeling that the toy, along with all the things they'd learned tonight, was coming home with them.

SNAKE EYES

....

Karin Kallmaker

I think I'm in the wrong place." Tendra's gaze swept the large suite again as she muttered under her breath. Yes, there were coffee and snacks on the side bar of the suite's main room. The sofas offered comfortable respite from a day of workshops and high-level networking. But the women in low-rider jeans and leather vests, fishnet stockings and mini-skirts were not adding up to the business of trauma surgical supplies.

A door to what she presumed was a bedroom opened and through it she glimpsed racks of lingerie. A compact blonde was adjusting the cups of a violet teddy until her breathtaking cleavage was properly arranged. She shook her full, golden hair into place over her shoulders and eyed herself critically in a full-length mirror. Frowning at what she saw, her gaze flicked out the open door to where Tendra stood staring.

That cool, critical gaze traveled up and down Tendra's body, then a lift of an eyebrow agreed that Tendra, in her baggy slacks and badly ironed white shirt, was definitely in the wrong room. With an elegant tap from the toe of a killer high heel, the blonde pushed the door closed, breaking the spell.

Tendra dug in her pocket for the business card-sized invite to the vendor's hospitality suite. Maybe it had been a mistake to treat herself to a day without her contact lenses. Holding the card as far away as she could, Tendra thought it said suite fifteen hundred, but that's where she was, and, well, the displays of certain items she could see through the other bedroom door weren't the kind of accessories used in patient treatment.

Her heart pounding in an erratic rhythm, she forced herself to stop looking at the coils of soft white rope, the gloves with everything from faux claws to sandpaper on the fingertips, and leather buckled items made to restrain any part of the human body. Peering at the card, she decided it must say suite sixteen hundred, and she turned toward the door.

"Can I help you?" The soft voice stopped Tendra in her tracks.

She knew it had to be the blonde before she even turned around. "No, but thanks. I know where I'm supposed to be."

Crystal green eyes appraised her coolly, though Tendra detected a hint of humor. "You're not the first person to get the wrong floor. You don't look like a doctor."

"You don't look like an…escort." At least not in the street appropriate black slacks and simple silk tee, Tendra could have added.

The eyes darkened. "Are you trying to insult me?"

"No more than you were me." Tendra shrugged. "I'm five years older than I look, and no, I don't stand on a box in the operating room." She was used to being shorter than her colleagues, and it was no surprise that as petite as the blonde was, she was still an inch or so taller than Tendra was.

"I run a cyber-escort service, and no, I don't fuck men for money."

Tendra gave a little nod. Her brain was too fogged and tired to exchange barbs and flirtations.

"I fuck women for fun, though," the woman added. There was a blatant invitation in her eyes. "You look like you could use some extreme relaxation. If you twist any tighter you're going to break."

Stunned by the woman's perception, Tendra fumbled for words. "I don't—I'm just in the wrong—I'm not—"

"Don't tell me you're not into women. Not after the way you looked at me. And at the toy room."

"I'm late for drinks—I was meeting someone—"

The cool, firm voice silenced her. "Have a drink with me in my room."

Tendra couldn't believe how much she was tempted. She hadn't had a sexual impulse for at least a week, and yet her entire body was screaming *yes* in seconds. She'd had the psych courses; she knew why she was looking for an escape from life, through any means possible, including far too much Scotch every one of the last seven nights.

"I'm Vette." The woman held out her hand, her expression cool except for that lingering gleam of humor in her eyes. "Short for the kind of car I'm sure you'll someday own."

An electric shock ran through Tendra the moment their hands clasped. "Corvettes aren't really my style."

Vette didn't let go of her hand. "But wouldn't you like to drive one, just once?"

She knew the color was draining out of her face. Blood was rushing to her sex, which was swelling and pulsing like a second heart. She had resented having to come to this convention instead of taking a badly needed few days off. Her mentor Reilly had said she would be better for the distraction, but Reilly had Liz, and that made her outlook on life a lot rosier than it used to be. Distractions? Tendra hadn't arrived here wanting more than a steady supply of Scotch and a lot of sleep.

Vette moved just a little closer, still holding Tendra's hand. "Actually, they say a Corvette isn't a car you drive. It's a car that drives you."

She trembled, unable to breathe. The woman's eyes were mesmerizing and Tendra felt as if a spell were stealing over her, and she was falling. Falling, and willingly.

"I want to fuck you," Vette whispered. "Jesus. I took one look at you, and that's all I can think about. Fucking you until you forget your name."

I just walked in the wrong door, Tendra wanted to say. She wasn't into this kind of scene.

"Breathe." Vette's voice sharpened with command. "Breathe before you faint."

Tendra sucked in air, and her vision narrowed to Vette's face. She felt pierced by those eyes, pinned in place, and far too much of herself was exposed.

Maybe if they'd had to wait for an elevator she might have found the wherewithal to extricate herself. Vette's grip on her hand wasn't tight. A simple twist would have separated them. Vette had stopped gazing at her with that penetrating intensity as they walked down the corridor, so she could have just walked away.

Vette opened the door to her room and even stood back to let Tendra enter first. She could have backed off. But she didn't do any of those things.

She went in. It was a hotel room, like any other. Sunlight still streamed in through the open drapes. It wasn't a dungeon, or a staged set like in a porn movie, just two beds, a dresser, and a tastefully hidden TV. A bottle of Glenfiddich sat on the dresser, still nearly full.

The door snicked closed as Vette said, "Take off your clothes and get on the bed."

Why did every word Vette say seem to hit her with a physical force? Her skin jumped at the command, but her brain objected. "I'm not into—I mean, this isn't me. I think you have the wrong idea of what I like."

Vette looked up from pulling the covers off the bed. "No, I think I have you figured out. You're not normally submissive. Most of the time you're in absolute control of everything. Your last relationship, if you can call it that, you were definitely the top in and out of the bedroom, and she left because you didn't give her any space."

Tendra wasn't going to talk about what's her name. In the tone she reserved for first-year residents, she said, "Stop it. You don't know anything about me."

"You're right." Vette undid the fly of her slacks and they made a soft, sensual sound sliding to the floor. "Except that right now you need in the worst way not to be in control. You need to let someone else do the planning, the worrying, the protecting. And right now, I really want to be that for someone. We both get what we're aching to have."

Tendra tried not to look at the almost sheer panties that were clinging to Vette like a second skin. She closed her eyes and saw the massive amount of blood against the white of the surgical table. The tone of the flat line warning on the heart rate monitor had played in her ears for the last week, though at the moment the pounding of her own heart was almost loud enough to drown it out.

She'd been lucky, lucky beyond belief to have practiced as long as she had without losing a supposedly otherwise healthy patient. Sure, there had been the patients nobody could save, but a teenager with an unsuspected blood clotting disorder—it had all happened so fast. The first was the hardest, everyone said so. Even if she had done everything she should have, everything necessary, it was still hard. His whole life had been ahead of him.

"Come back," Vette whispered. She was standing in front of Tendra now, magnificently naked. In the teddy she had been sensual and inviting, in street clothes elegant and sexy. Naked, it felt as if some other kind of energy was shimmering around her. Tendra had visions of one hard, erect nipple playing against her clit, and shivered at the thought of those full, soft breasts massaging her ass.

She was breathing hard. She had to close her eyes. She wasn't sure she licked her lips, but if she did it was because the thought of losing herself in the act of worshipping between Vette's legs made her thirsty, and a bottle of Scotch was no substitute.

"Take off your clothes and get on the bed," Vette repeated.

Tendra obeyed. She felt tension fall out of her shoulders during the simple act of unbuttoning her shirt. She opened her eyes to find Vette watching her appreciatively. A few minutes where she didn't think, didn't remember…this wasn't how she would normally achieve a state of *tabula rasa*, but the opportunity was here.

Her jeans slid to the ground. With a tug, they ended up in a heap, along with her shoes and socks. In another half-minute, she had shrugged out of her shirt, unhooked her bra, and stepped out of her panties. All done automatically, as if she were getting ready for bed at home, on her own.

"Very nice," Vette said. "Now get on the bed."

She hesitated. "How?"

"Surprise me."

Something in Vette's voice told Tendra she wasn't moving fast enough. She got on the bed, on her hands and knees.

"Spread your knees." Vette's hands were already on her body, caressing her back and shoulders, then underneath to play with her nipples. Tweaking, pulling, not cruel, but sharply stimulating. "You're naked and on my bed, waiting for me to fuck you."

Tendra said nothing, not sure what she was supposed to do except wait. Vette's hands were firm and controlling.

"Do you want me to fuck you?"

"Yes." It was the truth, but it wasn't all she needed.

"Then get on your back."

Tendra rolled over and was just settling when Vette moved on top of her. She was pushed down the rest of the way, her legs nudged open, then fingers were inside her. Vette pinned her with the weight of her body and she pushed even deeper.

Vette had been right; if there was bedroom play, Tendra was a top. She'd never yielded to anyone before, not like this. Vette had some of her weight on one elbow, and her forearm was draped lightly over Tendra's throat. When she swallowed, she could feel that light pressure reminding her she was not in charge. She was on this bed to take what Vette wanted to give, to enjoy it, to please with her own pleasure. To forget her name, to forget…

"No," Vette said. She looked into Tendra's eyes, all that sharp, bright intelligence leaving no room in Tendra's thoughts except for the sensation in her cunt as Vette thrust and rolled, massaged and teased. "Stay open, stay with me."

Tendra could hardly breathe. Those eyes possessed her; they gave her no place to hide except behind her own closed lids.

Vette put pressure on Tendra's throat. Tendra immediately opened her eyes. "That's better," Vette cooed. "No hiding.

You're getting fucked by a complete stranger who doesn't even know your name. Let it feel good. Oh, that's better. You just got so wet."

Tendra knew sex could fill up empty places inside her. She'd loved, been washed over with tenderness. What Vette was doing to her was the opposite—it drained. The room was going dark, sounds were getting muffled. Even her own heartbeat, throbbing in her ears, was getting faint.

She wanted to beg to come. She wanted to beg for Vette to lick her, to fuck her harder, but she wasn't in charge. Whatever Vette felt like doing that was what would happen. She hadn't been told she could beg.

"There, there, right there," Vette murmured. "Put your hands under your ass."

It was hard to move with Vette's weight on her, hard to make her body do anything when Vette's fingers were touching everything, stroking from nerve to nerve, deep, shallow, twisting, thrusting. She wriggled, trying to obey, aware that Vette wasn't making it easy. She had to get it right or Vette would stop.

She was about to say that she had done as she'd been told when Vette said, "That's right, I'm fucking you."

Her eyes glowed like green fire, burning into Tendra.

"We met ten minutes ago, and now you're getting fucked. There's nothing but my hand, my body, and your hungry cunt liking what I'm doing to you. I wanted your body, to own it, to use it. That makes you mine."

The words were running together. She wasn't sure what Vette was saying, but she didn't have to know. She hung suspended from the jewels of Vette's eyes, the world shrinking inward until those eyes were the only light, and letting Vette's hand enjoy her depths was the only reason she existed.

Vette shifted her position slightly and the feel of hot, wet pussy on her thigh distracted her from Vette's eyes. But Vette's words brought her focus back to the sharp gaze. "I thought you might want to know what you'll get to lick, if you please me."

The tension in her shoulders, across her breasts, was unbearable. She felt tethered to Vette's eyes, swinging with each thrust, afraid she would break free, fall, get lost forever. There was something that wouldn't let her go, but she needed to escape it, so she pushed up, thrust up to meet Vette, to give herself to those eyes.

Her orgasm shattered her. She was empty, turned inside out.

The past dissolved, everything went away. Only her body remained, a ragged collection of trembling muscle, shaking nerves and so much wet…so wet.

The green eyes softened, filled with matching tears. "It's okay," Vette said. "It'll be okay."

She curled into the welcoming arms, said thank you for the tissue. She'd never come like that before in her life. She wasn't sure she wanted to again, but even as the thought formed, her body told her otherwise.

Vette asked softly, "What's your name?"

She looked at Vette blankly for a long moment.

Vette smiled. "Good."

LET IT RIDE

....

Radclyffe

I've always wondered what limo drivers did while they were waiting for their clients to finish doing whatever they were doing," a woman said as she slid up beside me.

I dropped my last quarter into the slot machine and watched two cherries and an orange jiggle into position on the horizontal bar, then turned to the redhead I'd first seen that morning at the airport. The company I worked for had sent a fleet of six limos to pick up arriving members of Escort Services International, and I was driving one of the black stretches assigned to the group for the next five days. I hadn't been quite as lucky as a couple of my fellow chauffeurs. My client was one of the corporate executives—a friendly enough guy—but I would have much preferred to drive the escorts to the Palace. My current companion had been one of a group of sleek, sophisticated women who deplaned looking as if they'd just stepped out of the pages of *Cosmo*. Even though they were all great looking, she stood out for me. I think it was her obvious confidence and self-assurance. She clearly didn't think being a high-class call girl was anything to apologize for.

I motioned to the beeper on my belt. "These mean we don't have to lurk at the curb any longer."

"What do you do instead?"

"Most of the guys congregate in the lounge and talk about sports or girls," I replied. I'd shed my black suit jacket and loosened my tie when I'd started feeding the one-armed bandit an hour ago. I saw her give me a slow once over, and I hoped my white shirt wasn't wrinkled. She looked just as good as she had earlier. Her shoulder length red hair was wavy and thick, and she'd left it loose. She'd changed into a casual pair of black Capris and a sheer pale blue blouse, and the lacy cups of her diminutive bra were visible as they cradled her full breasts. I think I must have stared a little too long because when I glanced up, she gave me a knowing smile. I'm sure she was used to people assessing her body, and I suddenly didn't want to be relegated to the category of those who mindlessly lusted after her. Even if I did have a flash of mindless lust imagining what it would be like to get my fingers inside those frothy bits of white lace and lift her breasts out into my hands.

"You don't care for the topics?" she asked.

I struggled to remember what we had been talking about before my brain dropped into my crotch. Oh, right—sports and girls. "I like them both, in the right circumstances. But I prefer action to conversation."

She signaled to a cashier and bought a paper container filled with 400 quarters and set it on the narrow shelf in front of my slot machine. Without taking her eyes off me, she started dropping coins into the slot. "And what's your favorite sport?"

"Poker."

"You live in the right town then."

"That's what I thought when I moved out here," I replied. "I still do."

"And what about the girls?"

"What about them?"

"If you don't like to talk about them, what do you like to do with them?"

I caught her wrist as she was about to slide another coin into the machine. Her face registered surprise, then interest as I pulled the coin from between her fingers and dropped it back into her bucket. "It depends on how much time I have."

"Some things don't take a lot of time."

"And some things are better if they do."

She nodded, as if liking my answer. "Why did you stop me?"

"I was afraid you'd get lucky and we'd be tied up collecting your winnings."

"You have something else in mind?"

"My client said he wouldn't need me until after midnight. That's a little over four hours."

"That's a lot of time."

I picked up the cardboard container and tucked it under my arm. Then I took her hand. "That's just enough time. Would you care to join me for a drink?"

"I'd love to. I'm Erica, by the way."

I told her my name and led her away. We'd gotten halfway across the casino floor before she pulled on my hand to slow me down.

"Something wrong?" I asked.

"I was just wondering where we're going, since the lounge is in the other direction."

"I thought somewhere private would be nicer." When she didn't reply, I drew her through the crowds, down a long hallway, and outside to a small private lot where the limos were parked. At eight in the evening, there was enough light for me to see her clearly, and I could tell she was surprised. Her eyes, which were very nearly turquoise, shaded to a darker blue and her lips parted wordlessly when I opened the rear door of the stretch and motioned her inside. I imagined she was used to feigning excitement and pleasure, and I liked the fact that she hadn't expected this. The tinted windows rendered us invisible.

"What would you like to drink?" I asked, rapidly running through the rear controls to turn on the interior lights and the sound system. The auxiliary systems in the limo ran off a self-contained power unit, so I didn't need to start the engine. I found some sensual jazz, then opened a small refrigerator built into the rear of the partition dividing the front compartment from the spacious area reserved for clients. Two leather bench seats ran at right angles along the rear and the side opposite the doors. Erica sat in the center of the forward facing seat and crossed her legs.

"I would love a martini. Can you do that?"

"I can." I reached for the vermouth.

"Full service chauffeur?"

I hesitated for a second, then reached for the Stoli. Somehow, I knew she'd be a vodka martini woman. I wasn't sure how to phrase this without suggesting criticism of her. "I'll pretty much do anything the client requires."

"Does that include providing specialized services?"

"Not personally, no." I handed her the drink after dropping in an olive.

She sipped it, murmured appreciation, and regarded me over the rim of the glass as I settled on the seat next to her. "You don't perform sexual favors for your clients."

"No, but part of my job is to arrange an escort for them if called upon."

"I see." She cradled the martini glass in one hand and drew my tie through her fingers with the other, tugging me closer with each stroke. When her mouth was a fraction away from mine, she whispered, "What if the client requests you?"

"It depends on the client." I licked the surface of her lips which were tinged with the taste of alcohol.

"What if the *escort* requests you?"

She tilted the glass toward my lips and I sipped her drink. "None ever has."

"Until now."

Erica straddled my lap and wrapped one arm around my neck while she sipped her drink. At some point, she'd kicked off her heels, but I hadn't noticed. She settled her ass on my thighs, swallowed the rest of her martini, and deposited the glass on the small tray above the adjoining seat. Then she hooked a finger around the knot of my tie and dragged it down until it hung in two thin black lines down my chest.

"I'm on vacation. Well, not really a vacation," Erica amended. "A working holiday."

"Working?"

"Not in the usual sense of the word," she said with a smile as she slowly unbuttoned my shirt. "There's talk of a union and health benefits and other organizational details. I'm here to advocate, not see clients."

I raised my shoulders and Erica pushed my shirt down my arms, but when I would have pulled my hands free of the still buttoned cuffs, she stopped me, leaving me with my arms tethered at my sides. The unexpected restriction caught me by surprise, and so did the quick pulse of excitement that shot through my body and coalesced between my legs.

"Do you mind?" Erica asked lazily as she kissed my jaw, then my neck. "I so very rarely have a chance to call the shots."

"I'll bet you're always in charge," I said, my breath coming fast as Erica played her fingers over my chest, "except...no one knows it."

Laughing, she pushed her hips further back on my legs and curled forward to kiss the center of my chest. "It is possible, of course, to pretend to be led while really leading, but it's so much more fun not to be in the closet about it."

"I want you to have fun."

She regarded me seriously while rolling my nipple between her fingers, very slowly and very hard until my stomach contracted and my hips raised off the leather bench. "That's very nice of you."

"Not nice." I thrust my hips, hoping to bump my clit against her crotch. I ached for a little contact to diffuse the building pressure. "Pleasing women is what I need to make me come."

"Maybe we'll both try it differently tonight."

She sucked my nipple, scraping her teeth around and around the edges until I was so wound up only the back of my head and thighs were still making contact with the seat beneath me. When she slipped one hand between us and squeezed my crotch, I shivered and jerked away.

"I'm sorry," I gasped, "but I'm not used to this."

"You don't like it?" She covered my breasts with her hands as she slid off my legs and knelt on the floor. I opened my thighs without her asking and she licked a warm, wet trail down the center of my stomach.

"I like it. I'm just, I can't...I was afraid you might make me come. And I don't usually...that way."

She shook her head, obviously pleased, and unbuckled

my belt. Again, without being asked, I lifted my hips and she pulled my clothes down until she could get in close between my thighs. She kissed my clit. "Of course you're going to come."

When she sucked me, I made a sound that didn't sound like me at all. I didn't want her to stop. I loved the way her lips closed around me, hot and incredibly soft. She probed and teased me with the tip of her tongue, a torture so sweet I closed my eyes and prayed she kept going. And then there was nothing except her mouth, her lips, her tongue, and a pleasure so deep I begged out loud for more. When she moaned, the vibration shot through me as if a switch had been thrown on an electric current. I ripped my hands free and gripped her head, tangling my fingers in her hair, and wrenched her mouth away.

"Stop," I groaned. "Too much."

Stunned, she stared at me, her expression nearly pleading. It was then I realized she had opened her slacks and was masturbating while she pleasured me with her mouth.

"Please," she whispered, "you're close."

"So are you." I grasped her shoulders and coaxed her upright. "Come first. For me."

For a second, I thought she would refuse, and although my mind was hazy with the nearness of my orgasm, I realized she wasn't used to putting her pleasure first. I hooked my fingers in the waistband of her slacks and eased them down. "Straddle me. I want to touch you."

Her eyes never left my face as she bared herself and knelt on the leather seat with her legs on either side of my thighs.

"Open your blouse," I whispered, spanning her narrow waist with my hands, my thumbs almost meeting in the center of her abdomen. I dragged my hands down her sides and watched her fingers tremble as she worked the buttons loose on her blouse. As I danced my fingers over her smooth, tight thighs, I leaned forward and sucked her nipple through the lace of her bra. She moaned deep in her throat and drove her fingers into my hair, holding my face firmly against her. I cupped her with my palm between her thighs and she rocked back and forth on my fingers. She was hot, so hot, the way only a woman aroused can be. I spread my fingers and let her slide her clitoris between them, setting the pace.

With a flick of her hand, she opened her bra and let her breasts fall free. I rubbed my cheek over one, then the other, and sucked the smooth skin. Her thighs trembled on either side of mine, and I wrapped an arm around her waist to support her.

"I'm almost coming," she whispered, rocking erratically in my hand.

"Hold on, if you can." I steadied her hips between my hands and guided her forward until I could cover her clitoris with my mouth.

"Oh God," she cried in surprise, and I felt her jerk between my lips. "Oh, I'm coming."

I sucked and licked her, one arm around her waist to keep her cleaved to me, and grasped my clitoris with my other hand. She rubbed herself over my mouth, coming for a long time while I came fast and hard with only a few strokes.

"What happened?" she murmured as she dropped into my lap, turning sideways so I could cradle her in my arms. "That didn't go the way I planned."

"I guess I'm just used to driving," I answered, resettling her blouse around her shoulders so she wouldn't get cold. I kissed her as she relaxed against me. "Sorry. I know you had something else in mind."

"No. I liked it. I liked exciting you. I liked you exciting me." She looked up at me. "I didn't really have any plans beyond seducing you."

I laughed. "Well, you definitely succeeded. I'm sorry I have to go back to work later."

"Maybe we can do something about that." She reached behind her and between my legs, sliding her fingers over me. I was sensitive from coming, and when she fondled my clitoris, I groaned. She murmured, "Oh yes. We should definitely do something about that."

"I don't think so," I said, practically choking on the words. "I have to take your boss somewhere later."

She stopped what she was doing, but kept her hand over me. Then she kissed me. "He's not my boss. He's my operations manager."

"What?" I wasn't thinking very clearly because if she kept pressing where she was pressing, I was going to come again.

"I'm not an escort," she whispered with her mouth against my ear. "I'm the owner."

"Uh…I…"

She laughed, and as I started to come, she added, "And you're my new driver."

THREE OF A KIND

....

Karin Kallmaker

*I*can't believe you're making me do this." Farrah Fotheringay turned quickly into a nook as she strained to hear her agent's reply over the din of slot machines.

Her state-of-the-art cell phone was worthless; Ling sounded like she was on the far side of Jupiter, not cozy in her New York office. "Your squeaky clean image needs some serious tarnishing."

"But does the photo shoot have to be with *her*?" She faced the wall when a group of women emerged from the restroom. She enjoyed conventions and she liked talking to fans, but not on the way to the bathroom.

"Cindy Crawford was never so hot as when she was shaving k.d. lang's face. What's the matter? Are you afraid that more than Barrett Lancey's reputation will rub off on you?" Ling said something to someone that Farrah couldn't make out, then the connection cleared. "Her girlfriend is the photographer. What could happen?"

I could make a fool of myself, Farrah wanted to say. She hadn't been fighting these feelings for all these years to lose her reputation now. Maybe it was shallow, but she worked hard, and she intended to stay at the very top of romance best seller lists where image, image, image was everything, everything, everything. Farrah Fotheringay was romance's most eligible bachelorette. A long-nursed rumor of a love lost to a tragic, early death had hidden her secrets so deep even she didn't remember what she was. That is, until she looked at Barrett Lancey, her gorgeous girlfriend, and women like them.

Managing to complete her business in the restroom without being asked for an autograph, she tried to shake herself out of her poor-little-me state of mind. Makeup repaired, she made her way across the Palace Casino to the meeting rooms where there was already a queue at the doors for "Farrah and Barrett in Conversation."

She ought to be annoyed they were even paired on a panel like that. She had fifteen years in the business and Barrett only four. Farrah Fotheringay was her publisher's cash cow, and so far, while sales were strong, excitement in the existing fan base was the only thing Barrett Lancey was generating. Meow, meow, meow, Farrah thought. She's generating plenty of excitement in you.

What really annoyed her was that Barrett Lancey had groupies, both lesbian and straight. "Lance" could snap her fingers and any of the cute young dykes would crawl over cut glass for her. She needed to keep some distance from the shaggy-hair, dark-eyed woman, needed to downright hate her if she could, otherwise her racing pulse might become obvious to the woman who caused it. Even worse, Barrett's equally dynamic girlfriend could notice, and the last thing she needed was for Racie Racine to decide that her lens would highlight Farrah's crow's feet, cellulite, and suspiciously silver highlights.

Barrett and Racie—honestly! What kinds of names were those? Didn't lesbians have names like Mary or Jane or Patty? Oh stop it, she told herself. *Fotheringay* might be fake, but she was a closet-case lesbian named Farrah with no room to cast stones.

The groupies were clearing a path for the couple, who walked *everywhere* arm-in-arm. From the very start of her skyrocketing career as the new breed of romance writer, Barrett had made her sexuality plain in dedications of her work to her girlfriend. She could get away with that in this day and age, but Farrah hadn't had that option when she'd broken into romance publishing fifteen years ago. Back then a virginal aura meshed with that handy broken heart had been her only choice if she didn't want anyone wondering why she never married, never had children, lived alone.

She had only to look at Carly Vincent's rapid descent from A-List to B-List when she had come out fifteen years ago for proof. She wondered if Carly was as bitter as she was that these newbies, with no history, no baggage, could burst on the scene, peccadilloes and all, with nary a consequence.

Fifteen years ago, she had had to play it straight, and her heroines had to faint at least once every book. They couldn't be kick-ass super spy martial arts Navy Seal ninjas who spoke five languages while curing cancer and racing thoroughbreds.

So Barrett got everything she wanted, Farrah thought viciously, while other people were stuck accepting a career as a substitute for love, as if a stack of bestsellers could warm a bed. Well, it didn't warm one bed. It warmed three, including the one in Kauai, thank you very much. Three empty beds were better than one empty bed—oh, you're blathering, she scolded herself.

"Farrah!"

Crap. Barrett had seen her and the groupies were making room. Flashes popped as they did cheek kisses, then more photos were snapped as the smooches were repeated with Racie.

Those of Barrett's groupies that weren't hot for Barrett were hot for Racie. Where Barrett was just a bit scruffy, just a bit dangerous and rough, Racie was sleek and elegant, like a supermodel, except she had cleavage and muscles. Her long black hair stretched past her shapely backside. Farrah could be hot for Racie, too. Face it, you idiot, you could be hot for anything right now.

"How have you been, Farrah?" Racie held her just a little bit longer than the exchange of cheek pecks. The question, in her sexy contralto and the glance from her dark bedroom eyes made Farrah feel slightly confused, dazzled. That was one thing Racie and Barrett had in common. Both of them had the same alluring gaze that suggested that if were you in private, you'd see a very different woman, and not a woman who was necessarily clothed.

It was a ridiculous thought, she told herself. They were oozing sex appeal for the fans.

Farrah gathered her wits and answered, "Absolutely wonderful. I love it when conventions are in Vegas. There are direct flights out of Honolulu."

"Isn't this insane?" Barrett took her by the arm, and suddenly Farrah was in between the two of them, arm-in-arm. "When I found out we were doing a session together it blew me away. I'm so not worthy. They're all here to see you."

"You're too modest." Farrah found herself glancing back

and forth between Racie's suggestive warmth and Barrett's bold admiration.

"I'm just making sure the lovely Miss Fotheringay makes it safely to the podium," Barrett assured someone in the crowd. Her warm hand tightened on Farrah's arm.

In a heartbeat Farrah was back in San Antonio at the convention six months ago when she'd stumbled going up the stairs to a dais and Barrett, right behind her, had pulled her close to save her from a nasty fall.

The contact had been pure electricity, and the moment had disturbed Farrah's sleep for weeks. The Internet mania over the amateur photo of Farrah Fotheringay swooning in Barrett Lancey's arms was what had given Ling the idea for this photo shoot. Well, Farrah had her misgivings. Internet mania needed to translate to sales, didn't it, or what was the point? Hell, they both had warm hands.

The session moderator introduced them both with suitable flattery, and after some patter, their "conversation" got underway.

The questions weren't surprises, and as she and Barrett chatted, Farrah was even more aware of the animal charm that Barrett exuded. She was doing it on purpose. The look in her eyes was so blatant at times that Farrah inevitably glanced at Racie, wondering if she noticed. The event was over in what seemed like no time, and Barrett's efficient groupies limited the number of lingering fans until the three of them could finally have a few semi-private words.

Racie touched the light cashmere tunic that Farrah was wearing. "That blue makes your skin look like fine china. Were you going to wear that for the photos?"

"I could," Farrah said uncertainly. "I also have a silk dress that has Asian styling to it. Mandarin collar. It's a similar shade of blue."

"Speaking purely as a photographer," Racie said carefully, "I would love to see you in scarlet, and off the shoulder. I've got things staged for a sort of fainting couch pose." Her gaze was so intense that Farrah could feel it on her breasts. "Your round cleavage contrasted against Barrett's square shoulders, I mean, composition-wise, it'll be stunning."

It was just what photographers did, Farrah told herself. They all made their subjects feel beautiful and desirable. She'd done photo shoots before. She knew how the game worked. The trouble was she was going to be smashed up against a damnably sexy woman, a woman who made parts of her feel swollen and hot. And she was going to be watched by another damnably sexy woman the whole while. Racie Racine was an excellent photographer, and after all this time, Farrah didn't want her secrets divined from a photograph that captured something real, deeper than the persona she'd nursed all these years.

"What will Barrett be wearing?"

"A black vintage gambler's vest," Barrett answered, "and tuxedo trousers."

"The color of bow tie will depend on your dress," Racie added.

"Well, I don't have anything off-the-shoulder in scarlet."

"This is Vegas." Racie's smile was conspiratorial. "I actually saw the perfect thing in the window at Yves St. Laurent."

"I'll think about it," Farrah said. So she was going to be half-dressed while Barrett, lucky Barrett, got to be fully clothed. With one eyebrow lifted, she said, "Unless we want to play with gender roles. I wear the tux and she wears the dress."

Barrett made a low sound of approval. "I'd probably pass out if you wore a tux."

"She gets faint whenever she watches *Victor/Victoria*—
Julie Andrews in a tux." Racie chuckled. "But she hasn't worn
a dress since the fourth grade."

"I suspected as much." Farrah hoped her expression
was archly flirtatious, something, anything that didn't reveal
that Barrett's and Racie's frank assessment of her body was
causing a riot of pleasurable sensations between her legs. How
long had it been since she'd had sex, anyway?

That you even have to ask, she told herself, meant it had
been too long, and it had been a risky one-night stand, so
hardly satisfying. Well, she wasn't going to find sex in all the
wrong places, and Barrett Lancey's suite was at the top of that
list. There was a meeting of escort workers in the hotel—she'd
pay for it first.

"Well," she assumed a bright tone, "I think I have some
shopping to do. Are we still on for four p.m.?"

"Four it is," Racie confirmed. She moved into the casual
circle of Barrett's arm, still giving Farrah that you-gorgeous-
thing-you look at which photographers excelled.

Farrah made her way out of the meeting room, convinced
she could feel the gazes of both women on her back. Her feet,
of their own volition, turned toward the shopping concourse.

❖

At four p.m., the door to Barrett and Racie's suite stood
open. A couple of groupies were just inside, sipping wine as
they chatted.

"How wonderful to see you," one said. The other, in the
same uniform of jeans and a polo shirt, pointed toward the
suite's expansive main room. "They're set up in the master
bath."

"The bathroom," Farrah echoed. She resettled the dress

bag over her arm and tried not to show her puzzlement. Since when were there fainting couches in bathrooms?

It was fortuitous that she saw Barrett before anyone else realized she had arrived. The black raw silk vintage gambler's vest fit her like a glove, and tuxedo slacks were cut loosely over her slender hips.

Nobody had mentioned that Barrett wouldn't be wearing a shirt.

For several seconds Farrah had a lightning fantasy of licking her way across Barrett's hard-as-granite shoulders. She hoped the momentary weakness she felt didn't show in her face because she realized that Barrett had seen her. There was no sign of Racie, thank goodness, because that tight silk vest didn't hide the fact that Barrett's nipples had hardened.

"I'm waiting to be coiffed and made up. What do you think so far?" She turned in a slow circle.

"Gorgeous," Farrah said honestly. She was too breathless to say more.

"Do you need to get changed? How about the other bedroom?" Barrett led the way. "This suite is ridiculously large."

Finding her voice, Farrah strove to match the bantering tone. "As are most things in Vegas. I feel like I should car pool just to get from one end of the hotel to the other. I feel lost in suites like these, so I usually opt for a small setup."

Barrett turned from the door to the second bedroom. "Racie and I usually find a way to make use of the space." Her gaze flicked to the centerpiece round sofa in the main room as she gestured an "after you" to Farrah.

It was almost impossible to shake the image of Barrett and Racie entwined in various positions on the furniture. She knew nothing about them, not really, but her imagination supplied accoutrements for Barrett and a leather bustier for Racie while her ears were filled with a full-scale orgy soundtrack.

"Do you have everything you need?" Barrett lounged in the doorway, the vest pulled tight across her chest.

"Yes, thank you," Farrah said automatically. She clamped her mouth shut before she added, "But not everything I want." Instead she made a show of shooing Barrett out of the doorway. "Away with you. I have to get ready."

Barrett didn't move. "Ready for what?" Her eyes were openly suggestive.

Farrah didn't know where her answer came from. "Anything you've got." She planted both hands on the rock hard shoulders and shoved.

Barrett faltered back a step and Farrah closed the door in her surprised face.

❖

There was no point to false modesty. Farrah looked at herself in the mirror, assessing the fit and drape of the scarlet dress she'd bought to please Racie. The off-the-shoulder bodice swept forward to cup her breasts. A technological marvel of a bra lifted her bust to create cleavage where gravity had long since won. The bra had been so gorgeous she'd gotten the matching thong, not that she was going to let Racie photograph it. Tapering in at her waist, the heavy fabric flared at her hips and fell to the floor. Once she had on her shoes, it would just brush the ground. With every step, the twin slits would expose her bare legs from ankle to four or five inches above her knees.

It wasn't her usual look, but Racie's eye for style had been perfect. The dress was sizzling hot. She fought down a blush thinking of what it would do to Barrett's composure. Surely Racie, of all people, would see the crackle of chemistry between them—all fine and good for the sake of the photo shoot, but when that was over Racie might have second thoughts.

She answered a knock at the door, but it was only the makeup artist. Within five minutes she even had powder on her cleavage. Her eyes went from a sweet honey brown to a smoky, sultry topaz. Twenty minutes with a hair sadist transformed her shoulder-length blond hair into a high class French knot. Alone again, Farrah looked at herself in the mirror as she clasped a strand of pearls with a deep blue pendant around her neck. Matching drop earrings completed the outfit. Well, she still had to put on the shoes. She wasn't sure she could walk in them, so she'd wait.

The stilettos dangling from her fingertips, she took a deep breath and opened the door.

One of the groupies whistled.

Someone said, "Damn." Then Farrah realized it was Barrett. A scarlet bow tie had been artfully tied around her bare neck, and all Farrah could think about for a moment was undoing that tie with her teeth.

"Will I do?" She tried for the happy, virginal smile that graced the back of every paperback romance she'd ever sold.

"You'll do." Barrett sounded hoarse. "Did you need help with those shoes?"

"No, I was waiting—it's not—oh…" Before Farrah knew it, she was seated on the round sofa with Barrett kneeling at her feet.

The Ferragamo satin and patent stilettos were in Barrett's hands. She slipped the left on first, one warm, strong hand cupped behind Farrah's calf.

Her voice pitched low, she said, "You're going to be taller

than I am in these gorgeous shoes."

"Would you rather I didn't wear them?"

"Of course not." She slipped the right shoe into place. "I want you to walk on me in them."

Farrah batted her eyelashes. "I didn't think you were into that."

"Do you have any idea what you're doing to me?" Barrett looked up, the vest straining over her shoulders and against her taut breasts. She wasn't smiling.

"You started without me!" Racie swept into the room, her camera already clicking. "Jesus, you two look incredibly hot. Keep talking."

Farrah felt her cheeks stain with color. Barrett looked a little flushed too.

"Oh, you've both frozen up. Okay, everybody else out. There's work to be done. You two stay put." Racie shepherded everybody out of the suite, even the groupies who looked like they were going to faint. She flipped the safety latch on, then said, "Now it's just us."

Farrah wanted to ask Barrett what she'd meant, but it wasn't appropriate. She shouldn't be flirting. Barrett's hand still cupped her calf and Farrah took a deep breath, wondering what Barrett would do if she shifted the toe of the pump just a little to the left.

Maybe her intention showed in her eyes, or maybe it was just the way she shifted her shoulders, but when Barrett's jaw went slack, Farrah felt herself blush again. Femme fatales don't blush, she told herself fiercely.

Racie was saying, "Just the three of us. Baby, lean a little closer, and Farrah, can you incline your shoulders toward her, but look over this direction? Get closer."

"Someone said we were shooting in the bathroom."

"That's the cover shot," Racie explained. Her camera clicked and whirred like a slot machine wheel. "If these turn out, they could go inside. *Vanity Fair* is going to love this look. Barrett, honey, put your tongue back in your mouth and smile a little."

A nervous laugh escaped Farrah, and she couldn't help but glance at Barrett.

Barrett muttered, "I'd rather put my tongue in your mouth."

Farrah broke out in goose bumps. "Why do you think I'd let you?"

One expressive eyebrow lifted and a smile emerged at last. Still in that low, sexy voice, she answered, "Because I can smell you. You're as turned on as I am."

"Okay, let's move to the bathroom where the light is set up." Racie breezed away, scooping a second camera off a table as she went.

Barrett rose to her feet and extended a hand to Farrah. "My lady?"

Easily lifted to her feet, Farrah said, just as Barrett leaned toward her, "We can't ruin the makeup."

"Good thing you reminded me." With a distinctly regretful look in her eyes, Barrett led Farrah through the master bedroom and into a palatial bathroom, gripping her arm tightly when Farrah stumbled a little in the unfamiliar shoes. She wouldn't be able to walk twenty feet in them.

When she took in the layout for the photo shoot, Farrah laughed. The bathtub, easily capable of holding three people, was filled with white cushions.

"We're taking a bath together, sort of?"

"That's the idea."

Racie posed them several ways over the next hour and

took preliminary photographs. Farrah straddling Barrett, Barrett spooning Farrah from behind, Farrah looking as if she'd fallen across Barrett's lap, and so forth. Each pose included careful arrangement of the folds of Farrah's gown and the set of Barrett's shoulders.

Racie paced and muttered, mostly to herself, then announced, "I'm liking this one so far. Let's do a full set with it."

Barrett was resting back in the tub, the heels of her men's dress shoes up on the lip farthest from the camera, ankles crossed and looking very devil-may-care. Farrah was on her side, her head on Barrett's shoulder and her dress was spread over the cushions, exposing her legs as the dress covered Barrett's.

"A few little things," Racie said. She tweaked the dress again, then leaned over the tub to lift Farrah's pendant from where it had become trapped between her breasts. Racie's fingertips brushed over Farrah's chest as she set the pendant where it would be seen. Farrah couldn't help but stare down Racie's loose-fitting tank top. She wore no bra and the erect nipples of dusty rose made Farrah's mouth water. "Now don't move."

The camera shutter clicked, batteries were swapped, the lights shifted. Racie had to dab their faces with more powder as the temperature kept going up. Farrah lost track of time. The lighting didn't allow for any change in the sunlight, though it had to be early evening, and she was intensely aware of Barrett's pounding heart and taut body.

The suite's doorbell rang and Racie went to answer it, saying, "I bet that's the room service you preordered, baby. You two relax. I think we're just about done."

"Thank God," Farrah muttered.

"Could you get off my shoulder?"

"Sorry!" Farrah wiggled around, her legs feeling stiff.

"It's not your fault. Racie can be a real…taskmaster."

Farrah managed to get herself onto the side of the tub. "Do you really think we're done?"

"I hope so, because I really want to kiss you."

Having had the past hour to think about it, Farrah said, "Do you make all the girls feel this way at these conventions?"

"Do you think I have a woman in every port, or something?" Barrett looked offended.

"You're a natural born flirt."

"So what if I am? And exactly how am I making you feel?"

"I think you know."

"I know what I want to be true." She leaned close, her lips only an inch from Farrah's. "I want you to be as wet and as aching as I am. I've been like this since San Antonio. Touching you was unforgettable."

"Barrett, stop it." Farrah glanced nervously in the direction of the door.

"Why?"

"Your *girlfriend* will be back any moment."

Barrett's eyes had no business crinkling with such charm. "I certainly hope so. We play as a couple."

Farrah's heart nearly stopped. Not just Barrett, with the hot, eager eyes, but sultry, sexy Racie too? They both…wanted her?

"Racie thinks you're confused and just need a helping hand to show you what you really are." Barrett brushed her lips against Farrah's.

Say something, Farrah thought desperately. *Nice girls do not have threesomes.* Say no, that's right, say no. Say it now.

"But I read between the lines in your love scenes, and I

think you already know what you are. You're just afraid to live it."

Her voice taut with panic and excitement, Farrah asked, "Is that supposed to goad me into saying yes?"

"I don't want you to say yes." Barrett undid the first button on her vest with a dexterous flick. "I want you to scream it."

Racie re-entered the room, licking her fingers. "I'm sorry, guys. If you eat something you'll ruin the makeup and I realized there's one more pose I want. The crab dip is delicious, and there are apricot crepes with burnt sugar." She seemed oblivious to the telling angles of Farrah's and Barrett's bodies. "If you've eased those tired muscles, I want to use the sunset lighting in the hallway. We have to move fast."

Farrah leaned on one shoulder against the nondescript wall where Racie pointed. After Racie finished fussing with her camera, she gave Farrah one of those oh-you're-edible looks.

"Stand here," she practically purred, placing Farrah's feet a good twenty inches from the wall. "Now lean like this." Her hands were warm and firm.

The position, with her shoulders flat against the cold wallpaper, was awkward, requiring her to bend backward at an extreme angle.

It got less awkward when Barrett's thigh was pressed between her legs to hold her up. One arm supported her back, requiring Barrett to lean into her, their faces only inches apart.

"That's fantastic." Racie's shoulders and neck were flushed by the time she had Barrett posed to her satisfaction. She snatched up her camera. "Your bodies are in the light, your faces in shadow—this will be a totally hot black and white shot. It's just like the covers of all our books, the big clinch."

Farrah could feel Barrett's heartbeat against her breasts. It was all she could do not to rub herself on the hard thigh. Aware that Racie might be able to hear her, she dropped her voice as low as possible. "You weren't making it up, were you?"

"Making what up?"

"That you both…you know."

"Play? No, it's the truth." If anything, Barrett leaned closer. "Racie is so turned on right now I'm surprised she can focus her camera. But she always manages. She's all about the visual, and you are so wicked hot."

"I don't—why? Why me?" Farrah realized she was stammering like a teenager.

"Damn, woman. You're intelligent, you're funny, you're incredibly sexy. Of all the characters you write, the ones who ring the truest are the good girls with a wildcat in their soul. Do you think all those hot-for-Farrah posts on the fan lists are just flattery? If I were a guy I'd have a hard-on the size of Montana around you."

"Barrett." Farrah breathed out the name, knowing she had wanted to say it for a long time.

"I'm not a guy, but right now my clit feels like the size of Montana." With a little growl, she pushed her thigh more firmly between Farrah's legs.

"Perfect," Racie said. "Just like that." She circled them slowly for several minutes, camera whirring.

Finally, Racie put the camera down, then approached them. Farrah expected more posing, though it seemed to her that the shadows were getting long and low for any more photos. Racie had gotten all the desert's summer sunset could give.

Leaning in to look at Barrett, Racie said, "Now I think you should kiss her."

Farrah gasped.

"God knows, I want to. But it's up to Farrah." In spite of her words, Barrett buried her lips into the hollow of Farrah's throat.

Racie's lips were at Farrah's ear. "I know you want her. It's okay. I love her, and I love watching her."

Farrah struggled to find her voice as Barrett nuzzled at her other ear.

"I'm a visual person," Racie went on. "When she's making love to me I can't watch her the same way. So I watch her with other women and it's incredible. I get to enjoy all her beautiful strength, I get to see every nuance of her body when she comes, and I still get to be in her bed, too. I get it all."

"You dressed me for her." Farrah didn't resist the firm glide of Barrett's thigh against her very wet cunt.

Racie's tongue flicked her earlobe as Barrett slid slowly to her knees. "No, I dressed you so you'd look like the hot, sensual woman you are. And I dressed you for me. She would just as soon we were naked."

The heat of Barrett's mouth pressing through the fabric of the dress nearly buckled Farrah's knees. Racie groaned in her ear and one elegant, long-fingered hand caressed Farrah's bare shoulder, then moved to her breast.

"Barrett," Farrah managed to moan. Her head said it was too much, too sudden, but her body had decided that making up for lost time was imperative. She arched harder against Barrett's mouth as Racie pulled the dress downward to bare Farrah's breasts.

"Perfect," Racie breathed. Her hand came back to caress and tease Farrah's nipples while Barrett seemed intent on biting through Farrah's dress.

Racie leaned away just enough to look down at Barrett.

Farrah saw the ardent appreciation in Racie's eyes at the sight of her lover, abandoned in passion. With a fluid motion, Racie pulled her tank top over her head, leaving low-rider jeans clasped around her narrow hips. With deliberate quickness, she wound her fingers into Barrett's thick hair and pulled her away from Farrah—pulled her away to turn her head and bring her mouth to the crotch of the jeans.

"That's right, baby." Racie went up on her tiptoes as she rubbed herself on Barrett's mouth. "Two women to satisfy tonight."

Farrah realized she'd never said yes, but who was she kidding? She was so full and slippery she could feel wetness trickling down her thighs.

Barrett reared back with a deep groan. She scrambled to her feet then kissed Racie on the mouth, hard. In the next moment, she swept Farrah into her arms, carried her to the living room, and finally spread her out on the round sofa.

It was like a stage, Farrah thought, pleasing to Racie's eye. The drama wasn't lost on her, either. Barrett was a study in lines and angles, Racie in dark planes and muscle. She added pale curves. Barrett circled the sofa to caress first Farrah's calves, then her shoulders.

Watching Barrett prowl around her made Farrah dizzy. It took her a moment to realize that the hands pushing her dress out of the way were Racie's. Barrett circled the sofa again, to cup the back of Racie's head and guide her into Farrah's cunt.

"Does that feel good?" Barrett leaned over to brush her lips over Farrah's panting mouth. "You're so beautiful to watch. So is she."

The sinuous tongue was stroking places only Farrah's fingers had touched for years. All the build up, all the fantasizing had her on the edge of climax within seconds.

She jerked against Racie's mouth when Barrett tugged on her nipples. Her restraint was gone; there was no reason to deny what she wanted. She shredded the lie of Farrah Fotheringay in her mind and grabbed Barrett by the waist of her pants.

"Please," she said. "You don't know how long it's been, please."

Barrett stripped, and she was gorgeous, a body like a god that Farrah appreciated for the few seconds it took to pull Barrett onto the sofa. "Kiss me," she pleaded.

Barrett covered her lips in a heated rush, and Farrah pushed her tongue hard into the eager, welcoming mouth, realizing as she did so that she was matching the motion of Racie's tongue doing the same thing to Farrah's cunt.

"Damn," Barrett said against Farrah's lips. "Damn, it's as good as I thought it would be."

"Kiss me again." Farrah lost herself in Barrett's mouth while the pleasure between her legs grew unbearable. She bucked against Racie and Barrett's grip on her tightened.

"That's right, that's right, come for her."

Farrah struggled not to burst into tears. Racie's mouth felt that wonderful, her tongue that intense.

Barrett shifted to hold Farrah in place as she writhed in response to Racie. Farrah turned her head to find one erect nipple. She bit down, then sucked it into her mouth, drunk on Barrett's earthy groan blending with Racie's appreciative gasps. The two of them had unleashed her. She shoved her hand between Barrett's legs.

Barrett's elbows buckled as she pushed her cunt against Farrah's fingers. "Damn, woman, let me catch my breath."

"No," Farrah said. She curved her fingers, opening Barrett. "If you thought I would be a passive plaything, you were wrong."

Racie finally raised her head from between Farrah's thighs. "Yes, just like that. Fuck her. Just do it. That's how she likes it."

Barrett made a choked noise as Farrah pushed roughly inside her.

"Get me out of this dress," Farrah said to Racie, even as she twisted around to get a better angle. Racie fiddled with the zipper, then pulled the dress off, discarding her own jeans as well.

"You're so gorgeous, baby." Racie ran her hands over Barrett's body. "You're going to come, aren't you?"

Barrett nodded desperately.

Farrah whispered, "Please open your eyes."

Barrett's gaze was unfocused when she did as Farrah asked. The just-a-bit-dangerous woman had disappeared, leaving a vulnerable one behind.

"It's okay," Farrah said. "We've got you." She rolled to Barrett's side, her hand sliding even deeper. With her other arm she pulled Barrett close, cradling her.

"I know how long you've wanted her," Racie said. "It's okay, baby. God, I know you're this way with me, but I've never been able to watch you with a strong femme before. You're so strong, too, Barrett, honey…I love the way your back arches. It's okay, you can let go with her."

Barrett's groan was long and loud as Racie draped herself along her back.

Farrah bit Barrett's lower lip. "Do you like being a femme sandwich?"

After an explosive exhale, Barrett said between gritted teeth, "Fuck, yes."

Farrah no longer questioned if she ought to be enjoying herself, she only knew that she was. Racie's fingers were playing near where her own were plunging in and out of

Barrett, then Racie replaced her, reaching in from behind, and Farrah's slick touch concentrated on Barrett's rock hard clit.

Barrett panted into Farrah's shoulder, near climax but able to laugh between gasps for breath. "How did I get to be in the middle?"

"We put you there, baby." Racie kissed the back of Barrett's neck.

"Because we want to take turns fucking you." Farrah licked the notch in Barrett's collarbone.

With a guttural cry, Barrett jerked helplessly between them. When she finally went limp, her face was buried between Farrah's breasts.

"That's not exactly what I thought would happen first," she muttered.

"I'm pleased," Racie said. She looked at Farrah over Barrett's head.

"So am I." Farrah inclined her head and Racie leaned toward her so their lips could meet. Soft, sensuous, delicious. "And you can take my picture anytime."

Racie laughed into their kiss, then ended it by licking Farrah's lips. Barrett stretched in between them, her arms slipping around Farrah's waist.

"It feels wonderful to hold you like this at last," she said.

Farrah couldn't help it—she glanced at Racie to make sure it was okay.

Racie smiled reassuringly. "You don't put wild things in cages, and that's how I've managed to hold on to her."

"And vice versa," Barrett murmured.

"I think that means I'm just happy to be out of my cage," Farrah said. "That I'm with two incredible women is like frosting on the cake."

Racie kissed her again, at first with a smile, but it faded. "She's not the only one who has wanted to hold you. We read your books together. You talk about women, how they feel, the way that Barrett does. She does amazing things to me and I'm thinking you will as well."

Farrah shivered, and a luxurious feeling of letting go of all pretense washed over her. She melted into Barrett's embrace, her head half resting on Racie's shoulder. Tomorrow was a long way away. For tonight, she felt free.

LUCKY 7

Karin Kallmaker

*f*inally!" Tess threw her arms around Brandy the moment the hotel room door was closed. "We're on a real vacation, and together!"

Brandy tackled Tess and they landed on the bed with a delightful mashing of breasts and thighs.

After a long, delicious kiss, Tess stretched out in Brandy's arms. "What do you want to do first?"

"I thought I was making that clear," Brandy said. "Am I losing my touch or something?"

Tess bit the tip of one of Brandy's fingers. "Later."

"Why not now and then later?"

"Because later I won't be distracted by thoughts of blackjack and poker because I'll have played some by later."

Brandy laughed. "Okay, I see where I am in your priorities." Later was better, anyway. She had a little surprise for her lover.

❖

Happily getting into the groove of Las Vegas, Brandy returned from the video poker machines to find Tess exactly where she had left her, frowning over her blackjack cards. The dealer was a gorgeous black woman who was either a dyke or just really fond of women, because Tess's cleavage was getting plenty of attention. Well, someone would have to be dead and buried not to notice Tess. There were actually an amazing number of really beautiful women in the casino, but none held a candle to Tess.

"Hit me," Tess said. She gasped as the card came down. "Twenty-one!"

The dealer paid her off as Tess backed away from the table. "Taking the money and running?"

"I've just paid for our vacation." Tess flipped a chip back to the dealer. "Thanks."

"Thank you." The dealer pocketed the chip with a wink and Tess dragged Brandy across the casino to the cashier. "Let's get the cash before I change my mind. I'm lucky tonight."

And you're going to get lucky, Brandy wanted to say, but that would be a cheap joke and she was trying to be more subtle these days. They were now gainfully employed tour guides with the most successful lesbian tour group. Though their clientele could appreciate the occasional really bawdy joke, she was trying to learn some restraint.

"What shall we do for dinner?"

Tess turned from the cashier with a fistful of twenties. "Well, whatever it is, dinner's on me."

A group of fast-moving women in sensible shoes jostled Brandy into Tess, not that Brandy minded. "I heard it was an open bar," one said to the others, and if anything, their speed increased.

"How about dinner in that dark little place on the mezzanine?"

"Sounds delightful," Tess said. They were on the elevator, holding hands, when she added, "You've got quite the cat in the cream look."

Brandy shrugged, hoping she looked debonair and mysterious.

"Okay." Tess caught one of the male passengers looking at them. She gave up one of her mega-wattage smiles. "I'm going to get lucky tonight."

The women behind them spluttered with laughter. Brandy glanced over her shoulder—oh, dykes if they were a day old, and they were. One was no taller than she was, which was welcome, and the other was yet another gorgeous creature, tall and lithe, and about as well endowed as Tess. She gave the short one a solidarity wink, as they were both unquestionably lucky dogs.

The woman winked back as if to say, "Yeah, we both married up, didn't we?"

"Our floor, Marian." With a smile at them both, the taller woman pulled her girlfriend after her into the corridor. "If you're done flirting with the other cute little butch."

"I was not flirting, Liddy, it was—"

The doors closed and Brandy wondered if she was, in fact, giving off a butch vibe these days. She'd always considered herself on the girly side for butch, though she despised handbags and required pockets in all her clothes. She could don a little black dress and heels and not feel the least bit weird. Not that she was going to wear that tonight. She had other plans.

When she put the harness on the bed, Tess said, "I thought we were going to dinner."

"We are."

"Oh."

"Do you like that idea?"

"Is that why you suggested the dark little place?"

"Yeah."

Tess planted a huge kiss on her. "I really am going to get lucky tonight, aren't I?"

"I'm the lucky one, baby." Brandy kissed her back.

"You say the sweetest things."

"And that's not all." Brandy reached into her suitcase and withdrew the surprise. "Happy anniversary."

"It's not our anniversary—oh wow. That's...wow."

The toy was heavy and thick and long, the largest that Good Vibes carried. Tess was a size queen and Brandy loved finding new ways to make her eyes roll back in her head. "You like?"

"I think I'm going to like, yes." Tess's tongue darted over her lips and Brandy thought it was highly likely that Tess's beautiful little clit had just put on a party hat and grabbed the maracas. "How on earth are you going to hide that in your pants?"

"Those baggy gangster pants you hate."

"Is that why you brought them? I love those pants now." Tess was still staring at the toy. "I like that shade of pink, too."

"Thought you might."

"It's still not our anniversary."

"Sure it is. We've been together four years, five months and thirteen days."

"I love you." Tess gave the new toy one last fond look. "I'll just go get dressed."

Brandy fiddled with the harness and finally got Lucky 7—as good a name as any—into the O-ring. It was a bit of a pushing, pulling, rolling challenge, but it all sorted out and she set about getting into the harness. She still felt silly in the thing at such times. Never silly when she was actually going to get into bed with Tess, but wiggling around, dancing in circles trying to pull her pants up and the toy catching on everything, well it wasn't debonair.

After a one-legged Watusi, she finally had the pants belted around her waist. It really felt weird. She adjusted the pants on her hips, wriggled until the toy hung down one leg. Then she realized why it felt weirder than she'd expected.

She'd forgotten to put on the boxers. She didn't intend to go out of the room without some kind of underwear on—

Tess came out of the bathroom.

Breathe, Brandy told herself. Tess was a vision in a very short aquamarine dress studded with copper beading. The halter neck made Tess look even taller.

"I take it from the look on your face that you like this dress?"

Brandy nodded. She had just about found her voice when Tess turned around. Her bare back put Brandy back into the Land of No Breath. The high neck clasped with a twist of beads that dangled along Tess's spine. Undo the beads, Brandy thought, and she'd be naked in seconds.

All for you, you incredibly lucky dog.

She watched Tess put on her favorite sandals. They weren't made for walking, and had, in fact, never been out of their apartment.

Tess looked up when she'd fastened the last buckle. "Ready?"

"Uh-huh."

"Don't you think you should put a shirt on?"

"Oh! Crap." Brandy blushed furiously. "That dress is a walking crime."

"I just got it this morning. There was a guy selling dresses out of the back of his van. I only noticed because he had quite a crowd. Twenty bucks. I figured out later he was there to sell stuff to the escort service workers." She gave Brandy a worried look. "I don't look like I'm for sale, do I?"

"I will make it plain you've already been spoken for."

Tess gave her one of those serious looks that said they would talk about the subject again.

"You don't look cheap or available for the asking, darling." Brandy tucked in her shirt. "You look like the gorgeous, classy creature you are. Not to mention young and attractive."

"You found that gray hair the other day, remember?"

Was that still bothering her? Dunce, Brandy scolded herself. Next time don't point it out. "That was sun streaking."

"If you say so."

"How about this?" Brandy balled her fists on her hips and walked toward Tess like Yul Brynner's King of Siam. "Go out with me, and everyone will know you're mine."

"You look magnificent."

Brandy dropped the attitude. "No, really. Can you see it? Does it show?"

Tess hesitated. "Maybe a little."

"Well, what does it matter? Nobody is going to be looking at me."

Brandy repeated that to herself all the way to the restaurant. Of course it felt like the entire world was staring at her crotch. They were quickly seated and decided to share what turned out to be a wonderful apple and pecan salad, and a perfect steak with parmesan chips. Brandy enjoyed every moment of watching Tess sparkle in the candlelight. Her best friend, her lover—all the beauty in their relationship was on Tess's side of the table, as were most of the brains.

They shared dessert as well, and Brandy found herself a little disappointed. "Your brownies are better than this one."

"It looks like chocolate," Tess said. "But I don't taste it."

"Kind of like cruise ship chocolate. Remember, I told you about the food on the boat?"

"And you told me about nearly being borrowed by that hot butch."

Brandy grinned and shrugged. "She was awfully cute. But I really missed you, and I was thinking about your ankle and how you must be so sorry to be forced to sit at home. I know you wouldn't have minded if she'd borrowed me for a night, but…." Brandy hadn't been able to admit to Tess that she'd backed out because she'd realized that nobody could touch her, reach into her, the way Tess did. The okay-to-be-borrowed rule was Tess's, even if neither of them had used it so far. She didn't want to mess up a really good thing by appearing possessive all of a sudden.

Tess took her hand, her expression turned serious again, and Brandy wondered what was bothering her. There was something, but she trusted Tess would bring it up. Tess wasn't afraid to talk about anything, and Brandy had already unlearned many bad habits of resentful silence and passive-aggressive fighting that she'd picked up from her dysfunctional family.

All Tess said was, "I have a Snickers bar in my suitcase. We could go back to the room for dessert."

"Oh, I'm having dessert in our room, most definitely." For just a moment, Brandy didn't feel awkward as she shifted in her chair suggestively. Tess's quick little exhale was quite gratifying.

The check paid and their intentions declared, they were back in the elevator when a crowd of curvy, slinky, high-heeled, coiffed and elaborately made-up women of all heights and colors crowded on with them.

"I want to dance all night," a bright-eyed Latina said.

"Our own private disco, in the penthouse."

"Who has the invitation?"

The Latina made eye contact with Tess. "Do I know you from somewhere?"

Tess shrugged. "Probably from around."

"Is that your girlfriend?"

Tess tucked Brandy's hand under her arm. "Yep."

"She looks really happy to see you."

Brandy blushed to the roots of her hair. All the women were giving her the once-over now. "I'm always happy to see her."

"Lucky her," the Latina said. "Maybe I'll get a dance later?"

"We're not—" Brandy realized they'd missed their floor. The doors opened to a blast of music and the women poured out of the elevator with delighted whoops. The security guard looked helpless as they pushed past him.

Caught up in the rush, Brandy found herself jostled along to the parquet dance floor that had been laid out in the suite's living room. It was packed with women, some of whom weren't wearing much, not that Brandy minded.

"Do you want to stay?"

"Why not?" Tess tucked her little purse down Brandy's capacious front pocket. "Dance with me, baby."

It was heaven. They hadn't been on vacation in so long, and even when they did get to dance, they were almost always still on the clock—being a tour guide meant there was no "off."

She swayed in Tess's arms, pulling her close, and closer still. Other women were making out as the music pulsed around them, so Brandy felt perfectly natural pulling Tess down to her for the first of a dozen long, luscious kisses.

"You always wind me up," Tess said. "I'm so torn. I want to dance all night with you, but I also want to…" Her hand moved between them and Brandy shuddered as she felt

Tess gripping the toy through her pants. "What a wonderful dilemma."

"Just because we're getting older and wiser doesn't mean we have to be silly." Brandy took Tess by the hand, leading her away from the dance floor.

"If we leave we might not be able to get back in."

Brandy veered past the impromptu bar. Where there was a penthouse there had to be bedrooms. Before Tess, she'd had women in the fitness room storage closet, behind the pool house, once even on the back of a Sea-Doo. Sneaking into a bedroom for a not-so-quickie was positively tame.

"Oh, you are in a mood tonight, aren't you?" Tess didn't seem the least bit displeased when she figured out what Brandy was thinking.

The first door was locked, the second revealed another couple with the same idea. If they were even aware of the door opening, they didn't show it. A third bedroom was equally occupied, and the bathroom was usable only if one could ignore the noises coming from behind the glass shower doors.

Brandy sighed with frustration.

"Over here," Tess said. She pulled Brandy behind a not all that large potted palm.

"Baby, anyone can see us."

"Ask yourself who here is going to arrest us?"

Brandy's pulse reached a boil. "I see your point. So I'll fuck you right here?"

For an answer, Tess gave her a slack-jawed look and undid the neck of her dress. In moments it was puddled around her ankles.

"Baby." Brandy was stunned. Tess was in one of her moods, and she loved those moods, but this was more than... beyond even... She might have stood there, mouth hanging open, but fortunately a little voice inside her shouted, "Shut up and fuck her, you idiot!"

Brandy unzipped. "All for you."

"Now," Tess said, spreading her legs.

It felt like the first time all over again. Tess made a sound that had Brandy's head spinning. She pushed harder, paused when Tess reached down. "Is it okay? Damn, I forgot the lube."

"It's fine, just something…there. Oh fuck, yes, Brandy, please."

Tess's hands went down the back of Brandy's pants, squeezing and massaging Brandy's bare ass. The surge of erotic adrenaline drove every other thought out of her head.

She bit Tess's neck and fucked her. Held on, fucked her, lived all their nights and days over again, felt that electric current of memories that culminated in the promise of a future that went on like this, full of love and passion and play—fucked her through her first climax, knew there would be a second, and relished that knowledge. She loved this woman, loved being with her, and knowing her body the way she did only deepened the magic.

Tess said her name, gorgeous in her abandonment. "Don't stop."

"You know I won't."

"Damn it, it's filling me up, Brandy, you know, please…"

Their words danced back and forth, no pattern or reason anyone else would understand, but four years and more of working on their own language meant Brandy knew Tess wanted hard, deep, steady strokes now, then short ones, softer while she hovered on the edge of climax again. She listened, heard the sharp whimpers. She pinned Tess to the wall and fucked her, hard, fast, relentlessly, and Tess came again, words and little noises all jumbled together.

❖

They drifted in each other's arms on the dance floor, Tess covered, Brandy zipped.

"That was incredibly fun."

"It was," Brandy agreed. "Want to do it again?"

"In our room. In just a little while." Tess ground against Brandy with no rhythm that matched the music, and it was perfect.

A woman paused next to them as they swayed. Brandy recognized the attractive Latina from the elevator. With a direct look at Tess, she said, "Mind if I cut in?"

"As a matter of fact, I do." Tess arched one eyebrow at the woman that plainly said, "Go away."

"Sorry. I know you already got some of what she's packing, and you may have noticed that she's the only one. But if you're not sharing, that's cool."

"She's not for borrowing."

The woman shrugged expressively and walked away.

Brandy looked up at Tess, not exactly confused, but feeling like she wasn't sure why Tess had put it quite that way.

For a moment, Tess wouldn't meet her gaze, but then she did with her serious, open expression that Brandy had always found brave and wise. But at the moment it was tinged with chagrin.

"I didn't even ask you if you wanted—"

"I didn't," Brandy assured her. "I really didn't and I don't. You're right. I'm not for—"

"I want to make it permanent," Tess said, all in a rush.

"Are you sure?" Brandy's heart melted in her chest.

"No borrowing. No sharing. Just us. I want to be yours." Tess kissed her softly. "And I want you to be mine."

"Yes." Brandy kissed her back, then nuzzled at the pulse point of Tess's throat.

"I know it'll be the same old, same old, boring and..." Tess's voice trailed away.

Brandy stepped back to give her an incredulous look. "You're kidding, right? Boring? You?"

Tess shrugged a big fat it-really-doesn't-bother-me lie.

It was no time to be shy.

"You just let me fuck you in public, you got naked for me to do it, and we've done a lot of things, but that was the hottest so far, and if you think I'll ever be bored with your body, you're crazy, and right now I want to take you back to our room and do about five hours worth of the same-old-same-old, until we're both sore and exhausted and this new, very lucky toy, is worn down to a nub. Then I'm going to get out the lube so I can fuck you again because the favorite thing I love to hear you say is 'honey, I'm done' and that's what I live for, Tess, that's what I want, you, in my bed because you are every woman all in one, and I love you."

Brandy ran out of breath. Tess blinked tears out of her eyes.

Several women nearby had paused in their dancing, openly smiling. Brandy ducked her head in embarrassment.

"Time to go."

Tess didn't protest. She tucked her hand under Brandy's arm and nodded.

Once in the elevator, Tess slid her hand down Brandy's arm to intertwine their fingers. "Know what?"

Brandy risked a look and found Tess gazing at her with eyes like stars. "What?"

"I think today really is our anniversary. From now on."

TOP-BOTTOM TICKET

Karin Kallmaker

*A*re you Harmony Kincaid?" A woman with a shock of short red hair paused at the open office door, looking flushed and nervous. "*The* Harmony Kincaid, Assistant Director of Convention Services and She Who Makes All Happen?"

Harmony immediately knew who it had to be. The hair, wire-rimmed glasses, and gamine smile fit the description of the one person she'd been hoping to see since yesterday. "Yes. And you're Leona Madsen, Meeting Planner Extraordinaire. Come in. I can't believe it's finally the big weekend."

She's as cute as I thought she'd be, Harmony told herself. A million words in e-mails for the last fourteen months to set up the International Librarian Association's convention had let her form an impression of her primary contact. They'd never exchanged photos, but over time personal details, like Leona's needing a trim of her short cut every four weeks and Harmony's euphoria over a steal on a new pair of shoes, had leaked into their correspondence. Leona sent links to quizzes and personality tests and Harmony forwarded online questionnaires. She knew quite a lot about Leona, in an odd way, for someone she'd never met.

"I've been going flat out since we got here. I meant to stop in yesterday to see you, but your minions are many and efficient. It was non-stop till I dropped." Leona set a heavy satchel bulging with papers on the floor. "But I've finally got a break."

"Well, so far the staff loves librarians." Harmony got up from her desk to perch on the edge closest to Leona. It was friendlier and she could go on studying the fascinating reality of the woman she'd been talking with for over a year online. God, she was cute, all cherub. "I'm told they read their materials, show up to sessions on time, leave their rooms long enough so they can be cleaned, and they drink more than firefighters. Apparently they're too smart to play keno, though."

"That's my people!" Leona smiled brightly. "They're really a fun bunch, and I have to say, it's all about information with them. Access to information. Equal access for everybody. Books especially, but maps and notes and—sorry." Leona grinned. "For someone who isn't a librarian, I can get all worked up about it. I like doing their meeting planning."

"How long is your break? Can I take you to lunch?" Harmony glanced at the clock on her desk. She could sneak off for an hour now that she didn't have to cover for Jennifer at the VIP check-in.

"I've got about thirty minutes." Leona relaxed in the chair, and Harmony realized Leona hadn't yet really looked her in the eyes, as if she was nervous.

Well, she was nervous, too. They'd been mostly business-like during their correspondence, especially on their company e-mail addresses, but their hair had come down, so to speak, a little bit in the last month or two, when details grew overwhelming and Leona had been working night and day and at times resorted to her personal e-mail when the work server was unavailable. During the past twelve months they'd both gone through a break up, agreed that women could be shits, in the last month shared that dating wasn't really a priority, and then last week…

"I need to ask you something," Leona said abruptly. "I was, um… I e-mailed that stack of beverage order documents last week? And…"

Harmony wished Leona would look at her. "Do you mean that, um, word processing document I'm not sure you meant to enclose?"

"Did you read it?" Leona's cheeks flamed with color.

"Yes. Every last word." Harmony squirmed slightly on the desk. No girlfriend for months now, and a red-hot erotic story in her inbox had been too hard to resist. "I didn't want to embarrass you by telling you I'd gotten it in error."

Leona finally looked up. "It wasn't a mistake. I wanted you to know."

Harmony's corporate uniform was suddenly way too tight. "That you like to read erotica? Who doesn't?"

The blush was still very present, but the bright brown eyes were dancing. "Did you like it?"

"Yeah. Um, well, I'm not sure how you knew I liked that kind of story."

"Little things you said—especially after what's her name dumped you for that little bitch. Sex was the only decent thing you had left, and you predicted her new girlfriend would end up rather disappointed if she thought she was getting a hard-core top. Ergo, you were disappointed that she hadn't been that for you."

Harmony flushed. She hadn't realized she'd revealed her predilections quite so clearly. She went for a distraction. "They broke up last week—a friend told me yesterday. I feel vindicated. This time what's her name got dumped, and for a guy."

"Ouch." Leona grinned.

"I suppose that's not very evolved of me, delighting in her misfortunes."

"She fell for someone else and then went around saying you'd cheated on her."

"Oh yeah." Harmony laughed—she was nearly over it. Nearly. "I knew I hated her for a good reason."

Leona slid down in the chair slightly and crossed her ankles. "So I got the story right?"

Harmony swallowed. "Why do you want to know?"

Leona took a deep breath. The expression on her face transformed from a cherubic teddy bear to a sensual dyke whose gaze slowly caressed every inch of Harmony's body. "You have made me laugh every day, sometimes several times a day, for the past year and more. Because ultimately, we want the same things out of life, remember? You sent that fifty-things-your-friends-don't-know questionnaire that was making the rounds. I read yours, carefully." She undid the top button of her pristine white shirt. "And most of all, because I'm likely a better top than your ex, and you deserve being made to feel very, *very* good."

"Oh…" Harmony couldn't think of another thing to say. She'd pored over Leona's answers to every test, but tried to tell herself it was all about business, thoroughly knowing the person she was working with, even if all by e-mail.

"So I wrote you that story."

"You *wrote* that?"

"Yes." Leona smiled. "For you."

Details of the story—she'd read it at least a dozen times—burst into her memory like fireworks. It had been exactly the kind of scene she'd always wanted. "None of your quizzes or tests hinted that you were a writer."

"I write only for myself. And, well, for you."

"I'm honored." Harmony felt heat flare in her face.

"So," Leona persisted. "Did you like it?"

"I loved it." Harmony didn't look down, but she was pretty sure her suit jacket didn't hide the fact that her nipples had just gotten very hard.

Leona smiled, and her gaze once again swept over Harmony's body. "Does your office door lock?"

Oh, fuck, Harmony thought. That's how the story started. She nodded.

"Do whatever it is you do to tell people you've gone to lunch. Then lock the door."

Her hand shaking, Harmony forwarded her calls to voice mail, then put the inter-office away message on her computer for anyone who was looking for her. "Off hook for thirty" meant she was not reachable, and the next person in charge should deal with whatever the problem was if it was urgent. She only went off hook once a month, perhaps, but never for such a heart-pounding reason.

She dimmed the office lights that were visible through the transom over the doorway. Then she locked the door.

"Come here." Leona held out one hand.

Harmony knew without asking that she should straddle Leona's lap. She had to pull her suit skirt all the way up to do it, revealing her thighs.

"That was number twenty-four—nobody knows you like wearing garters and hose," Leona said. "They're incredibly sexy." She ran her hands along the inside of Harmony's thighs. "Very lovely."

Harmony settled on Leona's lap and felt the bulge immediately. She didn't know how she hadn't seen it before.

"I had it tucked," Leona said, as if Harmony had spoken. "I put it on in that handy bathroom just down the hall. Look at me."

Shivering, Harmony felt herself falling completely under Leona's spell.

"You're a bottom, and you're suggestible. You said as much in your answers to that what's-your-porn-star-identity test. I *know* I am pushing your buttons. Is it okay?"

Harmony nodded. She couldn't have formed the word *no* to save her life at that moment. She didn't know why she experienced sex this way, and she'd gotten hurt far too often, but sometimes it was glorious. Sometimes…maybe this time.

"Is it okay that we do this here? Are you going to get fired? I'm a top, but that doesn't mean I get to be destructive in your personal life and expect you to accept it. Being a top, to me, is not about hurting you, it's about protecting you."

"You can't tell anyone we did it here. Ever." She'd never let a business contact get under her skin this way, and Leona was under her skin, deeper even than that. A stranger, but not. A friend, but not. She'd made mistakes in the past about whom she could trust. Las Vegas was full of users. "I don't care if they know we fooled around, but not—"

"I'm not your ex. I won't be reckless with your reputation. Why would I tell someone else how vulnerable you are, and risk them figuring out what it took me a year to put together? No way, not when I want to be more to you than the hot, quick fuck we're about to have."

"Oh. Oh, my."

"That is, if you say yes."

All those e-mails, a dozen a day, short jokes, long, intense presentations of her position on some fine point of the hospitality contract, articulate, but never mean. Harmony dealt with a lot of people who thought resolution was achieved by yelling and insults. Leona had always been respectful of Harmony's position representing the hotel, even when they'd had tense exchanges about who was paying for the fresh flowers in the meeting rooms, or if the beverage allowance included mixed drinks or just wine. Discussions around money brought out the worst in people, but Leona had never crossed the line.

"Yes. Or no?"

Trying to take a deep enough breath to calm her nerves, Harmony asked, "If I say no, does that mean no forever?"

"Of course not." Leona reached halfway to Harmony's cheek, as if to caress her, then deliberately put her hands on the arms of the chair. "We'll resume this talk later, if you want to wait. I just thought…if you liked the story, that…"

"Yes." It came out as three syllables as Harmony failed to conquer the quaver in her voice. She hadn't been down this road before.

Leona gazed into Harmony's eyes for a long, long moment. "I promise that the way we are right now is not going to bleed over into who we have to be when the lights go on again, when you unlock the door."

Harmony wondered how Leona had known she needed to hear that. "Yes," she said more steadily.

Without a pause, Leona said, "Then take out my cock."

Her breath started coming in little gasps all over again. Harmony managed the button, the zipper, then reached inside. Leona's thighs were wet, lord she's as excited as I am, Harmony thought. She freed the warm silicone and greedily rubbed the tip against her panties, brushing her clit.

Leona helped Harmony slide out of her suit jacket, folding it neatly before resting it carefully across her satchel.

Harmony couldn't stop herself from shifting and grinding in Leona's lap.

"Do you have another pair of pants? I'm going to get yours all wet."

"I have that covered. Don't worry." Leona unbuttoned Harmony's standard-issue white business blouse, then smiled at the decidedly non-standard bra. "That's as lovely a sight as those garters. The staff uniform makes you look very professional, but I like seeing you this way."

Harmony shuddered as Leona trailed long fingers over the cups of her bra. She'd been expecting Leona's arrival yesterday or today, and had told herself it was only coincidence that she'd picked out her favorite lingerie. Her heartbeat was pulsing across her skin, responding to the simple caresses.

"Beautiful," Leona murmured. She unhooked the front clasp. "Show me."

Harmony ran her hands up her tummy, hoping she was at least a little bit coquettish, as alluring and sensual as the woman in Leona's story. She didn't want to be a fantasy, though; this was too real to her. Gazing into Leona's eyes, she eased her fingertips under the cups, slowly pulling them aside until it was Leona who looked down.

The sound Leona made when Harmony toyed with her nipples, then pinched them, showing how firmly she could be touched, that sound conquered what little trepidation Harmony had left.

"Thank you," Leona whispered just before taking one red, aching tip into her mouth.

Harmony ground down on Leona's lap, her fires at a full raging roar. "You have to…" She paused to find something like coherence. "You have to tell me to be quiet."

Leona looked up, a question in her eyes.

"If you don't tell me, I'll scream." That would be bad, she

wanted to add, but the deeply pleased gleam in Leona's eyes took her breath away, again.

"Oh goodness, you are turning into the woman I've been searching for all my life." Leona licked her lips. "Talk to me with your eyes. Tell me what you feel by the way you move on me. But no words, no cries, no moans."

Harmony looked her need at Leona, saying it all.

"Lift up," Leona said quietly, "and slide down on me. I want to hear you taking me inside you."

Harmony couldn't control how loudly her heart was beating, and she hoped that Leona understood that if she didn't gasp for air, she would faint. Even so, she was quiet enough, the room still enough to hear the wet sound of Leona pulling her panties aside, then the soft whisper of Leona's cock parting her folds, finding the place Harmony needed Leona to possess.

Leona thrust upward as if she could wait no longer to take Harmony all the way. "Hold still. Let me."

Harmony froze, her hands on Leona's shoulders. Leona pushed up again, harder then again, and again.

"Listen to you. Listen to your body loving what I'm doing."

Harmony nodded. She could hear it, inside and out. She was a bottom, but that didn't mean she craved wax or chains, or cleaning boots with her tongue. It wasn't about physical compulsion or dominance; it was about someone getting into her mind, working her brain from the inside so the outside could do what it was doing now. Giving by taking. Yielding every place in her by choice.

"Look at you." Leona gasped. "You're beautiful like this."

Sobbing in silence, Harmony came in convulsive explosions as Leona held back her own cry with gritted teeth. She collapsed into Leona's arms, her head on Leona's shoulder and they moved together again, slowly, rocking skin to skin.

Finally, Leona kissed her.

"Thank you," Harmony murmured. "I've never…" She didn't quite know what else to say. She stole a look at Leona's face and saw that the intense top was gone. The cherub, a little nervous and shy, was back.

"You get it, right?" Leona said quietly. "That I want this, but I want to see if we can have more than this, too?"

"I get it," Harmony said. "You've made me laugh every day for the past year, too. I think we'd be fools not to see if we can do that in real life. Because if you've got sex and laughter, you've got just about all you need."

Leona's arms tightened around her and she shifted just enough to wake up Harmony's stretched nerves and muscles all over again. She glanced at the clock on the desk, then realized Leona was doing the same.

The top came back. With deep pleasure, with joy, Harmony did exactly as she was told.

❖

"How are you going to explain what I did to your pants?" Harmony gave Leona another sheepish look as she fastened her bra and tried to regain her composure. She felt awed at the depths to which she had surrendered to Leona, and yet somehow powerful at the same time. The combination was new and very intriguing.

"I couldn't fit the toy *and* a pair of pants into the bottom of my satchel, so I decided honesty was the best policy." Leona picked up the cold cup of coffee on Harmony's desk. "Soon as you're ready, you're going to bolt for the bathroom for paper towels."

Harmony laughed. "Let me get my blouse tucked in."

"You really are beautiful," Leona said.

"Not everyone thinks so. My nose is too—"

"You're beautiful," Leona repeated. "Especially when you smile. And I would really like to take you out to dinner tonight."

She might just mean it, Harmony thought. "Dinner before or after that intimate buffet for one hundred and fifty, cash bar and slideshow A/V setup?"

"After." Leona grinned. "Dinner and breakfast."

"Yes." Harmony pulled on her jacket and adjusted the cuffs of her blouse. "There, I'm ready."

"Here goes nothing." Leona poured the coffee into her lap.

Laughing, Harmony unlocked the door and hurried to the bathroom.

SWITCH HANDS

Radclyffe

diting is such a bitch."

Jules Montgomery pushed back from the desk in her hotel room and rubbed her face with both hands. The generic black plastic digital clock on the bedside table read 7:45 p.m. She'd been working five hours—five hours that felt like fifty, and that's exactly what she'd accomplished, fifty pages of edits. After twenty-seven novels, she should have anticipated the fact that she could only manage ten pages an hour if she was truly, seriously editing. Critically appraising her technique, as opposed to just looking for spelling errors and egregiously repetitive language, took time. Time she was desperately short of. Why she had agreed to speak at this damn conference when she knew she had a deadline in ten days remained a mystery. Her agent would say it was because she always overestimated her abilities, and she would counter with the argument that she never missed a deadline or a scheduled engagement.

Still, alone in her hotel room on a Friday night—in Las Vegas, no less—even she had to admit that her life of all work and almost no play was wearing her down. No wonder she couldn't keep a girlfriend. No wonder she hadn't had sex with anyone, even a stranger, since that time three books ago that she'd hooked up with a bookstore manager one night after a signing. That had been an all too brief few hours that had left her physically satisfied but emotionally disquieted. She had to struggle not to ask herself, *Is that all there is?* She didn't want to believe she had nothing to look forward to except random encounters with attractive strangers, even if her recent experiences failed to suggest otherwise. She was, after all, a romance writer. She believed in fate and passion and love. If she didn't, she wouldn't be able to write about it, not as many times as she had.

"And this one's not going to write itself, either." She grimaced at her laptop. "Or edit itself."

She supposed she could slough off the edits for a while and work on her presentation for the romance panel the next afternoon, but that would be cheating. Putting together a thirty minute talk about something she loved to discuss wasn't nearly the same as wringing the last drop of emotion out of every single word on a page.

"Food. Food and a bottle of wine, and I can do anything. Even get through the last hundred pages of this manuscript."

Scrolling down the screen with one hand, Jules snagged the desk phone with the other and punched in the extension for room service from memory. One thing she loved about traveling was room service—not just the food, but the clean sheets and the fresh towels and the bed turned down every night. She'd never admit it, but she enjoyed being pampered. With the receiver tucked between her ear and shoulder, she deleted half a sentence and retyped it *without* the gerund as she listened to the phone ring. She'd have to run a search for the word suckle and expunge it from the manuscript. Whoever heard of a grown woman suckling anything, let alone a—

"Hello?"

Jules dragged her attention away from the screen. "Hi, this is—"

"You're late."

Frowning, Jules checked the clock. A few minutes to eight. The in-room dining menu stipulated full dinner service until eleven, and after that, "snacks" were available all night. If you didn't mind paying five dollars a potato chip.

"I'm sorry—"

"Sorry isn't good enough." A woman's voice flowed to her, low and almost playful.

Jules hesitated. "I just wanted to order—"

"You've suddenly acquired a taste for something new?"

"I'm sorry?" Jules realized she was repeating herself. Obviously, she needed an editor for more than just her manuscripts.

"Since when do you like to give the orders?"

"I'm sorry," Jules repeated, feeling like a parrot and not a particularly smart one. Didn't some of them have a vocabulary of five hundreds words? "Is this room service?"

"Well, that's one way of putting it."

Silence descended and Jules realized she was supposed to say something. Dialogue had always been her strong point, and now she was having trouble forming whole sentences. "To whom am I speaking?"

There, that came out nicely.

"You called me. Don't you know?"

"Uh…" Jules cleared her throat and looked around the room. Everything seemed perfectly normal. Just an ordinary $900 a night suite in an opulent Las Vegas casino hotel. Her shoes lay next to the bed, her trousers draped over a chair. Her briefcase sat open next to her on the floor. She was barefoot in boxers and a T-shirt, which was what she always wore when working. Everything was exactly as it should be, except some time in the last twelve hours she had developed a cognitive disorder of some kind and couldn't carry on a sensible conversation. "I just wanted a charbroiled hamburger and a bottle of Merlot."

"The last time we talked you wanted me to spank you until you came all over my silk stockings."

"That wasn't me," Jules whispered. And as she said the words, she suddenly wished it had been. She had a sudden image of being stretched over the creamy, bare thighs of a woman wearing a black silk camisole. A black lace bikini just covered the woman's shaved pussy, and black satin garters stretched taut to the top of black silk stockings. Jules's hard penis nestled between the woman's thighs. As a small hand struck Jules's ass sharply, she thrust downward, rubbing the flushed head against smooth skin. The swift stab of pleasure obliterated the pain and she knew with the next blow she would explode.

Jules blinked and the image disappeared. She looked down, almost surprised not to see an erection tenting her boxers. Her clitoris stiffened very nicely and rubbed against the cotton of her shorts. "I'm sorry. I have the wrong number."

"Are you sure?"

A foot away on the desk, the screen of her computer beckoned. She was used to escaping into other worlds, other lifetimes, other lives. Hers was a world of shifting boundaries, and sometimes reality was as fluid as a keystroke.

"Aren't you waiting for another call?" Jules asked.

The woman laughed. "He missed his chance, but the hour's paid for."

"Maybe he's trying to call right now."

"It will do him good to be disappointed. He's grown too confident."

"I feel sorry for him," Jules said.

"Do you?" Surprise. Curiosity. "Why?"

"I imagine he's been looking forward to this call all day."

Laughter. "He's been looking forward to it all week. I'm on a business trip, but I made a special date with him. After he begged."

"Are you going to punish him for being late?"

"Oh, yes. I'm going to tell him exactly what he missed."

The low, throaty voice washed over Jules as if hands were skimming over her skin. She heard rapid breathing and realized it was her own.

"Tell *me*," Jules urged.

"I'll do more than that. I'll show you." A pause. "Would you like that?"

"Yes. I would."

"Put this call on hold and take off your clothes. Then use the handset by the bed and tell me when you're lying down."

Jules pushed the hold button and sat for several seconds. She could disconnect the call and it would be all over. She could go back to her editing. She could prepare for the next day's presentation. She could spend the rest of the night alone. And she would never know the end of the story. Abruptly, she stood and pulled off her T-shirt, pushed her boxers down, and strode naked into the bedroom. She didn't turn on a light, but hurriedly picked up the phone.

"I'm here." Jules stretched out on her back, the phone resting on the pillow next to her ear.

"And what are you doing *here*?"

"I'm a writer," Jules said. "I'm here for a conference."

"I saw a horde of people with pens attacking several

women in the lobby the other day. Would one of those sought after women be you?"

"Probably not." Jules laughed. "I've signed a few autographs, but I don't usually incite a riot."

"What do you write?"

"Love stories." *No,* Jules thought, *they're more than that.* "Stories about women in love."

"And sex? Do you write stories about women having sex?"

Jules closed her eyes so she could concentrate on the voice. Alone in the darkness, the sound of the husky tones so very close to her ear created an intimacy that made her stomach tingle. "Yes. I write about women having sex."

"And you? Do you have sex with women?"

"Yes," Jules replied, feeling strangely relaxed. Almost languid. The room was warm and she lay naked on the sheets. "I have sex with women."

"And men?"

"No." Jules thought of the man who was supposed to be talking to this woman right now. She imagined him poised on the other end of the phone, having anxiously waited all week for the special call. He would be excited. Had probably been excited for hours, watching the clock, hearing the sultry voice in his mind, anticipating how it would feel when she whispered to him. "Do you only do this with men?"

"Do what?"

Jules brushed her hand over her belly and felt the muscles tense beneath her fingertips. Lazily, she circled her navel. "Have these private conversations with men."

"My clients want me to make them come. Usually they want me to make them *beg* to come. Men and women are all the same in that moment."

"I don't want you to make me come." Jules bent one

leg and rested the ball of her foot against her opposite knee. Lightly, she stroked up one thigh, over the delta between, and down the other.

"Aren't you excited?"

Jules tapped her finger lightly on her clitoris. She was hard and swollen and she had to force her hand away. If she started in on it now, she wouldn't want to stop until she came. "Yes. I am."

"Then you must want—"

"What do you do to make them beg?"

Jules heard the woman catch her breath, as if caught off guard. "I offer them the one thing they crave."

"What's that?" Jules skimmed her palm up the center of her stomach and then over her breasts. Her nipples tingled at the glancing caress. "What is it they want?"

"Permission. They want my permission. Permission to take pleasure. Permission to come, no matter what it is they need."

"When they come, do you feel the rush?"

"Yes," the woman said, her voice thick. "Yes, I feel it."

"But you don't come, do you?"

"No."

Jules rolled her nipple between her fingers, harder and faster until her clit jumped and her pelvis lifted from the bed. "When you hang up the phone, *then* you make yourself come, don't you?"

Jules could barely make out the choked reply. "Yes."

"It's hard to wait, isn't it? When you're so hard. And so wet." Jules slid a finger over her clit and between her lips. She was hot and thickly wet. She kept her fingertip pressed to the underside of her clitoris, but didn't caress it. The tense shaft throbbed against the length of her finger. Through the phone, she heard panting.

The woman had started masturbating, something she must deny herself during those other phone calls. Even though she wanted it. Even though she needed it. Self-denial was power, too.

"Sometimes you come without touching yourself, even when you don't mean to. Even when you don't want to."

"Yes." A strangled sound, half-sob, half-moan. "Are you making your clit hard right now?"

Jules pushed down against her hand and rubbed her clit rapidly for twenty seconds, then stopped. "No." But she couldn't smother her groan.

"You're lying," the woman laughed breathlessly.

"I know you're fondling your clit," Jules countered.

"Mmm. I am. God, I don't think I've ever been so big."

"Not even when you're making some poor guy come all over your black silk stockings?"

"They don't make me ache the way you do."

Jules curled one finger inside and massaged the spot that made her clit rigid. If she masturbated her clit at the same time, she'd orgasm right away. She pressed her finger to the hard core. "Ah. God."

"What are you doing?" The woman was gasping. "Are you making yourself come?"

"Is that what you want?" Jules's legs strained as her body arched off the bed.

"Yes. I want to hear you come."

"Will that make you come?" Jules started to work her clit between her fingers. Her stomach tightened and the telltale tingling began at the base of her belly.

"It will. You know it will."

"You don't come for them?"

"They don't want me to." Her voice sounded high and thin. "Their pleasure…oh, I'm getting closer." She gave a shuddering moan. "That's what they want. Their pleasure—not mine."

"Ours," Jules groaned. "I want ours. I'm coming. I'm coming now."

"I…I…"

A scream penetrated Jules's awareness as she writhed and twisted on the bed. When the last jolt of pleasure trailed away, she fumbled for the phone. "Don't go," she managed to croak. Seconds, minutes passed and only silence greeted her. Jules pressed a hand to her stomach, still aching from the powerful contractions. "Are you there?"

"Yes."

"Are you sorry you let yourself come?"

"I'm not sorry you made me come."

"I'm going to hang up soon and order that room service," Jules said.

Laughter, tinged with sadness.

"Will you join me?" Jules waited, utterly still.

"Should I plan on you switching hands on me again?"

Jules smiled. "I'd say that would be a safe bet."

"Then how could I possibly refuse?"

DEALER'S CHOICE

....

Radclyffe

"So, do you two want to come in for awhile?" Monica asked. "I'll break out some champagne and we can talk...or whatever."

I looked at my wife, Sheri, because Monica was her friend—well, work colleague, anyways—and this was Sheri's trip. I came along because I'd never been to Vegas and I wanted an excuse to get out of doing yard work for a week. Besides, Sheri and I hadn't had a chance to really cut loose since she'd taken the job as head librarian at the university at the same time I decided it was a good time to start my own business. Between the two of us, we'd been working fifteen hour days, six days a week, for over a year, and I couldn't remember the last time we had a night out that ended with us having wild sex until the sun came up. When we first got together, all-nighters, nooners, and quickies in the shower were daily fare. It wasn't that we'd lost interest; we just didn't end up in the same place at the same time, physically or otherwise.

We'd had plenty of sex since we got here, but after spending three hours in a strip club watching practically naked women slither around the stage, I was ready for more. Still, if Sheri wanted to spend some time with Monica and her girlfriend, Tate, I could handle it. When Sheri was ready, I knew I would be. I'd been pretty much ready twenty-four hours a day since the plane touched down.

"Well, if you're sure," Sheri said, looking from Monica to Tate then me.

"Fine by me," I said gamely.

"Oh yeah, it'll be fun." Monica, a small, tight-bodied brunette in a short, tight black skirt and clingy halter top, keyed the lock and held the door open. Tate, taller than Monica by half a head and far quieter, nodded in agreement.

Sheri took my hand, and we followed them inside. A sofa and loveseat sat at right angles in the lounge area of their suite. Tate sprawled on the sofa while Monica pulled bottles out of the minibar. Sheri snuggled in my lap on the loveseat. A minute later, Monica passed around champagne, then leaned down and whispered something in Tate's ear. Tate promptly set her glass aside, got up, and left the room.

"So what did you think of the show?" Monica asked, curling up in the corner of the sofa closest to us. I tried not to notice how high her skirt rode when she tucked her legs up under her. Her lean thighs were pale, smooth columns, and for just an instant, I imagined running my hand along them.

When I looked away, I saw Tate coming back. She grinned at me, and I had a feeling she was reading my mind. She was barefoot in jeans and a T-shirt and had a very respectable bulge along the inside of her left leg that hadn't been there earlier. I glanced from her crotch back up to her face and her grin grew wider. Automatically, I tightened my hold on my wife.

Tate dropped onto the couch next to Monica, slouching with her legs spread and her arm stretched out along the back of Monica's shoulders. While Sheri and Monica continued recapping the show, Monica casually settled her hand on Tate's thigh. Her fingertips came to rest an inch away from the head of Tate's cock, which was plainly outlined beneath the nearly threadbare denim. Sheri tensed in my lap, and I saw she was staring at Monica's hand. Or maybe she was staring at what was right next to Monica's hand.

"Don't you think so?" Monica asked brightly.

I jerked, realizing she was looking at me and expecting an answer. "Sorry, I missed that."

"I mean, I know it was all an act, but didn't you think it was kind of sexy all the same?" Monica smiled at me and slid her hand up to cover Tate's cock.

Sheri squirmed in my lap.

"Yeah," I said, feeling a little light-headed. "I thought it was sexy."

Monica leaned forward as if she were going to tell us a secret, affording both Sheri and me a good look at her breasts, which were small and firm and very nice. At the same time, she tightened her fingers around the length of Tate's cock and pulled enough to tent the denim. Tate half closed her eyes and my clit got so hard I wanted to leave right then.

"While I was watching those girls slide around the pole and touch themselves, I was imagining being up there on stage with everyone watching me," Monica confided. "It made me so horny."

"Teasing everyone," Sheri asked, "or being watched?"

Monica smiled and her hand moved a little faster between Tate's legs. Tate's fingers twitched on Monica's bare arm as if a fine electric current flowed through them. "Both."

"Baby," I murmured in Sheri's ear, "I think we ought to go."

Sheri shifted so she was sitting completely crosswise in my lap, her ass nestled into my crotch. She wrapped her arms around my neck and kissed me, her tongue deep in my mouth. Sheri's ass rolling over my clit felt so good, for a second I forgot about Monica and Tate. I sucked on her tongue and skimmed my hand over the outside of her breast. She purred her approval and I worked my hand under the bottom of her Lycra top. She wasn't wearing a bra, and when my thumb skated across her small, hard nipple, she moaned. I slipped my other hand down to her ass and heard another moan. Except it wasn't Sheri's voice. Still kissing her, I tilted my head and shot a glance toward the sofa next to me. Monica had Tate's cock out and was bent over Tate's lap, sucking her. Tate was watching *us*, her face slack as she caressed Monica's hair. Monica's head bobbed in Tate's lap as she followed her fist up and down Tate's cock, and I wondered if she'd forgotten about us.

I could tell Sheri was too into kissing me to notice what was going on a few feet away. I stopped kissing her and nodded in their direction. Sheri blinked and gaped as Tate fucked Monica's face.

"Baby," I whispered again, "we should go unless you want—"

"I want you to play with my nipples some more," Sheri muttered and dove back into my mouth.

The more I squeezed and tugged, the harder Sheri squirmed in my lap, and the less I cared what Monica and Tate were doing. When Sheri arched her back and yanked her top up to expose her breasts, I didn't think twice about latching on to her nipple with my mouth. I sucked her and she dug her fingers into my hair and chanted *oh, baby, yeah, yeah, that feels so good.*

Next to me, Tate finally spoke. "I'm fixing to come in your mouth."

Monica sat up, her dark hair swinging around her face. "You are not. You're going to come inside of me." She gripped Tate's cock in her dainty fist and grinned over her shoulder at Sheri and me. "Sheri, want to see which one of them can hold out the longest? I bet yours will come before mine."

Sheri laughed, a wild light in her eyes. "Want to play, lover?"

I knew *sh*e did, and that was almost enough to get me off in my pants. I might as well let her have it the way she wanted it. "Sure, baby. Whatever you want."

"Okay, what are the rules?" Sheri said to Monica.

"You suck her off while I fuck Tate. And you can't stop. The first one of them to come, loses."

"Tate will lose," Sheri said confidently as she climbed down from my lap and knelt between my legs.

Monica hitched up her skirt and swung around to straddle Tate's narrow hips, positioning herself above Tate's cock. She faced us with her ass against Tate's belly. "I'm going to make sure you don't cheat."

Sheri unzipped my trousers and I lifted my hips so she could pull them down. Then she got up tight between my legs, her hands resting against the inside of my thighs. Just seeing her there made my clit double in size. I didn't think Tate was going to lose. I thought I'd last about a minute once she started sucking me. I glanced over at Tate. She had one hand on Monica's hip and the other steadying her cock so Monica could slide down it. She was breathing fast and I didn't think she had too long to go either. Maybe I did have a chance.

"Let's go then," Monica said and settled down on Tate's cock, taking her all the way in with one smooth, easy glide. She shivered. "Oh God. She's big."

"So's she," Sheri murmured and closed her lips around my clit. She swept her tongue around me once and then started to suck.

My vision went hazy for a second, and I really wanted to let go and come right then, but I remembered I wasn't supposed to. I needed a diversion, something, anything to take my mind off the way Sheri pumped my clit in and out between her pursed lips like it was a lollipop. Next to me, Tate gripped Monica's ass and stared, transfixed, into her lap as Monica rode up and down the length of her cock. Tate grunted softly, open mouthed, each time Monica slammed down on her. I imagined how that must feel, the warm, firm base of the cock banging against her clit, and mine popped up and twitched like crazy.

"Watch it," I groaned, and Sheri backed off to give me a break.

"No fair," Monica gasped, "you have to keep doing her."

Sheri teased me with the tip of her tongue, and I gripped the edges of the sofa cushion and tried not to come in her face. Tate whined and I knew she was getting ready to come. Monica made little whimpering sounds every time she shafted herself, and I knew she was right there too. I just needed to hold on another few seconds. Desperately, I grabbed Sheri's head with both hands and held her mouth still with my clit just resting between her lips. It jumped against her mouth with every beat of my heart. She gazed up at me, her eyes hungry, and flicked at me with her tongue. She knew that would make me come and it did. I swore, but the curses were drowned out by Tate.

"Fuck," Tate yelled, sounding like she was in pain. "Fuck fuck fuck, I'm coming."

I pushed my clit into Sheri's mouth and let her suck me off the rest of the way. It hit me so hard I felt like I'd been punched in the gut. I didn't hear anything for quite a while except the roar of blood through my head.

"Who won?" I finally heard Sheri ask.

"It was a tie." Monica's voice high and tight. I forced my eyes open and focused on her. She was still riding, and her eyes were huge black pools of need.

"Want to see"—Monica grinned unsteadily at Sheri—"which of us can last the longest?"

Instantly, Sheri climbed into my lap and pushed my hand between her legs. She was hot and wet and her clit stood up between the slick folds. "Okay. But you have to rub your clit, too."

Monica's hand flew to her clit and she started circling. "Mmm. I'm so hard." She looked at me. "Is she hard too?"

I squeezed Sheri's clit between my thumb and forefinger, right at the base, where she liked it. I rolled it a little bit, and Sheri's legs trembled. "Very hard."

"Are you squeezing it?" Monica stopped pumping up and down the cock and eased back against Tate's body with it deep inside her. She rested her head on Tate's shoulder and watched us. Tate reached around Monica's body and started to play with her breasts. Monica fondled her clit, massaging it with one finger. Her clit was the same color as her blood red fingernail.

"Squeezing *and* stroking," I replied. Sheri was breathing unevenly against my neck, and I knew from the way her clit felt she was going to come soon. When she was this hard, she couldn't control it. I figured Monica had a head start and couldn't last long either. In fact, from the way her head twisted from side to side, she had to be barely holding on.

"I bet Tate's big, fat cock feels good inside you, doesn't it?" I whispered, hoping to push Monica over the edge a little faster. After all, I wanted Sheri to win this little contest.

"Oh my God," Monica moaned, "it feels so so good. Makes me want to come so bad."

Sheri whimpered and clamped her hand over mine, pushing and pulling my fingers up and down her clit. That wasn't exactly the response I had hoped for.

"Hold on, baby," I whispered.

"I can't," Sheri wailed. "I want to *come*."

Oh well, fuck the contest. If Sheri needed it, I was going to give it to her.

"Okay, baby, okay." I slid three fingers inside her and worked her clit with my thumb. "You go ahead and come right here in my hand."

"Oh yeah," Sheri whimpered, sucking on my neck. She was going to leave a mark. "Oh yeah, you're making me come."

Sheri jerked upright in my lap, both hands clamped around my wrist, holding me inside. Her eyes were wide and dazed as she stared at Monica. "Watch me. I'm coming."

Monica writhed on Tate's cock, her hand a blur between her legs, her lips parted in a silent scream.

I held Sheri around the waist as she bent nearly double, coming over and over on my fingers in gushing waves. Monica finally found her breath and started begging for Tate to fuck her. Tate dug her heels in and obliged, thrusting her hips and her cock in and out while Monica masturbated furiously, making herself come, from the sounds of it, one orgasm right on top of another.

"Oh God," Sheri sighed, slumping back into my arms. "I came so hard I thought I was going to break something. Are you all right?"

I eased my hand out from between her legs, happy I could still feel my fingers. "I'm better than all right."

Monica was finally winding down at last. Her lids fluttered open and she smiled weakly at Sheri. "Was that a tie?"

"I think it was too close to call." Sheri dragged my hand back to her breast and I obediently fingered her nipple.

"Maybe we should go another round," Monica suggested.

"What do you say, lover?" Sheri started to slow grind in my lap again.

"Sure. As long as I get to deal this hand."

Sheri glanced over at Monica. "Okay?"

Monica gave us both a slow smile. "Call the game. We'll play."

TWENTY-ONE

Karin Kallmaker

wear to freakin' god, look at this place!" Liddy did
a little dance as she ogled the big roulette wheel,
the recessed area where poker tables were lined up
like green jewels, the gleaming rows of slot machines, and
over there they were playing baccarat, craps, *everything*. "Kid.
Candy store. Me!"

Marian laughed and gave her an indulgent look. "I'll go
to my workshop and you play the tables. But stick within your
budget, okay?"

"I know." She gave Marian her most innocent look. "I can
stretch a dollar a long, long way." She glanced around—they
were a long way from the openness of Iowa City—and there
seemed to be plenty of coupled up women nearby. With a
resounding smooch, she bounded away to the change machine.
Video poker was her first stop.

Twenty minutes and twenty dollars later, she thought if
she wanted to just throw her money away, she could play keno.

Buy an Edge or Top-Bottom ticket and kiss ten bucks good-bye. Or she could buy tickets to one of the many shows. The ones she could afford were likely still more entertaining than slot machines that ate her quarters like Marian's dog ate kibble, and that included the Engelbert Humperdinck imitators. She wished she could win something and afford tickets to Melissa or Madonna.

Banish that thought, she told herself. Feeling desperate to win attracted losing. It wasn't logical, but it was true.

She had her employer's hundred dollars, a gift for "research" Dana Moon had said. She was to spend it on blackjack, then write down every last impression she had of being an unskilled player at a middle stakes table.

Ten minutes later, she tapped Loser from loserville, that's what it feels like into her PalmPilot. Swear to freakin' god, she'd never seen cards so bad. She'd had twelve, three times, and gotten a ten every hand. Nobody busts with twenty-two three times in a row, ka-ching, ka-ching. The dealer had looked a little chagrinned.

She glanced at her watch. Marian would be another hour at least. She would have gone along to watch her mostest favorite librarian participate on a panel discussion of cultural sensitivity in the labeling and display of young adult titles, but she was sort of banned from the proceedings because of last year. Not officially banned, but that idiot guy had *so* not known what he was talking about, and in her opinion any librarian who supported a censorship position ought to go to work at the department of motor vehicles alphabetizing license plates.

Marian had tried to calm her down after the altercation. "Liddy, honey, I know you love to ask questions, and I have never seen anyone who loves a good debate like you—"

Liddy had snarled in the general direction of petty fascists the world over. "Debate? I was kicking his ass, and if he calls you *little lady* one more time, I'm gonna kick his ass for real."

"Honey, I know you feel strongly about it, and I know you really can kick his ass because I saw you get your black belt, but you can't go around kicking the asses of the members of the board. Especially when you're not a librarian and you aren't even a paid attendee at the conference."

When Marian was right, she was right, and Liddy had learned to accept it. And when she'd asked Liddy not to go into any of the sessions this year, and hinted she was just passing on a more or less official request, Liddy had promised to be good.

The panel was probably boring Marian out of her mind. She could hear her love right now explaining that librarians did not act *in loco parentis*, and that any so-called child with the wherewithal to find a book ought to be able to check that book out, and any parents who wanted to keep a firm grip on what their children were reading had the perfect recourse of not letting their children have their own cards. It was that simple. But no, parents wanted to park their children at the library after school for a couple of hours, and then got upset when their children actually *used* the library to look up stuff that interested them. Number one search for males aged fifteen to eighteen was sex. Number two, sex. Number three, cars. Number four, cars and sex in cars.

So, she could see about making her next twenty dollars last an hour—unlikely—or she could think of something else to amuse herself.

Text messages were free, she thought. She punched up Marian's number and asked her if she was able to get texts.

Marian replied her bit was over and she was seated in the audience and asked what was wrong. Liddy loved the economy of Done, off dais, okay?

1 Liddy texted back. A walk in a thunderstorm.
?
2 Your shirt soaked to your skin. There was no reply, and Liddy was pretty sure she had Marian's attention. 3 My shirt soaked to my skin.

Well, maybe she should play a little bit more video poker.

Her next twenty bucks lasted longer because she stopped after every dollar or so lost to send Marian another text.

4 Chasing drops of rain down your throat with my tongue, followed an ill-advised attempt to draw to an inside straight.

She had drawn a spade to go with four diamonds when a reply from Marian arrived. She smiled fondly as she read: 5 You make love like you eat.

Maybe she could find a pint of ice cream and a spoon and invite Marian upstairs for a memorable lunch. A couple of clicks on the poker machine brought her a modest return in the form of three of a kind. For ten minutes, she played happily, not quite losing, then her fortunes took another turn for the worse.

6 Against the door.

Immediately she got back: 7 You naked. Me not.

She shivered. Five years and that still turned her on. Marian the Librarian was really playful, and the best part was nobody suspected, so there were no nympho-femmes trying to poach her girl. Liddy hadn't known she was a nympho-femme until Marian.

She looked down when her phone buzzed. 8 Shower?

9 Your favorite word, yes.

Marian didn't answer, so it was possible she had to actually talk to people or something. Liddy cashed out what was left of her money in the poker machine and carried the quarters to a good ol' Lucky 7 slot machine. Plink-plink-plink, spin-whirl-click, gone-gone-gone.

Maybe she should try a different casino, but she didn't want to leave. It was rather nice to have more women than men in the hotel, and there were librarians everywhere. Attendees for the Escort Services International group were also in evidence, and there were even some faces she recognized as famous romance writers.

Marian said that writers and librarians were natural pairings, and even if Liddy wasn't a writer, she did research for one, which made them even more ideal as mates. What Liddy couldn't find, Marian could. They'd lie in bed at night talking about search strings and cataloging, total geeks, then Marian would take off her glasses, take off Liddy's clothes, and in the morning there were towels and sheets to wash. Marian's favorite flannel sheets hadn't survived their first year.

Her phone buzzed. 10 All my fingers, all over you.

Well, okay, Liddy had started her little game thinking to make Marian crazy, but at the moment, Marian was getting the upper hand. She laughed, startling the man on the stool next to her. What else was new? Marian always had the upper hand, and they both really liked it that way. 11 plus your tongue.

12 Our first night together, you.

Oh, Marian was not playing fair. Liddy abandoned the slot machine as the memories of that first night washed over her. She'd not known just how multi-orgasmic she could be. She'd not been that way with anyone else, and wonderful Marian had decided that just because Liddy didn't know she *could*, that wasn't the same as knowing she *couldn't*.

Marian, again. 13 The next day and night.

Now she was just showing off. 14 Hours it took you to call me after.

15 Times I've said sorry.

16 Times I've said sorry for bringing it up. Oh dear, things were not going the way she intended.

17 Favorite thing: Make up sex?

Liddy laughed, relieved. Her steps turned toward the conference center. 18 Yes, please. Now.

19 Minutes I have left in this session.

20 Minutes till I see you in our room.

21 This afternoon, you.

Liddy blushed and was so glad no one else could see the display. When Marian got in these moods and wanted to see how often Liddy could... Nympho-femme, she thought, and don't say that like it's a bad thing.

She sent back: Game over. I've won all I need, all I want.

❖

"What I love," Marian whispered against Liddy's breasts, "is feeling like I make your fantasies come true."

Liddy was incredibly pleased with the status of the world, the cosmos, and the praline truffle ice cream that had not quite melted all the way. It had made for a wonderful snack before Marian decided they should shower and go back to bed. "You make fantasies come true that I didn't even know I had. That's the really amazing part."

"Want some more to come true?"

"Not right now—I mean, yes, actually." Liddy grinned at her lover.

"You have the most amazing eyes," Marian said. "The goddess was playing with the most beautiful blues and greens when she conceived you."

Liddy redirected Marian's hand from between her legs to her breast.

"If you don't want that, what do you want?" Marian tweaked Liddy's nipple, which responded as it always did even after the hours of fun.

"You." Liddy ruffled the short hair that curled ever so slightly on Marian's forehead. "You don't need the way I do, but I know that you need. I told you the first time we were together I wasn't a pillow queen."

"You never have been. That you let me play with you the way I do is one of the ways you make love to me."

Liddy tweaked Marian's nipple exactly the way Marian was touching hers. She'd learned that the confident lover who could be so aggressive and so thorough needed a few minutes to fade before a more vulnerable woman emerged, one who could let Liddy see her need.

Tapping into a patience she did not normally possess but had learned to nurture, Liddy stroked Marian's hair. They had already had five years of passion—passion for their work, their friends, each other. Learning to take and give had been so important.

"We're going to miss out on baseball theme night," Marian said. Her playful tone was at odds with the need now showing in her eyes.

"Don't let me be selfish," Liddy whispered. "It's not good for me." She touched the tip of her tongue to Marian's earlobe, then rubbed her lips along Marian's cheek and jaw.

Marian exhaled, a small sound that Liddy knew was surrender to Liddy taking control. With a purr of pleasure, Liddy peeled Marian's T-shirt off, glad that the skittishness that she had first encountered when making love to Marian was long gone.

"I love you," she said, knowing Marian needed to hear it. She slid one arm under Marian's shoulders, pulling her close while her other hand explored the wonderful, full breasts. She wanted to say, "Beautiful," but Marian's gentle butch objected to the word. Instead, she held the word in her mouth as she kissed Marian slowly, luxuriously. No one had ever made her feel as if she could read minds, interpret the most subtle body language the way Marian did. It was a powerful feeling that sprang from intimacy, not the mind games they had both endured in their exes.

Marian loved her touch, and it still went right to her head, a different kind of dizzy arousal than what she'd already experienced. She stayed close, drowning them both in kisses while her hand finally dipped between Marian's legs.

The explosion of wetness made her whimper. She drenched her fingers with it, brought them to her mouth, tasted and licked, then painted Marian's lips with the wonderful essence. More kisses, her fingers again dipping, pressing, then finally, sliding inside.

"Oh, yes." Marian arched into their kisses, shuddering under Liddy's hand.

"I'm right here, darling." Liddy breathed out the reassurance, felt it unknot the tension in Marian's shoulders, spreading down her body until her legs parted. She was suddenly so wet that Liddy's hand was swimming. "I know this is what you need."

She pressed inward, smooth and steady, drawing a hoarse, sharp cry out of Marian that turned into an ecstatic, exultant, "Yes!"

My favorite word, too, Liddy thought. *Our favorite word*.

After a few minutes of increasingly languid kisses and murmured reassurances, Liddy smooched away the faint hint of tears in the corners of Marian's eyes. "Love you, and I love doing that to you."

"Baseball night," Marian mumbled. "We're missing out."

"Sleep." She watched Marian's eyelids droop.

"But it's our last night. You wanted to gamble."

"Don't need to. I'm already the winner."

Marian's hand tightened on hers, then slowly went limp. Liddy smiled into Marian's hair, and after one more sigh of contentment, joined her in sleep.

NO LIMIT
....

Radclyffe

I wondered if she thought I wouldn't notice that she was staring. Even though I sat on a raised platform at a table with five other panelists in a crowded conference room, I could feel her eyes on me. All 300 seats were filled, being as *The Erotic Transformation of Romance Fiction* was a popular topic for writers, booksellers, and librarians—like me. I didn't write books, nor did I sell books. I just loved books. I loved the way they felt, the way they smelled, the way they looked lined up on a shelf with the spine text all neatly aligned. I loved the anticipation of the first page and the bittersweet pleasure of the final sentence. Most of all, I loved the adventure, the discovery, the wondrous revelations that held me captive and, every so often, if I was very lucky, left me wanting.

Someone in the audience asked me a question and I answered automatically, smiling by reflex after years of dealing with the public. I made eye contact with the questioner, before broadening my gaze to take in the entire room, including everyone in the discussion. But always, no matter where I pretended to look, I was aware of her standing at the back of the room, her face partly shadowed by the column she leaned against. She should have been too far away for me to see her clearly, but I could make out her features as distinctly as if she stood before me. I knew she was a stranger, just as surely as I recognized her in some deep, visceral way. Her eyes were dark, as was her thick, slightly wavy collar length hair. Her body was long and slender, almost thin, and the deep-charcoal tailored jacket and trousers accentuated her austere appearance. She stood with her arms folded across her chest, one shoulder tilted against the cool white marble support. A flash of gold winked at her waistline and on the small finger of her left hand. She had been watching me since the moment she walked into the room, her gaze like hot sunshine on my cheek.

"Thank you all so much for participating," I heard the session moderator say, and in an instant the stage was deluged by eager audience members. I answered questions, made reading recommendations, and handed out the bibliographies I had prepared for those who wanted to research the topic further. When we were finally forced to vacate the room for the next session, I made my way down the central aisle, my focus on the far corner of the room. She was gone, and I laughed inwardly at the sharp pang of disappointment. Of course she was gone, as far from my reach as the women in the pages of the books whose passion I guiltily took as my own.

With my briefcase in hand, I quickly crossed the lobby, skirting around the long line of conference goers that had formed to pick up a complementary box lunch. I preferred to eat alone, somewhere quiet, with my thoughts and, yes, my fantasies for company. Balancing the social requirements of an event like this against my innate need for privacy was a constant challenge, and one that tired me. Unfortunately, Las Vegas casinos were not known for quiet or privacy—everything was geared toward constant stimulation, feeding the adrenaline rush that kept people on the edge, kept people awake, kept people taking a chance. As I crossed the gaming floor, I envied the jubilant, almost frenzied gamblers. They were so alive, the very air reverberated with the collective pounding of their hearts. In contrast, I felt like a shadow, a closed book waiting to be opened so life could begin.

Shaking my head, I tried to dispel the unsettling images. I didn't often allow myself the luxury of self-analysis. Despite my frequent feelings of being not quite part of the world around me, I had work that I loved and pleasures that satisfied me. I spied an overstuffed chair next to a small table tucked into a corner of one of the many lounges bordering the main casino, and changed course to claim it. That was when she stepped out of the shadows as if she had been waiting for me. Even though it was the middle of the afternoon in August, inside the casino it was perpetual "any time," neither night nor day. With no clocks, no windows, and only the artifice of fabricated worlds as a backdrop, it was easy to lose touch with reality. Or whatever passed for reality anywhere but here.

"Chase Rogers," I said, recognizing her now from book cover photos that didn't do her justice. Up close, I was struck by the perfect pallor of her skin. Not so much the absence of color, but an ethereal translucent white that made her appear flawless and timeless and as nearly untouchable as Michelangelo's *David*. Nearly untouchable, because I had an overwhelming, completely irresistible desire to run my fingers over the faultlessly etched curve of her cheekbone. And I did, with just the tips of my fingers. Her skin was as smooth and cool as I expected. Carved marble.

"I'm sorry." I dropped my hand. "I have no idea why I did that."

"Perhaps because I wanted you to."

The rich timbre of her voice struck me deep inside, like tinder bursting into flame, and I knew I would do anything she desired. Distantly, I was aware of people passing by, but it seemed as if we existed in a circle outside the everyday realm of ordinary lives. Her gaze never left my face, and she hadn't moved closer to me, but I felt as if she was exploring my body in the most intimate of ways. My face flushed and I felt a stirring between my legs. Incapable of moving, I clutched at the gossamer strands of reality before they completely slipped away.

"I love your books."

"You don't find them too violent? Or too dark?"

"No, I don't find consuming passion too violent. I don't believe that needs so deep you bleed from them are dark, only powerful. After all, blood is life."

"And what would a vampire story be without blood?" Chase's pale, perfectly shaped lips thinned slightly, with what might have been regret.

"Incomplete," I said immediately and saw her eyes, which I had first taken to be a deep brown, suddenly become so black the irises nearly merged with the molten centers. I couldn't look away, and feared I would never want to.

"Are you here alone?" Chase asked.

"You know I am," I answered, certain it was true without understanding how.

She held out her hand. "Come."

Her long, tapered fingers were cool as they closed around mine, and as she clasped my arm close to her body, I felt the power in her deceptively slender frame. I was aware of hallways, an elevator, a door opening, but I viewed these commonplace things as if through shifting fog. A sharp, pungent odor swirled around us, like leaves burning on a cold autumn night. My skin tingled as if I had stepped from a hot springs into a frigid snow. My blood rushed so close to the surface, I felt more acutely alive than I ever had before. Beside me, Chase moved with effortless grace, her expression unreadable, at once intense and remote.

Then I was inside a room unlike any I had seen in the hotel thus far. The windows were covered with heavy brocade drapes, the dark, richly papered walls lost to shadow. The only illumination came from a heavily shaded lamp in one corner of the bedroom just beyond the room in which I stood. The bed was raised, with gleaming carved posts at each corner. The very air felt thick and languid against my skin.

I dropped my briefcase on a nearby chair and started forward without invitation, knowing my destiny as if I had been in this place before. Chase caught my hand and turned me back to face her.

"Do you know me?" she asked simply.

"I feel like I do." In the low light, her skin took on color and mine blanched until the hand I extended to touch her once again was the same shimmering white as her face. I wondered if my eyes had turned from blue to the fathomless black depths that looked back at me. "I recognized you this afternoon." I touched my breast, over my heart. "Here."

Chase made a sound low in her throat that was half moan, half growl before clasping my shoulders and pulling me to her. Her mouth on mine was hot in the way ice burns, and I opened to a heat that was not flame, but something far more dangerous. Through my half-closed lids the room took on a hazy red glow and I would have fallen if Chase had not wrapped one arm around my waist, cleaving me to her. Her body was hard, power beyond simple strength rippling beneath the surface. I

RADCLY/FE & KARIN KALLMAKER

pushed her jacket from her shoulders and she freed one arm, then the other, never letting me slip out of her embrace. Tilting my head back, I offered my throat while I pulled at her shirt, knowing I was tearing the fine linen and not caring. When I slid my hands beneath the pale weave, I touched perfection. Sleek, flawless skin, perfect breasts—as pristine and pure as driven snow. I caressed her, brushing my fingertips over her small, hard nipples until she groaned against the base of my neck. I felt the graze of her teeth, careful and restrained. When I gripped the back of her head and urged her to plunder, she pulled away.

"No." And for the first time, her implacable countenance faltered. She trembled as I stroked her breasts, and I saw hunger smoldering in her eyes, a hunger that went deeper than anything I might touch.

"Yes." I retreated from her embrace but gripped her arm, compelling her to follow me to the bed. I felt her reluctance but would not let her deny us what we both craved. "Yes."

I held her gaze as I unbuttoned my blouse, unzipped my skirt, and removed each article of clothing until I was completely nude. She watched me, strangely helpless, as if the slightest movement would break the spell and we would find ourselves once more in the brightly lit, noise-filled chaos of the other world. The world where we had never belonged but lived as exiles, incomplete and forever wanting.

"Please," I whispered, reaching for the gold belt buckle at her waist. I opened her belt, then worked the zipper down. Hooking my fingers over the waistband, I searched her eyes. I saw worlds in them, past, present, future, sliding around me and over me and through me until I was dizzy. "Please."

And then the landscape beneath the dark mirror of her eyes shifted, and flames leapt in them. She tore her shirt away and cast the remnants aside. Then she grasped my arms and pushed me down on the bed, following an instant later after she'd shed her clothes. When I reached up to draw her into my arms, she clasped my wrists, one in each hand, and forced my arms down to the bed. At the same time, she knelt between my thighs, forcing my legs apart, so that I lay exposed, arms outstretched, legs open to accept her as she curved above me, a specter of fire and ice.

"Touch me," I begged, and she brought her weight down upon me, roaming my neck with her mouth as she fit her sex to mine. My skin burned wherever hers touched mine, and I writhed beneath her, swollen and hot. Although she kept my arms pinned so I could not hold her, I wrapped my legs around her thighs. She was hard against my hardness, wet against my wetness. When I rubbed myself against her, she moaned and I felt the sharp bite of teeth at my throat.

"Take me," I urged, thrusting up as she bore down between my legs. Blood pounded, thick and heavy, in my loins, making my clitoris pulse in time to the beat of my heart. Our one heart. "Fuck me, please."

She released one arm and kissed me as she slipped her hand between us. I cried out against her mouth as she filled me with those long, cool fingers that heated me inside until I felt my body turn to flame. I cupped her neck, refusing to let her draw away as I thrust my tongue into her mouth, exchanging fire for fire. She pushed deeper inside me, and I felt my orgasm ripple and spread from the tight walls around her fingers to the base of my clitoris and down my legs. I tossed my head and felt a sharp pain in the side of my tongue. Then I tasted blood. My blood. My blood, her fire, our passion.

She jerked her head away, crying hoarsely, "No."

"Don't stop, I'm coming," I moaned, as she reared back. I reached for her as she knelt between my thighs, her arm as hard as stone between my legs. "I'm coming. Please."

"Remember me," she whispered as she bowed her head over my body and drove me to orgasm, once and then a second time, until the breath left my body and I pleaded helplessly for her to stop.

She was so beautiful, kneeling between my legs, and through the haze of my own pleasure, I thought I saw her eyes glow red, as if reflecting the passion she had unleashed upon my body. Reaching down, she began to draw the sheet over my body, but I found the strength to raise myself and still her hand.

"You haven't come," I murmured, cupping her cheek as I kissed her. My fingers were so hot now that she felt even cooler. "What do you need?"

"Nothing," she said, her voice thick and low. "You've given me everything I need."

I framed her face with both hands and searched her eyes. The fire still burned in them. "Not quite everything."

Finding her hand, I drew it to me and pressed her fingertips to the place where the pulse still beat hard and heavy between my thighs. "I need you, too. I need you inside me. I need to be inside of you. Please don't say no."

"You don't know—"

"I do." I kissed her, my hands in her hair, my breasts against her breasts, my tongue searching for what we both needed. I felt a small stab of pain again and then the clean, coppery taste of my blood. She trembled and would have pulled away, but I would not let her. She was so much stronger than I, but her need made her weak. Now, in the heat of our wanting, I was the stronger one. I guided her down as I lay back, until her face brushed the inner curve of my thigh.

"Take me," I whispered for the second time that night. "Drink me," I implored, for the first time in my life.

Still, she tried to resist, but I pressed myself to her mouth. Her tongue was soft, her mouth gentle, her hands careful as she entered me again. I caressed her jaw as she kissed me, her fingers taking me closer to coming with each stroke.

"I'm close, I'm close," I told her. "Please, come with me."

She groaned, and I felt the last of her resistance fall before the rising tide of our singular need. Then a wave of heat like nothing I'd ever felt before seared through my being, burning a pathway to my heart, to my soul, to a place beyond time. She filled me and I filled her, with all that we were.

When I awakened, the sheet covered me and she was gone. I bent my leg and saw the small shadow of a bruise in the bend of my thigh. In a few hours, it would be gone. In a few hours, she might be gone. But I didn't intend to wait that long. I swung my legs over the side of the bed and reached for my clothes.

I intended to find her. What is life, after all, if not the flame of passion?

HARD TEN

....

Radcly*f*fe

*J*ust as Micki Wright laid her chips on the Pass Line and held out her hand to accept the dice from the stickman, a deeply tanned blonde with ocean blue eyes and short, sleek hair edged up to the craps table opposite her and nodded as if they were acquaintances. They weren't. Micki had never seen her before. She didn't forget women built like her—etched muscles in her biceps and forearms, broad swimmer's shoulders tapering to a narrow waist—and all of it nicely showcased in a black silk T-shirt stretched tight over prominent pectorals and small, neat breasts. Micki couldn't see much of her black jeans, but she had no trouble imagining the toned thighs and firm ass that had to be there. After a few brief seconds admiring the very impressive package, Micki turned her attention back to the table.

"Dice are out, hands high," the stickman called, and the players around the long, narrow table lifted their hands off the rail. Micki shook the dice and let them fly. They bounced off the far rail, and the gamblers drew a collective breath as the small red cubes came to rest. "Natural seven," the stickman announced. Everyone cheered, and the dealers paid out the bets.

The blonde gave Micki an approving nod and a smile that said, *very nice*, and Micki's stomach did a little roll. The dice came back to her and she had to look away from the captivating face to place her chips and shoot again. Her come out roll was an easy eight, and excitement built around the table. She threw again—a fever five, then an easy four, and finally, a three and five.

The stickman announced, "Winner eight," and the guy in Bermuda shorts and Hawaiian shirt standing next to her clapped her on the shoulder, collected his chips, and left the table. The blonde took his place.

"Nice shooting." Her voice was chocolate smooth, dark and creamy with a rich aftertaste. Micki's stomach tightened a little more and her clit bucked in her jeans. She supposed anyone watching would think them mirror opposites, her with her dark hair and eyes and white T-shirt versus the blonde in black. Micki had worn a sports bra, but not a heavy one, and since her nipples were as hard as her clit, she knew they had to be obvious if anyone cared to look. Apparently, the blonde did, because she dropped her gaze for an instant, then looked into Micki's eyes. "*Very* nice."

"Thanks." Micki's throat was dry and her drink was empty, but she wasn't passing the dice while she was winning. Besides, she wasn't sure she was reading the signals right. She couldn't imagine she was the kind of woman the blonde would go for. Micki had almost as many muscles as her, and she gave off "top" vibes even though that wasn't always the case. And if she hadn't been planning to spend the evening in such a public place, she might have been packing. She wouldn't be surprised if the blonde had a little something extra behind the buttons of her 501s herself. No, the appreciation she was picking up on was probably just friendly approval from one stud to another.

Micki let loose the dice and rolled double fives—a hard ten. Next to her, the blonde placed a huge chip stack betting that Micki would hit the point. Micki wanted to win for her. She wanted to please her. Didn't matter that she didn't know her. She just wanted to see her eyes light up again. She rolled the dice, and a relieved sigh flowed around the table when an eight came up, and not a seven. She was still alive. She rolled a six. Then she glanced at the blonde, who nodded encouragingly, and let the dice fly. Double fives came up. Yes!

"Hard ten again," the blonde murmured, resting her hand in the small of Micki's back. "You're good."

It could be just a friendly gesture, but Micki's legs went weak. She pocketed her chips and passed the dice to the guy next to her. Then she turned to the woman whose hand still rested on her back. "Let me buy you a drink."

"I'd like that," the blonde said, "but I'm already late for an engagement."

"Oh, sure. Got it." Of course, she'd have a date. They stepped away from the table and others immediately took their place. People hurriedly brushed past them, anxious to get to their addiction of choice—the bar, the gaming tables, the slots, or just the teeming streets where anything goes and everyone keeps your secret.

"Listen, why don't you come with me?" the blonde said. "One of the sponsors is throwing this bash, and they always provide *all* the entertainment."

"What do you do?" Micki asked, stalling while she tried to get a read on the invitation.

"I'm a poker pro. One of the online franchises sponsors me." The blonde held out her hand. "Fenn Anderson."

Micki shook her hand, liking the strength in Fenn's long fingers and noticing that she seemed in no hurry to break their connection. Still, Micki wasn't sure about this "party" idea. "I appreciate the offer, but I'm not certain this is my kind of thing."

Fenn stepped closer and lowered her voice. "Unless I'm way off base, you and I probably have the same taste in women. There will be some great looking girls there, and believe me, they like playing as much as we do."

"I guess it's not your first one of these parties," Micki said, doubting very much that she and Fenn had the same tastes. Everyone assumed from looking at her that she was into femmes. That wasn't the case, most of the time, but Fenn sure looked and sounded as if *she* liked the lipstick girls. "Who else will be there? I'm not into guys. That gonna be a problem?"

"Nope. Unless you signal that you're into something, no one will pressure you." She grinned, her eyes dancing. "If you just want to watch, that works, too."

"Even for you?"

Fenn ran her hand down Micki's bare arm. "You can watch me all you want."

"Let's go then." Micki's rapidly swelling clit was already calling the shots, and watching would be better than nothing.

Fenn led the way through the casino and out onto the expansive rear veranda where individual cabanas as large as some middle-class family homes ringed an enormous free-form pool complete with waterfall and multiple hot spas. Parties seemed to be going on in all of the buildings, but the artfully arranged landscaping provided natural barriers that dampened the noise and obscured visibility from one cabana to the next. When they made their way down a palm-shrouded walk and inside to a large open room lit by flickering faux-flames in wall sconces, Micki saw the party had been going on for quite a while. Even in the low lighting, she made out the forms of men and women lounging on sofas and oversized chairs throughout the room. More than a few couples were sharing kisses and caresses along with their drinks.

"Looks like we're late," Micki said.

"How can we be late?" Fenn slung her arm around Micki's shoulder and gave her a squeeze. "We just got here."

Micki laughed and some of her tension dissipated. She might not be Fenn's date, but they were together somehow, and she liked that. As they made their way through the throng toward the bar, she tried not to stare, but considering the number of half-undressed people—of all sexual combinations and a few threesomes—flagrantly making love, no one would mind if she did.

"Is it always like this?" Micki asked, signaling the bartender for a beer.

"Yeah, these private deals are wild," Fenn said, taking a beer of her own. She glanced around the room. "You probably can't tell, but there are security people all over the place in here. The party's invitation only, and we were most likely scanned coming up to the front door. You got in because you're with me, but there are some pretty famous people in here who don't want the world to know about their party habits."

"And what are you looking for tonight?" Micki asked.

Fenn shrugged and tilted her beer bottle toward a redhead perched on the arm of a love seat on the far side of the room. The redhead, in a backless, skintight dress that just barely reached the tops of her thighs, stroked a woman's breasts as the woman busily kissed a third person. Male or female kissee, Micki couldn't tell.

"She looks wasted on that action," Fenn observed.

Not surprised that the sexy redhead would be the kind of woman Fenn picked out, Micki took a slug of her beer. She shouldn't have been disappointed, but she was. "So go for it."

"You mind?"

"Nope," Micki said, hoping for cool. "I'm good."

Fenn hesitated, her expression pensive, then she upended her beer bottle and drank it down in a series of deep pulls. She set it aside on the bar behind them. "Don't go too far."

"I wasn't planning on it." Micki wasn't interested in hooking up with anyone. The only person she was interested in clearly had different tastes. But she'd known that coming in, so she could hardly complain. She accepted a refill on her beer from the bartender and shifted along the perimeter of the room as Fenn cut directly through the crowd to the redhead. Fenn held out her hand as she leaned down to say something in the redhead's ear, and then the two of them moved off to a vacant sofa against the wall. Even though they were in shadows, Micki could see them clearly from where she leaned against one of the pillars in an even darker part of the room. She thought she saw Fenn glance around, imagined that their eyes met, but she knew that was wishful thinking. Still, she watched, because part of her enjoyed watching, and because Fenn had seemed to want her to. Maybe that was why she'd invited her.

It didn't take them long to get down to business. As they kissed, Fenn caressed the redhead's breasts, easing her hand inside her low cut dress. The redhead arched into Fenn's body, sliding one leg over Fenn's thighs, her dress pulling up to her hips. Fenn pushed flimsy fabric aside and lowered her mouth to the redhead's breast, tonguing her nipple while stroking the length of her naked thigh. Micki couldn't hear them, but she didn't need to. The redhead's eyes were closed and her mouth open. She had to be moaning as Fenn teased her breast. While Fenn seduced the femme, Micki watched Fenn. She was a practiced lover; that was clear. The redhead was really worked up, her hands all over Fenn, but when she reached down to cup Fenn's crotch, Fenn diverted her hand. The first time she did it, Micki thought it might have been an accident, but the second time it was clearly deliberate.

Fenn pulled back and murmured something to the redhead, then stared over her shoulder directly at Micki. She grinned fiercely, then gave the redhead a bruising kiss. Micki felt sweat trickle down her back. Fenn was getting off from knowing she was there. Being on the outside was exhilarating and frustrating at the same time. Micki glanced around and when she saw that no one was looking, she squeezed her crotch, pressing her thumb into her hard clit. It didn't help. It only made her want more. She wanted to do more than watch. And somehow, she knew Fenn knew that. She should leave, but just then, Fenn slipped her hand under the edge of the redhead's dress and pushed up between her legs.

Micki's stomach clenched as the redhead writhed into Fenn's lap, her mouth against Fenn's neck, her hips rising and falling to the stroke of Fenn's arm between her thighs. In her mind, Micki heard the redhead's cry as she climaxed, and the paean of pleasure mocked her.

"I can help you with that, lover," an exotic dark-skinned woman with a sultry voice said as she edged up to Micki and covered Micki's hand where she still gripped her crotch.

"Thank you," Micki rasped, moving both their hands away from between her legs. She hadn't intended to masturbate in public or have someone else do it for her. She mustered up a smile, and noted that the woman was more than just pretty. If she hadn't already had Fenn's face burned into her mind, she might have been tempted. "I'll keep for a while."

"I'll be here," the woman said, moving away with an indulgent smile.

Micki checked back on Fenn's action just in time to see the redhead curl up contentedly in the corner of the sectional and Fenn stalk rapidly toward a hallway at the back of the room. Uninvited, Micki followed. When Fenn ducked through a doorway, Micki pushed in behind her. She knew exactly where Fenn was going and why. She'd done it dozens of times herself. The restroom was small, with only two stalls, and they were both empty. Micki reached behind her and locked the door.

"Enjoy the show?" Fenn asked with a smug grin, leaning her ass against the granite-topped counter surrounding the sinks.

She looked cool and self-satisfied, but Micki knew better. "How long will it take you to get yourself off now? Thirty seconds? A minute? That's what you came in here for, isn't it?"

Fenn frowned. "Look—"

"No," Micki snapped, grabbing Fenn and spinning her around toward the counter so hard that Fenn grabbed the edge to steady herself. "*You* look." Catching the mixture of surprise and unmistakable arousal in Fenn's reflection in the mirror above the sinks, Micki's clit finished stiffening. "It's your turn to watch."

"If you're pissed—"

"I'm not." Micki kept one hand on Fenn's shoulder, forcing her forward and slightly off balance, and reached around with her other hand to unbutton her fly. "You wouldn't let her touch you. But you're going to let me. Aren't you?"

Fenn shivered lightly and spread her legs, her eyes meeting Micki's in the mirror. Her voice was barely a whisper. "Yes."

Micki angled her hips so her crotch rode against Fenn's thigh. The contact only made the spiraling pressure in her clit worse and her control slipped a little. She shoved her hand into

Fenn's jeans. "Oh, Jesus, you're so fucking hard already."

Fenn grunted softly, her hands white as she clenched the counter for support.

"Did fucking that pretty little girl turn your clit into this rock?" Micki grated, working her thumb and finger roughly up and down Fenn's clit. When she got no answer, she twisted.

"No," Fenn said, sounding as if she were strangling. "You watching me fuck her did that."

"And this is what you always do after, isn't it?" Micki picked up speed, sliding the slippery hard length between her fingers.

Panting, Fenn pumped into Micki's hand. Sweat flew from her hair and misted Micki's face. In the mirror, her eyes were dazed. "What?"

"Isn't this what you always do?" Micki demanded, her mouth against Fenn's ear. "Make the girls come and then go off somewhere alone and jerk off?"

"What do you think?" Fenn groaned defiantly.

Micki slowed down and gently massaged Fenn's clit with her fingertip. "I don't *think*, I know." She tapped rhythmically and Fenn twitched. "You do it because they don't know how to give you what you need and you won't ask." She tapped again and Fenn tried to pull away. "But *I* know." Micki bit down on Fenn's bicep and pinched Fenn's clit at same time.

Fenn threw her head back and roared. "Oh Jesus, Jesus. That's gonna make me come."

"Look in the mirror," Micki choked out. She rode Fenn's thigh and worked Fenn's clit in long, deep strokes. Her own clit beat restlessly, trapped and aching. "Watch me make you come."

Fenn's mouth twisted into a grimace, her eyes beseeching as they held to Micki's. "I need it hard. Please. Please don't let up."

"I know what you need." Micki kissed the rigid angle of Fenn's jaw, her face resting alongside Fenn's as she watched their reflections. "Keep your eyes open."

"I'm right there." Fenn sounded as if she might cry. "Do me faster?"

"Don't worry, you're going to come," Micki said with confidence, reaching around Fenn's chest with her free hand and palming her breast. She squeezed Fenn's nipple and pulled hard on her clit. Fenn's eyes rolled back and her legs buckled. "Oh yeah. There you go."

Fenn's eyes slammed shut and she sagged forward over the sink. "Uh uh uh uh."

Micki massaged Fenn's clit until it softened and her tortured groans tapered off to an occasional moan. As soon as Micki was certain Fenn was done, she pulled her hand free of Fenn's jeans and fumbled with her own. Then her fingers were on her clit and she was jerking off. It felt so good her legs gave out and she clutched Fenn to stay upright.

"Oh, *fuuck.*" Micki pressed her face to Fenn's shoulder, about to go off.

Fenn yanked Micki's hand out of her pants, grabbed her hips, and swung her around and up onto the counter. Before Micki knew what was happening her jeans were down around her ankles and Fenn was between her legs.

"I think this is mine," Fenn muttered, and went down on Micki's clit.

Fenn's mouth was so hot, her tongue so insistent, that Micki started to lose it right away. She thrust both hands into Fenn's hair and tried to push her off. "Fenn, baby. I'm going to come in your mouth."

Fenn grabbed her wrists and clamped them to the counter on either side of her body. She sucked harder, her mouth a vice, and Micki exploded into her. When she couldn't take the sweet beat of Fenn's tongue another second, she begged Fenn to stop. Fenn straightened up and pulled her into her arms. Micki dropped her head onto Fenn's shoulder and clung to her so she didn't slide off the counter.

"Fuck. I tried to hold out. Sorry."

"I don't remember me asking you to," Fenn said in a low, pleased rumble. She stroked Micki's hair and massaged the muscles in the back of her neck. "You know, there's probably a line outside the door."

"I hope they enjoyed it as much as I did." Micki laughed and wrapped an arm around Fenn's neck, dragging her head down to kiss her, hard and deep. "You'll have to leave me here, because I don't think I can walk."

"Not a chance." Fenn eased Micki down from the counter and kept an arm around her waist until she was steady. Between kisses, they tucked in T-shirts and buttoned up flies.

"Are you playing tomorrow?" Micki asked.

"Tomorrow's a bye day for me," Fenn said.

"So you don't need a whole lot of sleep tonight."

"I wasn't planning on getting much." Fenn threw her arm around Micki's shoulder as they headed toward the door. She unlocked it and when they stepped through, three or four women applauded politely and streamed past them into the restroom.

"There goes your reputation," Micki said.

Fenn stopped, her arm still around Micki, and regarded her intently. "If they got the idea I thought I was leaving with the hottest woman here tonight, they'd be right."

Micki grabbed the back of Fenn's jeans and curled her thumb through a belt loop. "I've been rolling the dice really well tonight. Looks like I've got me another winning come out."

"Roll 'em easy or hard, baby." Fenn kissed her. "Any way you want it, I'm game."

DOUBLE DOWN

·····································

Radcly*f*fe

*T*his is the best birthday trip ever," Jeannie Bryant said, stretching out her arms and twirling in the center of their suite. "I can't believe how much fun I'm having. Did you like the show?"

"Sure. It was super."

Randy Michaels stuffed her hands in the pockets of her best black trousers and figured there was no point in saying that she would have been just as happy to watch a movie in the privacy of their room, where they could kick back and eat popcorn and make out a little bit. She'd spent six months planning this surprise birthday trip, and she wanted everything to be just perfect for her wife of almost ten years. Jeannie deserved a whole lot more than that for putting up with her for all that time. Randy regarded her still smiling birthday girl with a mixture of pride, amusement, and pleasure. Five feet three inches of blond-haired, blue-eyed exuberance, Jeannie was the best looking woman in Cherokee County. Hell, probably in the entire state of Texas. Possibly the whole United States of America. She didn't look one minute older than she had at eighteen, when Randy had first laid eyes on her at the rodeo. Jeannie was barrel racing with the rest of her family, who had been on the rodeo circuit for three generations. Twelve years older and nothing much to write home about in the looks department, Randy couldn't believe that Jeannie had given her the time of day. But Jeannie always said it was love at first sight, and since she'd never even heard of Michaels' Oil, after a while, Randy had believed her. And here they were.

"You're lying to me, Randy Michaels," Jeannie said, her hands on her hips. She was trying to work up a frown, but it wasn't very convincing. "I know you hate listening to people sing songs you don't even know the words to." She wrapped her arms around Randy's neck and snuggled her soft curves into the lean planes of Randy's rangy body. "I know you'd rather be astride a horse, out riding around that ranch, checking up on the wells and scaring all the roustabouts."

Laughing, Randy looped her arms around Jeannie's waist. "None of them are scared of me."

"Uh-huh. I've seen their faces when you light into them for not sticking to the schedule." Jeannie leaned back, hooked her finger around the onyx and silver clasp on Randy's bolo tie, and pulled one leather strand free. Then she proceeded to pick out all the studs on Randy's tuxedo shirt. "And I know you don't like getting all duded up."

"What I like is putting a smile on your face." Randy nuzzled Jeannie's neck and kissed the special place just under the curve of her jaw that always made her eyes get soft and dreamy. "I want you to know how lucky I feel to have caught you when you could have had anyone."

Jeannie slid her hands inside Randy's shirt and worked her fingers into the tight muscles in slow, firm circles, sliding a little lower every now and then to brush her nipples. "I roped *you,* as I recall."

Thinking back to that time in the barn when Jeannie had tossed a lasso over her head and dragged her into the hayloft, Randy felt a sharp twinge between her legs. Dropping a hand down to Jeannie's tantalizingly firm butt, she pulled her tight against her crotch. "Oh yeah, I remember."

"And don't think just because you always get to me first, I'm not always thinking about hog-tying you and having my way with you again."

Randy frowned, trying to figure out if there was a message in there for her somewhere, but she wasn't thinking quite right because Jeannie had started in on her nipples. Just rubbing them between her fingers, casual like. Now the twinge down low in her belly switched to a steady pounding. "Is there something you want in the bedroom department you're not getting?"

Jeannie kissed Randy's throat. "When have you ever known me not to tell you just exactly what I wanted?"

"Come to think of it, never." Randy massaged Jeannie's butt with both hands, loving the way Jeannie made little purring sounds and rubbed herself up against her like a cat.

"Let's get out of these fancy clothes," Jeannie said, "and cuddle up in bed. We can watch a movie. I know that's what you'd rather have been doing all night, anyhow."

Randy figured there was no point in protesting, because Jeannie could always tell when she was shining her on. She kissed her, sliding the tip of her tongue back and forth over the wet, soft surface of Jeannie's lips. "It's your birthday, baby. We'll do anything you want."

"Well then, let's get ready for bed, and I'll see what I'm in the mood for."

By the time Randy got out of the rest of her clothes and pulled on an old pair of baggy blue cotton boxers she liked to sleep in, Jeannie had let her hair down, stripped off her makeup, and donned an equally old, thigh length white T-shirt. Together, they arranged the pillows and climbed under the covers. Jeannie scooted close to Randy and threw one leg over Randy's so her thigh snugged into the crotch of Randy's boxers. Then she grabbed the remote and turned on the television.

"What should we watch?" Jeannie asked.

"You pick this time." Randy really didn't care what they watched, because all her attention was on the way Jeannie was absently rubbing her leg up and down between hers. She'd been more than a little turned on from the way Jeannie had been fooling with her nipples, but now she was getting a right serious bit of stiffness in her shorts. She was pretty sure there'd be a nice big wet spot in the middle of the pale blue cotton pretty soon, too.

"I've always wanted to watch one of these," Jeannie said, selecting the adult viewing choices. "Oh, look. They've got one with just girls."

Before Randy could gather her wits to protest, Jeannie keyed in the selection. And sure enough, within a second, the screen was filled with half-naked women.

Randy stared while Jeannie laughed. "They're supposed to be sharing a day at a beauty spa. I've never seen anybody doing *that* at the one I go to."

"Geez, I should hope not," Randy said as the three "customers" shed all of their clothes and started oiling up each other's bodies in preparation for their group massage. "I didn't know you liked this stuff."

"What?" Jeannie said, shifting her thigh away from Randy's crotch. "A massage or X-rated movies?"

"The movies." Randy divided her attention between what was happening on the screen and trying to figure out how to get Jeannie's leg back where it had been. "If you told me, I could've—"

"Lover, look. They're getting right down to business. Shush now, and watch."

Randy's feelings might have been bruised if it hadn't been for the fact that Jeannie reached over and put her hand high up on the inside of Randy's thigh, just underneath the leg of her boxers. Knowing Jeannie's fingers were only inches from where she really, really wanted them made Randy's clit stand up. She had a second's worry that maybe Jeannie would think she was getting turned on by what was happening on the screen, but then she noticed her lover's rapt expression. Jeannie's lips were slightly parted and her eyes wide as she stared at the three admittedly great-looking women kissing and fondling each other's breasts and sliding all over one another in the middle of a big bed. Jeannie's breathing had gotten a bit fast and her nipples made two nice little tents in the front of her T-shirt, too. Huh.

Moving carefully so as not to distract her, Randy eased her arm behind Jeannie's back and reached around her side so her fingers cradled the curve of Jeannie's breast. It was a sneak-up-on-'em move she'd perfected when she'd been a lot younger and she wasn't quite certain how far her date was willing to go. Casually, she feathered her fingers back and forth over Jeannie's breast. Jeannie cuddled up a little closer and rested her head against Randy's shoulder, her gaze still riveted to the screen.

"Do you think her breasts are real?" Jeannie murmured.

"I don't know, maybe. It's hard to tell these days." Randy kissed Jeannie's temple and inched a little closer to her nipple.

"Mine aren't nice and perky like hers."

"Yours are perfect." To prove it, Randy cupped Jeannie's breast. The soft cotton T-shirt did nothing to dampen the heat radiating from Jeannie's firm flesh, and when Randy flicked her thumb over the taut nipple, Jeannie twitched and moaned softly.

"Maybe I should shave my pussy like that," Jeannie mused.

"Do you want to?"

On the screen, a blonde and a brunette were French kissing while a redhead played with the brunette's breasts. Randy twirled her finger around Jeannie's nipple the same way the redhead worked her tongue around the brunette's hard, flushed nipple.

"Mmm." Jeannie bent her legs into a vee and rocked her hips. Her T-shirt pulled up until the blond triangle between her thighs peeked out. "Hers looks pretty sexy, all pink and wet like that. I bet if I did, it would feel really nice when you licked me."

Randy's clit jumped around at the thought of how sweet Jeannie tasted. *Slow, go slow.* "If you want to, we'll do it."

"I don't know though. I always want to come as soon as you start licking me." Jeannie rested her index finger on the base of Randy's clit. "I might not be able to hold out at all if I get any more sensitive."

"Aw, Jesus, baby," Randy breathed, her stomach tying itself into knots. She kept massaging Jeannie's breast and caressed her bare thigh with her other hand. "Whatever you want."

Jeannie glanced away from the TV and met Randy's gaze. Her eyes were liquid, heavy lidded, and her mouth curved with pleasure. She pressed down on Randy's clit. "So will you do it for me? Shave me?"

"Sure." Randy was having a hard time getting the words

out. Her chest was so tight she couldn't take a deep breath. *Please stroke it. Please stroke it. Please please please, stroke it.*

"You'll have to put shaving cream all over me with your fingers."

"Uh-huh," Randy managed. Just when she thought she couldn't get wound up much tighter, Jeannie pushed her hand a little deeper inside Randy's boxers and took a hold of her clit. She thought the top of her head might come off, but she forced herself to be cool. Jeannie's birthday, Jeannie's call. Except, oh God, Jeannie wasn't doing anything with her clit, just gripping it between her fingers. Hard. It felt so good she wanted to cry.

"And you'd have to cover my clit with your fingers so, you know, you didn't hurt me."

"Uh-huh." Randy pressed her fingers on the clit in question, and Jeannie caught her lower lip between her teeth. One of the girls in the movie started to pant and moan.

Jeannie glanced over at the screen. "She's getting her clit licked. She's all swollen and wet. I don't think she's faking."

Randy pumped her hips; she couldn't help it. If Jeannie didn't do something soon, squeeze her or stroke her or just fucking move her fingers a fraction of an inch, she was going to break down and blubber like a baby.

"I bet if you were licking her she would have come already."

"Oh fuck," Randy groaned. She wasn't watching the movie, she was watching Jeannie get excited watching the movie, and the sound of a woman in the middle of a screaming orgasm was definitely having an effect. Jeannie squirmed and pushed Randy's fingers down until they were just at her opening. At the same time, she started that wonderful, miraculous, up-and-down sliding motion on Randy's clit that always made her come.

"Do you think you could fuck me?" Jeannie breathed, guiding Randy's fingers inside her. "Just a little?"

"Just a little?"

Jeannie nodded vigorously, her lips parted, her neck and upper chest pink with pre-orgasmic flush. "Don't make me come yet."

Randy eased just her fingertips inside and cupped her palm over Jeannie's clit, rubbing softly. "Good?"

"Uh-huh," Jeannie panted, working Randy's clit faster as the second woman and then the third started to come. Jeannie gripped Randy's hand between her legs and started to ride. "Oh, lover, I think I'm going to come soon. But I don't want to!"

"Watch the movie, baby," Randy whispered and glided all the way inside her. She knew Jeannie was going to come. She could see it in her face, the way her body quivered, the way her breath came out in tiny sobs. And the closer Jeannie got, the faster her hand moved between Randy's legs.

Jeannie whimpered. Randy shot another look at the screen and saw the redhead writhing on the bed while the blonde pumped her fist between her legs. Jeannie gushed around her fingers, and Randy gave it up. "Oh fuuck!"

"Me too!" Jeannie cried, slamming her hand down over Randy's, pushing Randy as deep inside as she could. "Oh, lover, I'm coming so hard."

Jeannie slumped against Randy, her thighs clamped tightly around Randy's hand, hers still between her legs holding Randy inside. "God, they're not even my type."

Randy started to laugh. "Jesus, I'm glad to hear that, because I don't look anything like them."

"Believe me, lover, if I saw one of them in the bar, I wouldn't look twice." She kissed the side of Randy's neck.

"I think it was mostly us watching it together that got me so horny."

"I liked watching you watch them," Randy confessed.

"Yeah?" Jeannie nibbled on Randy's earlobe. "I liked watching. Do you think that's weird?"

"Fuck, no. I think it's incredibly sexy."

Jeannie toyed with Randy's clit. "Did you see that big sign in the lobby about the Escort organization that's meeting here?"

"Uh-huh. Baby, cut that out or you're going to make me come again."

"And that would be bad, why?"

"Never mind. Shortage of blood to my brain."

"It's still my birthday, right? And you did say I could plan all our activities."

Randy nodded, a few seconds away from blast off.

"Movies are fun, but I think I'd rather see a live show." Jeannie obviously didn't expect an answer, which was good, because Randy was in the middle of a mind-melting orgasm. "Maybe I could hire an escort…or two."

UPPING THE ANTE

Karin Kallmaker

*Y*ou're in my seat, I think." Kitty showed her ticket stub to the elegantly turned out woman whose mink and large Gucci bag took up her own seat, therefore requiring her to sit in Kitty's.

With a disapproving sniff, the woman somehow managed to get her stuck up butt into her assigned seat on Kitty's left. Like it was a hardship, Kitty thought. The closed-circuit room seating was a series of wide, comfortable cushioned chairs, suitable for anyone's living room, and tiered to give every seat a prime view of the enormous flat screen TV.

She sank down into the cushions, aware that she'd already been checked out by the three frat boys seated behind her. Infinitely more pleasing was the nod of greeting from the brunette on her right. "Hi, you."

Wahine gave her a pleased look. "Glad you made it. How did those Prada shoes work out for you?"

"Haven't tried them yet. This weekend is vacation." She

settled comfortably into her seat. After shopping together on Thursday, she'd lost track of Wahine, but had relaxed knowing they'd meet again tonight. They were the same age; they both lived in the L.A. area, and were in the business for the same reason: money for college. UCLA and USC weren't cheap. "Did you go to any of the sessions on cyber opportunities?"

"I did. It's a lot of investment."

"But it's safe. Safer."

"Yeah, that's true. The best piece of advice was probably forming a partnership and sharing bandwidth."

Kitty nodded, and would have asked if Wahine was making a proposal—they lived about thirty minutes apart—but the broadcast began with a splash of music.

"Can I get you a drink?" Kitty rose quickly, wanting to be settled before the competition actually got underway.

"I'd love a rum and Coke. I'll get the next one." Wahine smiled her thanks and Kitty had the tantalizing thought that her lush form was as ripe as a peach in August, curving in all the right places. The moment they'd met, Kitty had thought the wide, red-lipped mouth was very, very kissable.

At least when she looked at Wahine her tongue wasn't actually hanging out of her mouth and she didn't rub her genitals either. The three frat boys, sprawled over their chairs with legs propped up on the arms, were giving her that kind of look. She wanted to plant the toe of her sedate sling backs right on Mr. Stanford's balls. She didn't think anything about her attire announced her part-time profession, but he was so certain of his animal charm that he looked at her boldly, like he'd already paid and there was no way Kitty could say no.

He didn't even bother to get out of his chair. "Hey, babe, can I get that drink for you?"

Kitty made a show of looking around, like she couldn't figure out who he could possibly be speaking to. The bartender gave her his attention and she ordered two rum and Cokes. She ignored a similar outburst on her way back to her seat.

The uptight woman with the mink gave her a look like she couldn't figure out how Kitty could afford to be in the same room with her. What was with the mink coat? It was August in Las Vegas, and four zillion degrees outside. Kitty returned the look with a sweet smile, thinking that she'd saved up for this treat of a trip, and worked extra hours at her job at the warehouse store, so when she found a cheap last minute ticket for something fun, she'd grabbed it. Money from her escort services went one hundred percent for tuition.

Just loud enough, she said, "Do you know what some people paid to get into this broadcast?"

"Way more than we did—that scalper was desperate." Wahine accepted the drink with a smiled thank you. "There's a full open bar and buffet in the Titanium room. For us, however, I have brought some peanuts."

"That's more my budget." Kitty curled into her seat, glad of her comfortable jeans. "This sort of feels like going to a ball game, doesn't it?"

"I know just what you mean." Wahine toasted her with the glass, sipped, and Kitty didn't linger too terribly long on the sight of those wonderful lips closed around the delicate straw.

The announcers began their patter, predicting the fates of the finalists in the Seven-Card Stud Tournament. Two of the players were women, Kitty was happy to see, and the dark-eyed Texan was immediately her favorite. She leaned toward Wahine. "She's yummy."

Wahine made a noise of agreement, but to Kitty's surprise the stuck-up woman on her left said, "Yes, she is."

Kitty gave her a look of amusement and entertained herself with visions of the Texan helping Ms. Mink with that stick up her ass. Her mother would have slapped her for having such a base and hateful thought, but it was exactly the kind of sass Kitty had learned eavesdropping on her mother and the other church ladies.

The poker got very interesting, very tense, very quickly. She and Wahine made their way through the bag of peanuts in short order, crack-peel-munch, crack-peel-munch. The motion of chips sliding across the green tables, the heavy snick as they stacked, it was mesmerizing. The stakes went higher, the bluffs got bigger, and by the halfway point, both the women had been eliminated. It broke Kitty's heart to see the Texan go.

She was telling Wahine as much when Ms. Mink collected her belongings and flounced out of the room. Maybe she'd had a big bet and lost it all.

"Maybe she's going to console the loser." Wahine drained the last of her drink.

"I don't know. She seemed too uptight to think of anyone but herself."

"Tightly wound women can be a lot of fun when they unwind. I wouldn't mind being a fly on the wall later." Wahine shifted her hips suggestively in her seat and Kitty had a wonderful moment fantasizing about getting down on her knees to see how much more she could make those hips move.

When the broadcast went to intermission, Kitty found she was stiff. "That was really intense."

"I'll get the drinks this time," Wahine said. She pushed her long black hair over her shoulder and the light sparkled off the large gold hoops that graced her ears. Earlobes, Kitty thought, are the softest part of a woman's body.

Kitty watched her get to her feet. Goodness, the woman filled out those slacks. "I'll go to the gift shop and see if I can get us some more snacks."

They walked together to the door of the viewing room to

find that Mr. Balls-in-Need-of-Squashing was blocking their way. "Surely you ladies could use a drink."

"No, thank you," Kitty said primly.

"C'mon, we're generous guys."

Kitty said sharply, "We're quite able to take care of ourselves. We don't need your…generosity."

He was too drunk to let it go, not with two buddies egging him on. "Didn't I see you going into one of the sessions for the escorts? What do you *ladies* talk about?"

Wahine sounded philosophical as she said, "How to fake it. That was a good class."

"Excuse me," Kitty said firmly. "I have already acquired this lovely woman's services as an escort for the evening, so you're going to have to find someone else. If you can."

She put a possessive hand on Wahine's back and arched her crotch suggestively. "Come on, baby, I need to relieve some stress before the game starts up again."

Wahine was still laughing when they reached the nearest of the hotel bars. "I'll get the drinks here to avoid those losers."

"Don't go back inside without me."

Kitty headed for the lobby gift shop, but her nose was tickled by a familiar aroma and she followed it to the convention hall. To her delight, there was a party underway for—she glanced around, checked out the sensible shoes—the librarians. Cash was being exchanged for hot dogs, popcorn, and pizza by the slice, so she got in line. From where she stood, she watched some very elegant women hurrying to the grand ballroom where some kind of awards event already appeared to be underway. For the romance writers or the surgeons, she wondered.

Hot dogs acquired, she scooted back to the upper floor where the sporting events were broadcast. Loud cheers were issuing from one room—sounded like boxing. Wahine was waiting outside their room, a drink in each hand.

"I have manna from heaven," Kitty said. She waved the hot dogs.

"Oh, you are an amazing woman."

"Why, thank you. Oh, wait." She stayed Wahine with a gesture. "You can't go in there looking like that."

"Like what?"

Holding the hot dogs with one hand, Kitty quickly mussed her own hair and undid the top button of her blouse with the other.

Wahine laughed again—Kitty thought the sound of women laughing was one of the best things in the world—and kept giggling while Kitty mussed her hair too, and made similar adjustments to her shirt. "Do we look like we've been up to no good now?"

"Not quite," Kitty said. "You still have too much lipstick on."

Wahine was passive until the moment Kitty's lips touched hers, then she made a little noise and opened her mouth to Kitty's eager exploration. When Kitty finally stepped back, she felt more than a little drunk. Those lips were just as soft and inviting as she thought they'd be. She wanted in the worst way to run her tongue over the coffee-with-cream skin.

"Now," she said quietly, "we look like we've been up to no good."

Wahine's eyes were slightly glazed. "I like my shade of lipstick on you."

"That's not the only thing of yours I want on me," Kitty said as she opened the door.

The men noticed their return but said nothing, thank goodness, or Kitty would have been tempted to let them see just what it was they'd never, ever have.

Once they were seated, Wahine leaned close enough to ask, "Was that comment for them or me?"

Time for a little honesty, Kitty thought. "I don't give a crap about them. I was just trying to figure out a way to kiss you."

Wahine's lips quirked to one side. "Pretty quick thinking for a UCLA girl."

"That means the ball is in your court, USC girl."

The second half of the broadcast was even more exciting than the first. By the time the last hand was on the table and only the final bluff and the final call was left, Kitty's heart was beating so loudly she couldn't hear the announcers.

It wasn't the hands on the screen that had her enthralled; it was Wahine's hand in her pants.

The motion had started subtly, but now had a steady, flowing rhythm that Kitty had no trouble imagining on her own clit. Wahine's breathing was growing increasingly shallow, and the outline of her nipples, large and full, was obvious. Subtle, responsive jerks of her thighs made it easy for Kitty to follow her rising excitement, and she envisioned her tongue alongside Wahine's fingers, enjoying the journey. She wanted in the worst way to smell her.

There was a gasp and scattered applause from the others in the room as something happened with the game, but Kitty was caught by Wahine's liquid gaze seeking out hers. A few more strokes and her hips shuddered in the chair. All the while she stared into Kitty's eyes.

"That was the best finale ever!" The people in the row ahead of them were standing up.

Kitty had no idea who had won the tournament. Wahine pulled her hand back into sight, and Kitty swore she could see silken wetness coating the sleek fingertips.

Neither of them moved. Wahine had her hand on her

abdomen, looking disoriented. Kitty was dizzy because all the blood in her body had drained right to her clit. She wasn't sure she could stand up.

How strange, she thought, that every time with a woman I feel like I've not really ever been turned on before. It's not that strange, she answered herself back. Escort service is with men. And you love women. It had been a long time since pleasure had been a part of the equation.

Wahine finally stirred. With the room now mostly empty, she said, "I think the ball is back in your court."

"How about in my room?" She managed to get to her feet without revealing how dizzy she was, but she was afraid when she moved that Wahine would hear how wet she was.

Well, what if she did? She fully intended Wahine to *feel* how wet she was. And soon.

They passed the three losers on the way to the elevator, but if they had anything to say, Kitty didn't hear it. The fountains in the corner of the grand lobby, the paintings, the murals, all of which had delighted her for the last several days—she saw none of them. She was going to love a woman tonight and had no attention to spare on irrelevant things.

Kissing a woman was full of sound. The resonant *oh yes* in her head, the pounding of her heart, the rustle of eyelashes brushing against a rounded cheek. Though she knew those sounds, Kitty recorded them again in her memory, because being with a woman didn't happen often enough.

Though Kitty wanted to get to the bed, at the moment there was no reason to move from the wall just inside the door. She leaned into Wahine as their kisses explored and deepened. When Wahine's hands moved to her hips, pulling them closer together, Kitty felt the heat flowing into her pelvis, through her skin and her bones. Firm, gentle hands, the fingers long and purposeful—a woman's touch.

"It's been way too long since I've done this," Wahine murmured. "Can we take our time?"

"I was hoping to take all night."

They kissed again to seal the agreement. Kitty ran her fingers the length of Wahine's hair, anticipating the heavy silk of it on her stomach, against her thighs.

Each button undone on the blouse displayed new skin to be licked, and at last she tasted the faint hint of salt as her nose appreciated the cologne Wahine wore, with its faint notes of sandalwood, oak, and rose.

What had begun as an evening watching a competition of nerves had turned into a deeply welcome exploration of different nerves, nerves that sent shivers of delight, shocked awake memories and created fantasies. Her imagination painted lusciously evocative pictures of Wahine in a hundred poses, and composed a symphony of cries and moans as Kitty explored the inside and outside of her.

Wahine rolled her onto the bed, removing clothes in between languid kisses. They were both naked now, and Kitty relearned the difference between the muscles of forearms and the melting softness of breasts. The bumps of ribs under her fingers made her mouth water with the desire to count them with her tongue. She pushed Wahine onto her back to brush her nose against a gloriously full nipple, and marvel at how the tender underside of a breast could yield to tightly puckered skin that begged for her teeth to tease, her tongue to lick, her mouth to close down and lightly suck.

The crass frat boys, the rude woman—dealing with people was an everyday trial, sometimes, and the irritations of daily life had conspired with the stress of living to blot out how wonderful, how natural it was to pause in reverent anticipation just before dipping her tongue into a wet, full cunt. She inhaled the sensual smell, and drank in the sight of gleaming, wet folds, red and ready. Men tried to wound with the word, but their opinion of her, and her cunt, was of no importance. She knew its beauty, though sometimes she forgot. She was reminded of it now, gazing at the tight, sleek folds of Wahine's cunt. She kissed it wetly, rubbed her lips along the beckoning, opening slit until the inner folds were revealed, and then she used her tongue.

Wahine's groan of welcome was exactly what Kitty wanted to hear, and she tasted, savored, licked up the wetness that was only found in the beauty of a woman's cunt. She rolled it around on her tongue, savored the sweetness, the hint of salt, and went back for more.

She sank fully to the bed, pulling Wahine's legs over her shoulders, slipping her hands under Wahine's ass to tip her up. The more she feasted the more there was to enjoy until Wahine's cries peaked. Less direct attentions, wet kisses on the still pulsing clit, appreciative noises—Kitty didn't stop her adoration until fingers brushed her hair.

After a long minute of ragged breathing, Wahine said, "I think you really wanted to do that."

"I did." She gave Wahine a philosophical smile. She remembered the first woman she'd ever touched, the last woman she'd been with, and kneaded those memories together to unveil her fantasy of a future where time and mutual inclination brought her nightly to the same bed, with the same woman. "This is the food of my life and I forget that I'm hungry."

Wahine pulled Kitty up to feather her fingers over her face. "Then I think you'll be pleased to know that I'm starving."

INSURANCE
....

Karin Kallmaker

xcuse me, I can't believe I'm doing this, but can I ask you a question?" Pepper paused for breath and hoped she didn't sound like an insane person. She didn't often walk across a hotel lobby to approach a beautiful woman standing at a bar.

The cool, elegant redhead gave Pepper an exaggeratedly patient look. "Sure, go ahead."

"Are you doing anything tonight?"

"What?" She began to turn her back, but paused when Pepper tried to explain.

"See, there's this fancy awards thing tonight, downstairs. It's like the Year of the Lesbian or something. I mean, I just found out who's getting the Lamplight Award and who's giving it away, and I want to get published. It won't hurt for people to see me with a gorgeous date, you know?"

The redhead blinked at her.

"I really am a lesbian."

Leaning slightly closer, the redhead asked, "Are you drunk?"

"No! Seriously, I want to out myself. Tonight."

"And what does this have to do with me?"

"I need an escort. Or to be with someone I'm escorting. Your name badge says you're with ESI. That's the escort service people, right? How does that work exactly?"

With a narrowed gaze, the redhead said carefully, "I charge for my time according to what kind of escorting you want. Strictly legal—I'll even give you a receipt."

"Well," Pepper explained, "you'd need to look gorgeous and lesbian and maybe act like we were the hottest couple ever."

The woman was going to laugh at her and tell her to get lost; Pepper could see it in her eyes. She didn't know why she was having this conversation except, well, Carly Vincent was *the* one, the one who'd set them all free, and she hoped by the end of the night that she'd be able to say she'd shaken Carly Vincent's hand. And if Amelia Wainwright was presenting the Lamplight Award like it said in the copy of the program she'd pinched from the boxes being carried into the ballroom, well, that was incredible. Amelia Wainwright and Bryce Ambrose were an item, and everyone was buzzing about it. Not to mention that incredibly sexy Barrett Lancey and her terminally hot girlfriend Racie Racine. The lesbians were freakin' taking over and Pepper wanted to stand up and be counted.

"I'll pay you; I mean, I don't know what you charge. But even if all I could afford is to have you mingle at the cocktail party before you get called away—maybe we could say you were a doctor or something. What do you think?"

"I think you're crazy."

"That's okay," Pepper assured her. "I get that a lot."

"I'm sure you do."

"So what do you think?"

The woman shook her head in disbelief. "Well, I'm already dressing for the night, so I suppose we could do the cocktail party thing. An hour of glamorous lesbian flirtation for fifty bucks."

"It's a deal. Just the insurance I needed. Thank you." Pepper hurried away, really embarrassed and all, and not really believing she'd just hired an escort, then she turned right around and went back to where the redhead was still standing, all long legs accentuated by linen crop pants, and a sexy wrap shirt that really, Sophia Loren would envy. "What's your name?"

"Cara."

"I'm Pepper. You should probably call me that so people will figure we're on a date."

"What time and where should I meet you, Pepper?"

"Oh yeah, hey, can you tell I don't do this very often? It's a good thing you've got experience." Pepper gulped. "That didn't come out right. I'm sorry, how about over there, next to the reader board?"

"Time?"

"Oh, make it seven."

"I'll be there." With that, Cara turned on her lovely sandal heels and walked away.

Pepper stuffed the purloined program into her goodie bag. Crisis handled. Imitating Cara's elegant departure, Pepper spun around. There was a thud on her head and a shock of bright lights.

"Ow!" Pepper tried to pick herself up off the floor because nobody looked good knocked flat like that, but her head smarted too much to get back on her feet quite yet.

"Are you okay?"

"I will be. I'm sorry; I wasn't watching where I was going."

"No, I'm sorry. I was reading while I walked, and that has gotten me in trouble from the time I was eight."

Pepper looked up at her victim. Short, curly brown hair was the first thing she noticed, but then the brown-yellow eyes—was that topaz or amber, she wondered—had all her attention. Nice eyes, really warm. "What were you reading?"

"Bryce Ambrose's latest." The woman showed Pepper the cover.

"Oh, so you're a romance fan here for the book signings?"

"No, actually, I'm a librarian, but when I saw who was there, I got in line. There's a lot of overlap between librarian and reader. Do you need help getting up?"

"I got it." Pepper hoped she looked more graceful than she felt. "I really am sorry."

"It's okay. You got the worst of it, I think."

Now that they were eye to eye, Pepper could see that they were, well, eye to eye. That made the librarian the same height as she, around five-three. Wait—she was wearing two-inch heels and the librarian had on sensible shoes. So the librarian was taller. Not that it mattered. If this meeting was something she used in her writing she could make up anything she liked. She could make the librarian into the six-foot raven-haired beauty so popular of late. But she hadn't a clue what it would be like to kiss someone that tall.

Would finding out come under the topic of research?

It was a matter she was struggling with. How could she write a love scene when she hadn't actually done most of the things she'd write about?

"I'm Sally." The librarian held out her hand.

"Oh, sorry. I'm Pepper. Pepper St. Laurent. I think."

"How hard was that bump on the head?"

"No, it's a pen name. My first name really is Pepper, but I can't decide on the rest."

"Ah. Are you going to a session right now?"

"I don't think so. I think there's nothing happening because it's lunch time." Pepper squinted at the schedule.

To her surprise, Sally reached over to pluck Pepper's glasses from her face. She produced a small squirt bottle of cleaning solution from one pocket, then a soft cleaning tissue from another. A minute later she put the glasses back.

"Wow. Thank you." Amber, Pepper thought. Sally's eyes were amber.

"If you don't have a session, would you like to have lunch with me?" Sally gestured at the escalators that lead down a flight to the concourse that connected several of the hotels on this side of the Strip.

"I'd love to," Pepper said.

The world's best cheeseburger was followed by the world's best frozen custard, as proclaimed on the storefronts.

"That's just it," Pepper explained. "I think lesbians know a woman's heart better than anyone. She has to understand her own, first of all, and then if she falls in love, she has to understand a second one, and that's twice as many."

Sally nodded solemnly. "How long have you wanted to be a writer?"

"Since forever. Evidently, I was telling stories when I was just a toddler." Pepper paused in the act of licking another dollop off her scoop of vanilla bean custard. "I'm really excited to be here. I'm not usually quite so scattered."

Sally's eyes said she wasn't convinced, but Pepper decided to ignore that for now. The important thing was that

Sally looked really quite engaging with a dollop of custard on the end of her nose. Pepper used her napkin to dab it off.

Somehow, they forgot to go to their afternoon session. A stroll through the main art gallery had led to a discussion of art history and Sally had explained how cataloging non-fiction worked.

"We've got a baseball theme party in about an hour," Sally explained as they reached the Palace conference area again. "What are you up to?"

"Oh, it's the big awards night. Everybody who's anybody. I have two tickets, I bought a spare in case I had a date, and I guess I do."

"You have a date?"

"Yes, her name is Cara, but it's not like that. Would you like to join me? I'm sure she'll understand. Especially if I still pay her the fifty bucks."

There are situations, Pepper reflected later, that were out of control before they were even begun, but there was no way to know it.

First off, who would think that Bryce Ambrose would remember Sally from that afternoon, and stop to speak to her as they waited near the reader board for Cara to show up? Sally quickly introduced Pepper, who stammered out her own nervous praise as they shook hands and, really, Bryce Ambrose had very warm, strong hands. She and Amelia Wainwright were most certainly an item—the tender, melting looks would inspire an entire chapter for Pepper.

And that was all fine, all good, more than Pepper had hoped for the evening, really, and she'd waited contentedly next to the reader board with Sally, talking about everything. It was the place to be, because Barrett Lancey and Racie Racine stopped right next to them to adjust the straps on Racie's Grecian-inspired sandals.

While she and Sally watched Barrett's amazingly articulated hands move up and down Racie's calves—which was really a treat—Cara arrived.

"Sweetie," Cara cooed, and she wrapped her emerald-sheathed body around Pepper. "I finally woke up. You left me so exhausted."

"Um." Not the best start, Pepper could admit that, but before she could say anything else, Cara looked at Sally, very nicely turned out in black dress slacks and a brocade vest, and asked, "Who's this?"

"My date," Pepper said and that was quite possibly the stupidest thing she'd said all day, even if it was true.

Barrett Lancey looked up from Racie's legs, and Pepper hadn't really ever aspired to be outrageous to the point where she could distract Barrett from something so lovely.

"Your date?" Cara blinked, and she seemed to be trying to play along, but how could she know, Pepper had to allow her that. "Since when are you into butch?"

"I'm a librarian," Sally said.

Cara spread her hands. "I don't have a clue. I'm sorry."

"Here." Pepper reached for one of the flailing hands, did the two-hand clasp shake, leaving the folded bills in Cara's palm. "I'm really sorry it has to be this way."

"Women, women, women," Cara said. "You writers are all alike." Her dramatic sniff was somewhat undercut by her puzzled expression as she walked away.

Sally, looking highly amused said, "Since when are you into high femme?"

Barrett Lancey got up off her knee and smooched Racie. "Does that work better?"

"Yes, darling, thank you."

Pepper tried to think of something smart to say, something that would supplant Barrett Lancey's impression of her as a

RADCLY∫FE & KARIN KALLMAKER

womanizer. "I'm not into butch or femme, I'm into brains."

"Oh." Sally looked very pleased.

"It's true," Pepper added, and she realized it really was.

Barrett Lancey tucked Racie's hand into the crook of her arm, but before they walked away, she leaned over to Pepper and said, "This is when you kiss her." And she winked.

Sally liked the kiss, or Pepper guessed she did because she kissed back, blushing.

By the time the awards program started, they'd dispensed with what Sally termed *poulet du rubber* and two glasses of wine. The expected people won the expected awards, but the big moment for Pepper was Amelia Wainwright's tearful speech about Carly Vincent's brave decision to come out more than fifteen years ago.

So Pepper had only a drawer full of rejections for her first novel, and maybe she'd never publish one, but she was a lesbian, and she was proud to join in the thunderous applause. She made mental notes in case she should ever, like in her wildest dreams, be in the same position, and she hoped she was as gracious and kind as Carly was. Thank your partner, Pepper made especial note of that.

Sally liked to dance, that was also noteworthy. Sally liked to make out in the restroom stall; that was also something Pepper would never forget. By the time she was in Sally's room, naked and halfway to the Land of Happy, several of Sally's distinct likes were indelibly written on Pepper's brain.

Sally liked fingers, right there, and when Pepper added her tongue, it was clear Sally liked that, too. The inside of her was hot silk on Pepper's fingers, and when Pepper asked if Sally was okay with three fingers or should she go back to two, Sally said, "Don't you dare stop."

"I don't want you to think I believe big is better or anything like that."

Sally wound her fingers in Pepper's hair and said, "Shut up and fuck me."

Clearly, when you get that kind of direct instruction, it's wise to do as you're told. Pepper kept herself from talking by kissing Sally so hard there was no breath left in either of them.

"I'm really kind of surprised," Sally said later.

"By what?"

"I thought I was in the seventy percent of women who don't orgasm from penetration. But evidently not."

Pepper smiled, pleased. "How do you know stuff like that?"

"That I don't usually enjoy what you just did quite that much?"

"No, silly." She smooched Sally on the tip of her adorable nose. "The seventy percent stuff."

Sally blinked. "I'm a librarian."

"Are you going to say that every time you want to win an argument?"

Sally just smiled.

ON THE HOUSE

....

Radclyﬀe

When I noticed the little redhead check me out in the mirror for the third time, I grabbed my beer and slid off the bar stool. After four days of a predominately male-populated medical meeting, I was ready for a little female companionship. As I traversed a path between the sofas and chairs to where she sat alone in the lounge with her drink, she gave me a surprised look and then quickly glanced away. Hmm, mixed signals it would seem.

"Hi, I'm Tristan," I said as I dropped into a plush wingback chair across the small dark wood coffee table from her. "Are you here for one of the conferences?"

"No," she said abruptly, not meeting my eyes. She hastily finished her drink, grabbed her shoulder bag, and stood up. "Sorry, I've got to be going."

As she spoke, I noticed her look pointedly behind me, and I shifted in my seat to see who was there. I didn't have any intention of getting in the middle of someone's relationship.

Turned out not to be a who, but a what. A security camera perched in the far corner of the room, one of the hundreds that were discreetly placed throughout the casino, the lobbies, the elevators, hallways, and just about everywhere else, panned in our direction. I guess when an establishment deals with millions of dollars on a daily basis, they get pretty serious about security. I hadn't thought much about the spy cams until now, but something about that camera was freaking her out. She looked to be a few years younger than me, maybe twenty-five, and her low cut, very clingy emerald green dress went well with her red hair. It also displayed some very nice cleavage and a shapely ass in a tasteful but enticingly flagrant manner. The green eyes that had frankly appraised me a few minutes earlier looked anxious now, and I was curious. Curiosity tended to get me into trouble at times, but what fun was life without a little risk? Women endlessly fascinated me, and at the moment, this one had my antennae—and quite a few other parts of me—abuzz.

"Are you in some kind of trouble?" I asked, making a leap of logic of the sort that had, on occasion, very nearly gotten my face slapped. This time though, I could see I'd hit the mark. When I stood up to walk out with her, her expression became even more uneasy.

"I'll be fine," she said, "as long as you stay put and let me get out of here."

"Are you staying here at the hotel?" I didn't move as she sidled around me to leave. I didn't want to make her situation any worse, but I didn't want her to just disappear either. I wasn't sure why, but I knew I'd be thinking about her the rest of the night if I didn't learn her story.

"No. Goodnight."

"Goodnight." I waited until she disappeared onto the casino floor, and then I sprinted across the lounge to the exit on the opposite side of the bar, hustled through the casino, across the lobby, and out to the street. She was just flagging down a cab.

"Hey," I called, hurrying over to her. "If you're not comfortable inside, how about we take a walk?"

After staring at me for a second, she signaled a waiting couple to go ahead and take the cab and then grabbed my arm. I followed as she dragged me half a block down the street. She stopped in front of the huge fountain that fronted the casino hotel. Intersecting arcs of water, highlighted in rainbow hues by the hidden spotlights focused on them, created elaborate patterns against the night sky.

"Why are you following me?"

"Look," I said, holding my hands up at chest level. "I'm harmless, and if I'm bothering you or scaring you, I'll walk away right now. I saw you look at me back there in the lounge, and I thought maybe you might want some company for a while. I know I do." When she didn't turn around and disappear, I pulled my wallet from my back pocket and handed her my driver's license. "Like I said, my name is Tristan. I'm from Philadelphia, and I'm here for the trauma meeting."

She shook her head as she regarded my license, then handed it back. "You're a doctor?"

I nodded. "Yeah. An anesthesiologist."

"Here alone?"

I nodded again. "You?"

"I live here."

"Are you a professional gambler?" I pocketed my wallet.

"No." She stepped a little closer to me as a crowd of raucous tourists passed by. "I was waiting for someone who didn't show."

I shook my head. "Foolish of…her?" I said hopefully.

She shook her head.

"Ah, sorry. My mistake." I grinned. "Wishful thinking."

She smiled then, and the look she gave me as her eyes swept up and down my body said I hadn't been wrong in my first assumption. "It was a business meeting."

"So then, back to my original proposition." Taking a chance, I reached for her hand. "We can take a walk, or I can buy you another drink, or we could go somewhere quiet and talk."

"Talk?" She emphasized the word in such a way that let me know she knew I was hoping for more than a conversation.

"Would that be a problem?"

"Unfortunately," she sighed, "yes."

"Because you're in some kind of trouble."

"I could be. It's complicated."

I tightened my grip on her hand. "I've got all night. In fact, I've got all night and half the day tomorrow. I also have a sister who is an attorney…"

"No," she said quickly. "It's not that kind of trouble. It's not even trouble the way you're thinking of it." She glanced around as if to be sure we weren't going to be overheard. "Look. It's like this. I was in the casino working. Meeting a man. For the night."

"And he didn't show?" I'd never met a call girl before. I've seen plenty of prostitutes in the ER or hanging out on street corners in Center City, but this woman did not resemble them. If she was selling her body, I didn't think it was because she had no place to sleep tonight.

"He should've called me to let me know where to meet him. He didn't."

"Is that unusual?"

"Very." She smiled a little ruefully. "The appointment isn't cheap. But, sometimes a wife shows up unexpectedly. That kind of thing."

"So you're free for the night then?"

"That's just it. I'm really not. And the casino has a thing…" She grimaced. "I can't be seen in there unescorted."

I worked that around in my head for a few seconds. "You don't want anyone to think you're freelancing."

"I'd lose my job."

"But if you're there on a job, someone in hotel security knows?"

"Yes. I shouldn't even have stayed to finish that drink when he didn't show up, but…" She pressed her palm to my chest. I'd blown off the afternoon session to play poker and had on jeans and a cotton shirt with a T-shirt underneath. I was way underdressed compared to her. "I happened to see you at the bar and I guess I got distracted."

"So you can't go back inside with me unless someone tells security you're there on a job."

"Right. And I need to report back in and let them know my client was a no-show."

"Will they arrange another client for you tonight?"

"I don't know."

"I'll hire you."

She laughed, and then when she realized I was serious, she leaned into me and kissed me. She tasted a little like cinnamon and she smelled of something dark and lush and decadent. When her tongue skimmed my lips and inside my mouth for just a second, I was instantly and completely aroused.

"Why would you do that?" she asked.

"Because I want to spend the night with you."

"Enough to pay for it?"

"Why not?"

"You're serious." She rolled her hips, soft and slow, against my crotch. "I appreciate the offer, but that's not why I kissed you."

"I didn't think it was." I held her tight to me with one arm around her waist. "We need to go somewhere more private. Tell me who I should call or what I should do so you can come to my room."

When she just stared, I added, "Please."

"Just a second."

Without taking her eyes off mine, she fumbled in her big shoulder bag and pulled out a cell phone. She turned in my arms so her ass was against my crotch, punched in a number, and spoke quietly for a minute. While she talked, I tried hard not to rub against her, but my clit was a mile long and every inch was throbbing.

"They'll arrange it," she said, closing her phone. She leaned her head back against my shoulder and looked up at me. "We can do the business details later. Okay?"

I kissed her neck. "Let's go."

I held her hand until we were almost to the hotel lobby, and then I released it, conscious of the cameras everywhere. I doubted that anyone in Las Vegas with a secret ever really kept it secret, but I wasn't going to be anyone's show. And I didn't want her to be either.

"I've been calling you Beautiful in my mind," I said as we stepped into the elevator, "which is true, but I think a first name would be nice, too."

"Have you done this before?" Her question came out sounding seductive, not accusatory.

"No, why?"

"You're awfully smooth."

I put my arms around her and kissed her. To hell with the cameras. "You're beautiful and I am seriously turned on. Believe me, I'm not working a line."

"It's…" she hesitated for a heartbeat, then said, "Meg."

And I knew she was telling me her real name. I kissed her

again. "Meg. Like I said, beautiful."

The doors opened and I led her down the hall to my suite. Once inside, I didn't quite know what to do. I'd brought women who I'd just met back to my apartment or my hotel room on occasion, but never under quite these circumstances. The one thing I didn't want it to seem was businesslike. I shoved my hands in the pockets of my jeans and rested back on my heels. Meg walked to the side of the bed and put her shoulder bag down near the side table.

"There's a couple of things you should know," Meg said as she sat on the side of the bed and removed her shoes.

I walked over and stood in front of her, unbuttoning my shirt, since it seemed like that was something I was going to have to do sooner or later. I pulled it off and untucked my T-shirt. I wasn't wearing anything under that, or under my jeans, come to think of it. I waited to take my cue from her.

"You didn't ask me anything about my work," she said.

"What do you want to tell me?"

"I don't have intercourse with men."

I don't know why, but the frank talk about sex was making me even more horny. I popped the top button of my jeans and unzipped my fly.

"But you said—"

"My client was a man, yes, but my clients ask for me for a certain reason." When I didn't say anything, she explained. "They don't fuck me. I fuck them."

I caught my breath and couldn't help but look at her shoulder bag next to the bed.

"Usually when they're restrained," she added as she reached behind her back and unzipped her dress. The thin spaghetti straps fell from her shoulders and her breasts were bare. She wasn't a large woman, but her breasts were slightly oversized for her slim torso. They were a little too heavy to stand completely upright, but they were lush and full and I wanted to hold them. If she hadn't said what she'd just said, I would have reached for them instantly. Instead, I held back.

"Is that the way you like it?" I sounded hoarse and had to clear my throat before I finished, "Being in control?"

"Most of the time I don't like it or dislike it." She stood and let the dress fall to the floor. She was nude, her slim, pale body curved in all the right places. "It's a job."

She grabbed the bottom of my T-shirt and yanked it up so I had no choice but to lift my arms and let her drag it over them and off. Then she gripped the waistband of my jeans and pushed them down my thighs. I stepped out of them along with my shoes and socks.

"I'd like to fuck someone for the pleasure of it." She caressed my sides, brushed her fingers over my breasts, and touched my face. "You. I'd like to fuck you."

"I…uh…" What could I say? That's not my thing? It's not my style. It's not the position I'm used to. All true, but in that moment, the idea of her, of Meg, taking pleasure in doing to me whatever it was she wanted to do sent a jolt through me so intense I almost doubled over. "Do you have what you need in that bag?"

She smiled. "I do."

"What should I do?"

"Lie down and let me make you feel good."

The picture I had of us together was nothing like the reality when, a few minutes later, I was on my back with my arms stretched above my head and my wrists locked together with soft leather restraints that Meg had somehow secured to the frame. She'd obviously done this before, because it only took her a few seconds. Now she was kneeling on the bed between my legs, running her fingers up and down the insides of my thighs. I'd turned the room lights down when we'd walked in, but I could see her clearly in the dim light. Her mouth was curved into an amused smile.

I didn't doubt for a second she could tell exactly how turned on I was, because I could feel the wetness on the inside of my legs and I knew my clit was already full. She let me know I was right when she casually brushed her fingertips over it and my whole body went stiff as a board. She kept her fingers there and dragged her bag up beside her. When she pulled out a harness with a long fat cock attached, she gave my clit a quick shake. I tried not to let my eyes roll back in my head.

"Do you know what's going to happen next?" she whispered, her thumb and forefinger slowly stroking my erection.

"Pretty good idea," I gasped. What I was really hoping *wouldn't* happen was me coming all over her in the next ten seconds. "Can you ease up a little bit?"

She did, and I craned my head to watch her strap on. The idea of a cock on her lusciously female form had my head spinning and the rest of me twitching. "I'm going to come the minute you're inside me," I warned.

"Don't be so sure."

Then for the hundredth time it seemed, she surprised me. She worked one loop of the harness over *my* left leg, then my right. "Raise your hips."

My legs barely had enough strength left to do it, but I dug my heels in, braced my shoulders, and lifted my hips so she could slide the harness all the way up. The cock was double headed, and she opened me with one hand and glided the short c-curved end inside me before cinching down the straps.

"Oh fuck," I gasped. "That's gonna make me come."

"You can come if you need to," she said as she straddled my hips. She cupped herself, then lubed the cock with her own clear, thick essence. Gripping the shaft, she rubbed the head between her lips and watched me watching her. "I don't care when you come or how many times you come. I'm going to fuck you until I can't move."

Then she slid down on it to the base, her eyes closing as she took it deep. The pressure of her weight on me with the cock inside both of us drove the smooth head against the spot inside me that always triggered my orgasm. This time I fought it, because I wanted to feel her fuck us both.

She opened her eyes and leaned forward, bracing herself with her hands on my shoulders. Rotating her hips in slow circles, she stared into my eyes. "When I fuck them, I don't care if I come and I usually don't." Her voice caught and her throat trembled. I tried to raise my head to kiss her, but I couldn't reach her.

"Tonight I'm going to come," she whispered.

I couldn't touch her with my hands or my mouth, but we were connected. I lifted my hips and pushed into her as she rotated, and when I pulled out she gave a little cry. She circled, I thrust, and her fingers dug into my shoulders. Every time I pumped, my clit struck the flared base and the fat curve inside me massaged the spot that made my clit even harder.

"You want to come," she murmured, her eyes glazed. "Don't you?"

"You know I do."

"Bad?"

"Real bad." I whined a little but I couldn't help it. I needed just a stroke or two on that one special spot. I needed it…god, I needed it.

I must have said it out loud, because she laughed and moved her hands from my shoulders to my breasts and squeezed.

"Go ahead and come. I'm going to." Her fingers quivered on my nipples and her words were barely a whisper. "Soon. All over you."

She was fucking me and I was fucking her and I couldn't keep from exploding. I felt my clit go off and my stomach lurched and my hips jerked and I yelled. Then I was pounding into her while I came out of my skin and she reared up and screamed at the ceiling, and I knew she wasn't holding anything back.

I went limp after the crazy contortions stopped, and she fell forward over me. After a second, I realized she'd released my wrists and I wrapped my arms around her. The cock was still inside both of us, and it moved back and forth inside me as she moaned and rubbed her breasts and her belly over mine. The pressure kept my clit hard, but she was the one out there on the edge.

"Feels so good," she moaned.

I cupped her ass and started to thrust inside her again. I tossed her line back at her. "You want to come. Don't you?"

"Yes," she whimpered against my neck. "Oh, yes. And I'm going to. Now. Now."

She shivered in my arms while her hips danced on the length joining us and the sound of her coming against my throat sent me off like a rocket. When I stopped coming, I was pretty sure I'd never walk again because every muscle in my body had turned to jelly.

"I love the way you fuck me," I groaned.

She laughed and burrowed her face against my shoulder. "Ditto."

"Can you stay until tomorrow?"

Wordlessly, she nodded.

"Is there someone you have to call or something I have to—"

"No." She kissed me. "The only thing you have to do is get ready to come again. Because all the rest is on the house."

BETTING BLIND

·····································

Radcly*f*fe

*T*his wasn't what I signed up for," Ari Bianchi muttered under her breath as she watched a naked woman fold back the coverlet and sheets on a king-sized bed, arranging them in a precise diagonal from top to bottom like a half-opened envelope. When she stretched out on top of the crisp, unwrinkled sheets, the space beside her remained closed, effectively signaling she didn't welcome company. Ari recognized the pattern, because she'd observed exactly the same thing the last three nights. Although the image on the monitor was black and white, it was crystal clear. One thing a casino could be counted on for was top-of-the-line surveillance equipment.

When she'd joined the security service at the Palace after opting for some kind of active duty—hell, *any* kind of activity—over remaining a deskbound cop, she hadn't planned on spending her time spying on guests. She didn't mind watching the tables for players who beat the house just a little too often or escorting drunks and belligerent patrons back out to the strip, but shadowing a woman through the casino and into her bedroom made her feel sleazy. And that's what she'd been doing every night from midnight until eight a.m. for the last three nights. After the first two uneventful shifts, she'd considered telling her boss she wanted off the detail. Then she thought about Mulrooney and Williams, the other two officers assigned to this target. They were okay-enough guys. Her being a cop pretty much canceled out her being a woman in their eyes, and they treated her like a colleague. Meaning they felt free to tell off-color jokes and make sexual observations about women in front of her. Of course, that might be because she was a lesbian and they knew it and somehow thought including her in their sexual byplay was a form of bonding. It was hard to figure out what went on in a guy's head, but she knew exactly what Mulrooney and Williams would be thinking if they were sitting where she was, watching Melinda Baker arch her back and trail her fingertips delicately down the center of her abdomen.

"Jesus," Ari breathed, glad that her surveillance station was separated from the main security area. She was alone in an eight by eight room, sitting in a swivel chair in front of a twenty-inch monitor watching a beautiful woman touch herself. She knew what Melinda Baker looked like in the flesh. Five-ten, shoulder length, honey blond hair, long legs, full breasts, and an intense, focused expression that gave her almost too perfectly sculpted features a sexy edginess. So it wasn't much of a stretch to translate the stark black-and-white image into living, breathing—Christ, *very* rapidly breathing—Technicolor. Ari touched a fingertip to her earpiece, intending to turn down the sound from the microphone connected to the video camera in the corner of Melinda's room. The urge to protect Melinda's privacy surprised her, but she hadn't seen

Melinda do anything the slightest bit suspicious in three and a half days. In fact, the longer the surveillance went on, the less she liked it. Something wasn't right—this woman wasn't any threat to the casino's operation.

At the moment, the only threat Melinda Baker posed was to Ari's sanity. Melinda lightly scraped her nails, shining with polish, in long, languid arcs between her navel and her pubis, moving lower with each sweep of her hand. Ari shivered. Before she could press the small button on her receiver to mute the sound of Melinda's breathing, a soft moan froze her in mid-motion. God, there was nothing like the sound of a woman's excitement. The first hint of that low, earthy purr always made her wet, and tonight was no exception. She shifted uncomfortably in her chair, embarrassed to feel her clitoris stiffening. The rounded contours of Melinda's full breasts curved over the edges of her slender torso, and it was easy to imagine their weighty softness in the palms of her hands. Ari tightened her fists and willed herself to look away, but she couldn't. Melinda flicked a tight nipple with her fingertip and her lips parted with a soft sigh.

Mmm, so nice.

Ari groaned, her own hard nipples chafing against the inside of her bra. It was all she could do not to pinch them to ease the almost unbearable pressure. Melinda wasn't in a hurry. She ran both hands over her chest and belly, returning to her breasts again and again, fondling them and fingering her nipples. She panted softly, her legs indolently twisting in the sheets, her head gently rolling from side to side. Minutes, hours passed without Ari taking a breath. Her stomach ached from the merciless pounding between her legs. Still, she remained motionless, her gaze riveted to the monitor, her clenched hands turned to stone on her thighs.

She should look away. There was no one else in Melinda's

room; there was no reason for her to watch. Melinda's fingers plucked faster at her nipples, and her stomach hollowed as her pelvis lifted.

Oh, I want to come.

Ari could taste her, sweet and hot on her tongue. Melinda pressed the fingers of one hand into her pubis and circled her clitoris with a finger of her other hand. She breathed in Ari's ear, small gasps and whimpers, and her finger twirled faster. The muscles on the insides of Ari's thighs quivered, and the aching pressure at the base of her clitoris spread deeper into her pelvis. Melinda twisted on the bed, her thumb and index finger rapidly pinching the swollen prominence in the cleft between her legs.

Oh god, I'm going to…oh god. Oh god oh…oh.

Ari grabbed the receiver and yanked it off her ear as a high, thin wail filled her head. She threw the small device onto the counter in front of her and buried her face in her hands, deeply ashamed and so horribly aroused her whole body shuddered.

"Jesus Christ." Ari reached out blindly, switched off the monitor, and lurched to her feet. Her self-loathing was matched only by her fury. She shouldered through the door into the main security station where one of the other night operatives glanced up at her, surprise written across his broad, florid face.

"Problem, Bianchi?"

"No," she barked on her way to the door. "My target's decided to go for a stroll. I'll be mobile for a while."

"Roger that," he called after her in a bored voice, turning his attention back to the craps tables displayed on his monitors.

It took her close to five minutes to ride the jammed elevator down to the main floor, cross through the always-crowded casino floor, and take the exterior glassed-in elevator to the twentieth floor of the tower. Five minutes during which she hoped Melinda Baker was still luxuriating in the afterglow.

If by some miracle her target decided to jump up and go for a brisk walk to cool down, Ari would be looking for a new job. As it was, she likely would be anyway.

"Crazy," she murmured as she approached Suite 2011. Halting in front of the unadorned door, she eyed the bell set into the doorframe and asked herself what the hell she thought she was going to accomplish. All she was likely to achieve was getting herself reassigned or fired, and someone else, probably Mulrooney or Williams—she shuddered mentally at the thought—would end up watching Melinda Baker for the rest of her stay. Watching Melinda do whatever she did when she had no idea anyone could see her. *Not your problem,* she warned herself. Besides, there was probably a very good reason why the woman was under surveillance, and it wasn't her job to demand explanations. It was her job to follow orders.

That thought had her reaching out to press the doorbell. Following orders was exactly what had gotten her here in the first place. While she waited, she tried to formulate a plan since she hadn't been thinking of anything except the sight and sound of Melinda's gratification and her own illicit pleasure in it.

"Who is it?" a surprisingly musical voice asked from the other side of the closed door.

"Security, Ms. Baker."

Ari heard a solid *thunk*, and then the door was opening, and she knew she'd made a big, big mistake. She stared, and the casino and everyone in it faded into the far reaches of her consciousness.

Melinda Baker held the door open just enough to look out into the hall, her expression a mixture of question and concern. Even though the wall sconces in the hallway were muted, the residual flush of sexual satisfaction on her throat and in the triangle of pale, perfect skin where her black silk robe parted between her breasts was plain to see. Her blond hair was tousled, the way it would have been if a lover had run her fingers through it as they kissed. If Ari hadn't just observed her alone only moments before, she would have concluded she'd interrupted the room's occupant in the midst of lovemaking. As it was, her own body still resonated with the aftermath of almost sharing Melinda's orgasm.

"Is there some problem?" Melinda's eyes dropped to the breast pocket of Ari's navy blue blazer. "Ms. Bianchi?"

"No," Ari said, then quickly added, "Yes. May I come in?"

Melinda unconsciously drew the silk more tightly closed between her breasts with one hand, and after a moment's hesitation, stepped back. "Certainly."

Ari turned sideways as she stepped into the narrow foyer that led to the main part of the spacious suite. She did not want to brush against Melinda's body. Not only would it be inappropriate, she didn't think she could stand the contact when her nipples strained to be touched and her stomach rolled with the still-urgent need for release. The room was exactly as she had seen it moments before, the far bedside lamp dimmed to barely a glow, the bed covers precisely turned down, and the faint impression of Melinda's body pressed into the sheets where she had just climaxed. Ari turned her back to the bed, hoping to banish the visual memory, and found Melinda only a few feet away, one hand in the pocket of the robe that came just to mid-thigh. With her other hand she brushed strands of loose blond hair back from her face.

"I'm sorry to disturb you," Ari said, glancing up to the crown molding that edged the ceiling, knowing the camera lens was situated just at the end of the entrance foyer as it opened into the main room. She looked into Melinda's eyes, noting the blue had turned gunmetal gray. Was that what happened when she came?

"That's all right," Melinda said quietly. "What's wrong?"

"There's a camera in the ceiling on that wall over there." Ari tilted her head, but Melinda did not look around. Instead, she kept her gaze fixed on Ari's face. "For some reason, you are under twenty-four-hour surveillance."

"And you know this how?" Melinda's voice was low and steady.

"Because I'm one of the security officers assigned to observe you."

"Is someone watching now?"

"Probably not. It's my shift."

"Can you...disable it?" Melinda asked.

"Temporarily, but it will eventually be repaired."

"Turn it off, please." Melinda turned away and walked quickly to the wall of windows on the far side of the room. Beyond, the fountain lights lit up the night, and sprays of water, sparkling like chains of diamonds, floated through the air.

Ari dragged a chair against the wall, climbed up, and shined her penlight along the junction of the crown molding and the ceiling tiles. When she found the minute opening, she pushed the tip of her pen into it, taking care not to enlarge the hole. When she met an obstruction, she kept steady pressure until she felt it give, and knew that the end of the fiber-optic cable had shifted. Now the image would be distorted or obliterated. Mechanical problems happened sometimes when doors were slammed, heavy objects were dropped on the floor above, or just from subtle shifting of the building itself. Cables became crimped, dislodged, or sometimes completely severed. She stepped down, replaced the chair, and stood in the middle of the room, not knowing quite what to do. Melinda Baker remained looking out.

"Are you in trouble?" Ari asked at length.

Melinda turned, smiling sadly. "I'm not in danger, if that's what you mean. I suspect my soon-to-be ex-husband is behind this." She shrugged elegant shoulders. "He's convinced I'm having an affair." She laughed softly. "And everyone knows that Las Vegas is a hotbed of infidelity."

"I suggest you change hotels." Ari grinned. "Although I'd prefer you didn't mention my name if you do."

"The conference I'm attending is here, and it's much less convenient for me to stay elsewhere. Besides, what's to say my husband won't simply have me watched somewhere else? It won't be difficult to find out where I am."

"That's up to you," Ari said. "I just thought you should know."

"That I'm being watched."

"Yes."

"Even in here."

Ari's throat was suddenly dry. "Yes."

"And you were watching. A few minutes ago?"

"Yes. I'm sorry."

Melinda moved closer, so close there was less than an arm's breadth between them. "And if I stay here, will you be the one watching me at night?"

"Yes." Ari knew she should back up. Her head was swimming. Melinda's scent was sweet and earthy, like crushed flower petals after a hard rain.

"Are you the kind of woman who likes to watch other women while they orgasm?"

"Sometimes." Ari felt her hand lifting completely of its own volition, or perhaps she'd simply lost the last fragment of her control. She caressed Melinda's cheek with the backs of her fingers. "But not when they don't know it."

"Then perhaps I shouldn't tell you that it excites me to know that you were watching." Melinda cupped Ari's hand, angled her head, and kissed the tips of Ari's fingers. "I've imagined a woman touching me, making me come, for a long time. That's one of the reasons I'm leaving my husband."

"Is there someone? A woman?" Ari sifted strands of silky blond hair through her fingers, her palm sliding along the curve of Melinda's neck.

"No. When I finish, I'm always alone."

"Not tonight," Ari whispered. She leaned forward and very gently kissed Melinda on the mouth. "You weren't alone tonight."

Melinda circled Ari's shoulders with both arms and leaned against the front of her body. Her breasts were full and firm against Ari's, her hips softly insistent as she rocked between Ari's thighs. Ari skimmed both hands down the silky plane of Melinda's back and cupped her buttocks, holding her so she could press more firmly into her. Melinda tilted her head back and gave her throat to Ari's mouth. Ari kissed her way from the soft spot below Melinda's ear to the pulse pounding wildly at the base of her throat. She touched the beating point with the tip of her tongue and tenderly bit down.

"Oh," Melinda breathed, tightening her fingers in the taut muscles of Ari's shoulders. "When you watched me," she whispered into Ari's ear, "did you…"

"No," Ari gasped. She raised her head and cradled Melinda's face, kissing her again. "You excited me, but I couldn't take advantage of you that way."

Melinda smiled crookedly, sliding her hands from Ari's shoulders inside her blazer and over her breasts. Ari shuddered and Melinda laughed with quiet delight. "Would you take advantage of me now, if I asked you to?"

"Right now, I'll do anything you want."

"I understand now why men want women, and why women do, too." She caught Ari's hand and guided it from her face inside her robe, molding Ari's fingers to her breast.

Her pupils widened as her nipple hardened against Ari's palm. "The power is wonderful, isn't it?"

"You are wonderful," Ari said thickly, freeing the sash at Melinda's waist and opening her robe. She bent her head and took the offered breast into her mouth. Melinda gave a startled cry and sagged against her. Ari caught her around the waist and continued to suck until Melinda tugged her head away.

"Please." Melinda's lids were heavy, her mouth soft and vulnerable. "I so want you to touch me. Everywhere. Will you?"

By way of answer, Ari guided her to the bed and gently lifted the robe from her shoulders. "Lie down."

"Take your clothes off, too. Please."

"Are you sure?" The part of Ari's brain that was still functioning reminded her that Melinda's fantasy might not have included having a naked woman in her bed. "I'll be more than happy just to touch you."

Melinda smiled. "Oh, I want you to touch me. And I want to feel your body against mine when you do."

Ari kicked off her shoes, shrugged out of her jacket, and shed her shirt, pants, holster, and underwear in record time. Despite the flurry of activity, when she moved to the bed she slowed, leaned over Melinda, and kissed her again, her breasts barely brushing Melinda's. "Are you sure?"

"Yes." Melinda reached up and circled Ari's shoulders once more, pulling her down against the length of her body. "Please."

Ari slipped her thigh between Melinda's legs and slowly let their bodies merge. She kissed her, both hands in her hair, caressing her face and her neck as she explored her mouth. Dimly, she felt Melinda's nails course up and down her back and finally grip her ass, urging their hips together, harder, faster. Ari felt herself start to climb and eased away.

"What?" Melinda asked. "Did I do something wrong?"

"No," Ari said quickly, kissing her. "I didn't come earlier and I'm...I'm close."

The corner of Melinda's mouth lifted in a smile. "I *did* come earlier, and I'm close, too. Will you let me touch you while you touch me?"

Ari shifted onto her side so they could look into each other's eyes, then she caressed Melinda's breasts as they kissed again. Slowly, she dipped lower, smoothing her fingers over the silky skin of Melinda's belly, brushing the soft strands between her thighs.

"I'm not delicate," Melinda whispered, her breath hot against Ari's neck. "And I'm very certain that I want you to do this." As if to make sure Ari understood, Melinda swept her hand up the inside of Ari's thigh and stroked through the wetness between her legs.

"Jesus," Ari blurted, her hips jumping. "God."

"Oh, I think you might be just a little closer than me."

Nerve endings jangling, Ari rested her forehead against Melinda's and slid her fingers on either side of Melinda's clitoris. She squeezed gently and Melinda did the same. When she pressed and circled, Melinda echoed her, and she was lost. "I'm going to come in about one second."

"Oh, me, too." Melinda nipped at Ari's lip and sucked the tip of her tongue. "God, it's so good. So good."

Ari forced herself to keep her eyes open, watching Melinda's face as her orgasm flooded her, just as she had watched her on the monitor. Melinda was so much more beautiful now, her eyes shimmering with tears of pleasure and something Ari couldn't name, her body flowing hot and silky under Ari's fingers with each surge of pleasure. Ari climaxed, her own release so much less essential than Melinda's. When Melinda finally quieted in her arms, only then did Ari close her eyes.

"I'd love to come for you again," Melinda said, her voice drowsy and satisfied. "Like I did earlier, with you watching. But I don't think I'll be able to, if I don't know that you're the one looking at the monitor."

"How about I just watch you here?"

"And the other things I might want to do?"

"Anything."

"I'm not...I haven't...I might not be all you bet on." Melinda suddenly sounded shy and uncertain.

Eyes still closed, Ari kissed Melinda's temple and lazily caressed her back. "Don't worry; I know all I need to know. After this, I'd bet on you blind."

ALL IN

·················

Radclyffe

D r. Saxon Sinclair contemplated her Scotch rocks and watched the third man in five minutes try to pick up the blonde sitting opposite her at the horseshoe shaped bar that occupied one corner of the Palace casino lounge. She didn't ordinarily spend her nights in a bar, at least she hadn't for the last five years. But she couldn't sleep and her suite, although spacious, felt claustrophobic. She wondered briefly if the blonde, a fellow trauma surgeon she'd seen at the meeting just that morning, was having similar difficulties. She obviously wasn't there to find company for the night, because she quickly dispatched anyone who seemed to be interested. It was possible, Sax supposed, that the only other single woman sitting at the bar was looking for a different sort of companionship than what the men were offering, but Sax hadn't gotten that vibe the few times their eyes had met. No. She and the blonde were probably both sitting alone at three in the morning for exactly the same reason. A kind of loneliness that went deeper than any physical diversion could assuage.

"No, really, I'd rather just sit here and relax." The blonde's low, musical voice carried surprisingly well despite the cacophony of bells and whistles and constant rumble of voices coming from the gaming floor just beyond the lounge.

Sax narrowed her eyes as a heavyset middle-aged man in an expensive suit put his arm around the blonde's shoulders and leaned down to say something else, crowding her at the same time as he made it difficult for her to move away. Again, she murmured no and shook her head, her expression one of forced pleasantness. Sax imagined the woman was trying to avoid a scene. She knew the man, another surgeon. She had met his wife earlier that week at one of the trauma conference social functions that she hadn't been able to get out of, and remembered him mentioning that his son was a surgical resident somewhere in California. When the blonde signaled no for the third time, Sax felt a surge of anger that brought her to her feet. A woman shouldn't have to say no even once just because she was sitting alone at a bar. She certainly shouldn't have to say no three times. Just as Sax took a step forward, one of the Palace's security guards, recognizable from her understated uniform of dark blazer, white shirt, and dark trousers, as well as by the name tag over her breast pocket and the radio receiver clipped to her ear, appeared as if by magic and tapped the aggressive surgeon on the shoulder. Whatever she said brought a flush to the man's face and he rapidly strode away. As Sax reclaimed her barstool, she saw the guard murmur a word to the blonde, who fleetingly touched her arm, allowing her fingers to linger for just a moment on the sleeve of the blue blazer. Then the guard, too, disappeared. The exchange had been so brief, Sax doubted anyone would have noticed, but to her, the connection was unmistakable. Her chest tightened and she ached for just a simple touch, just a few seconds of feeling as if she weren't hopelessly, helplessly adrift.

"Hey," a deep voice said as a hand dropped heavily onto Sax's shoulder. "I called your room and you didn't answer. Listen, I have to go home."

Sax glanced up at her friend and former resident, Quinn Maguire. Some people said they looked alike, but Sax couldn't see it. They both had black hair and blue eyes, sure, but Quinn was an inch or so shorter and more muscular. And more importantly, Quinn always had an air of calm, steady focus about her that Sax rarely managed, especially lately. Right now though, Quinn appeared anything but calm—her cotton button-down collar shirt was rumpled and untucked, hanging out over her jeans. She wore loafers with no socks and had an expression Sax had never seen before. Panic.

"What's the matter?" Sax asked.

"Nothing," Quinn exclaimed. "Nothing. Honor called." Quinn's face widened into an enormous grin. "She's in labor. Two weeks early. I gotta go. Sorry to leave you hanging with the panel tomorrow."

"Don't worry about it." Sax stood to give Quinn a quick squeeze on the arm. "Give Honor my love and call me with an update, okay?"

"Yeah. Okay. I will." Quinn turned to go, then looked back, her expression unexpectedly serious. "You're okay, right?"

Sax worked up a smile. "Sure, I'm okay. Jesus, you think I can't get through a twenty minute presentation without you?"

"That's not what I meant," Quinn said quietly.

"I know what you meant." Sax knew she sounded gruff, but it suddenly felt like she was pushing her words out through ground glass. "Just go, already."

"You'll call me too, with any news, right?"

Sax nodded.

"She's okay, you know," Quinn said.

"Yeah," Sax said roughly. "Sure."

Then Quinn was gone and Sax was alone again. Even the blonde was gone. She sat back down, drained her Scotch, and signaled for another. Three weeks. She hadn't heard from Jude in three weeks. It wasn't unusual for her to go days, sometimes a week or even a little longer, without hearing from her, but this was the longest it had ever been. If she knew where she was, or even where to start looking, she would have flown to Iraq four days ago instead of Las Vegas. She knew where Jude had been eleven weeks earlier when she'd started out from Fallujah, one of three embedded journalists with a mobile division of the second Marines. After that, Jude's e-mails had been brief and sporadic and absent of any detail. After five years of being married to a documentary filmmaker, Sax recognized Jude's attempts to play down just how bad whatever particular natural disaster or human horror she was investigating really was. She was used to Jude being gone, too, sometimes for weeks at a time. This time it was different. This time she felt their connection, which was always so strong no matter where in the world Jude was, grow thinner and thinner until she feared it had snapped. And as the ties to Jude slid through her fingers like so many infinitesimal grains of sand that she tried so desperately to hold in her closed fists, she watched the world around her fade to a gray unreality, as if she were watching life on the screen of an old black-and-white television. She knew Jude would be pissed at her for losing her grip, so she tried to pretend that life went on. She was at the damn conference, wasn't she?

She rubbed the back of her neck, tired and so damn lost.

"Here, why don't you let me do that?" a husky voice said from behind her as Sax's hand was replaced by two smaller ones.

Sax gripped the rounded edges of the shiny black bar top with both hands, struggling for balance. Her head felt as if a bomb had burst inside it. Her voice came out barely a whisper. "Jude?"

"For your sake, it better be." Jude's breasts pressed against Sax's back as she leaned down and kissed her just below her ear. "Because I'd find out otherwise, and you'd be dead meat, Sinclair."

"How?"

"I saw Quinn grabbing a cab out front. She told me where you were."

Sax hadn't yet glanced back, almost too afraid to discover that she might be hallucinating. Still, when she reached back she grasped a warm hand, rougher than she remembered, but just as strong.

"No, I mean, how are you here?"

"Military transport. I got lucky and there was an extra seat at the last second. It was either get on the plane without calling you, or miss it all together. I've been traveling about two days."

Finally, Sax swiveled on the seat and faced her lover. Right before she left, Jude had cut her shoulder length red hair short. It was shaggy and needed a cut now, falling just above her collar in thick waves. She wore a tan T-shirt and faded khaki camos, and even in the low light of the bar, Sax could tell her pale skin had tanned in the unrelenting desert sun. Clearly exhausted, she appeared wraithlike, and Sax saw the haunted expression her lover tried to hide with a welcoming smile.

"Hi, baby," Jude Castle said, leaning in between Sax's spread legs and slipping both arms around Sax's neck. She kissed her firmly, but far too briefly, and then leaned back. "I know you hate these conferences, so I thought I'd drop in and distract you."

"Working pretty good so far." Sax rose and slid her arm around Jude's waist. "Let's head upstairs. You look a little tired."

Jude laughed shortly. "I look like hell." She frowned as they started to walk. "You look a little thin, too. And what are you doing up at almost four in the morning?"

"Hoping to get lucky," Sax murmured, kissing Jude's temple.

"Did you?"

"Oh yeah."

Once upstairs, Sax stripped, lowered the room lights, and turned down the bed while Jude took a quick shower. When Jude walked naked out of the bathroom toweling her hair, Sax's only thought was to get her into bed and hold her. Hold her where she could rest and be safe. Then she registered the scar, immediately assessing in her surgeon's mind the barely healed wound on Jude's abdomen. She was across the room in three long strides.

"What is this?" Sax demanded, unable to keep her fear from translating into anger. A seven-inch long, angry red ridge wrapped around Jude's left flank just below her ribs "You didn't tell me you'd been injured."

For a second, Jude seemed confused, then she reflexively covered the area with her hand. "God, I'm so tired I forgot about it. It wasn't anything much. Just a glancing—"

Sax spun around and stalked to the far side of the room, which suddenly felt even smaller than it had hours before, when it held only her loneliness. Now there wasn't enough space to contain her rage, but it wasn't Jude she wanted to lash out at. With her back still turned, she snarled, "That's a bullet wound. Do you think I don't know that? Do you think I don't know if the trajectory had been slightly different you'd be dead right now? Jesus Christ, how could you not tell me?"

"I knew you'd worry, and I knew I would be all right," Jude said softly, suddenly right behind Sax. "Baby, you're shaking."

Sax pulled her shoulder away when Jude caressed her. "Don't. Just…" Her hand was shaking as she swiped the tears that had come out of nowhere too fast for her to stop. Every lost and desolate moment of the last three weeks crashed down on her, and she had a soul-destroying image of what life would be if Jude had not come back. "I'm sorry. I can't…just get in bed. You need to sleep."

Jude wrapped her arms around Sax's body from behind, pressing her breasts to Sax's back and her cheek to Sax's shoulder. "That's not what I need. That's not what I traveled around the world for. Turn around."

Sax had never been able to say no to Jude, and she couldn't now either. But she didn't want her to see what must be in her eyes. Desperation, and devastation. Not quite looking at her, Sax grasped Jude's hand and led her to the bed. Then she drew her down and pulled the covers to their waists as they faced one another. Stroking wet strands of red hair back from Jude's cheek, she whispered, "Close your eyes. Sleep will be good for you."

"When I first got…hurt," Jude said, her eyes wide and never leaving Sax's, "the first thing I thought was that I was still alive, and there were others near me who weren't. I was glad, glad it was them and not me, and part of me knew that was wrong."

"No," Sax said, the agony of imagining Jude wounded making her voice sound harsh. "There is no such thing as justice in war. You were lucky, and it's okay to be glad."

"And then for awhile I didn't have time to think at all." As she went on, Jude caressed Sax's face and Sax gently stroked Jude's body, taking care not to disturb the freshly healed wound.

"When I got my turn with the medic and he was stitching me up, I thought of all the times I'd filmed you doing the same thing. Saving lives. I missed you so much right then."

"I would've come over there, if I'd known you were hurt."

Jude smiled and traced her fingertips over Sax's mouth. "I know. But I really wasn't in danger. After a few days, I wasn't even sore. It just looks bad."

"You forget who I am," Sax grumbled, capturing Jude's hand and rubbing it against her cheek. "Don't try to snow me."

"Baby, I'll never forget who you are." Jude shifted closer, pressing her breasts to Sax's and tilting her hips until their lower bodies fused. "I'm sorry you were scared."

"Terrified," Sax said hoarsely.

"When it was bad," Jude whispered, "worse than bad, and I felt things inside of me breaking…"

Sax groaned and cradled Jude's face against her throat, stroking her hair. "It's okay, baby. It's okay."

"I knew," Jude said, her mouth against Sax's skin, "you'd heal me." She tilted her face up, trembling in Sax's arms. "Please, baby. I don't need sleep. I don't need food. I don't even need you to take the nightmares away. It was hot, always so hot, and I'm still cold. I need you to make me feel again."

"I need you in order to live," Sax murmured, gently pushing Jude onto her back. She settled her hips between Jude's legs and held her body above her, braced on her forearms. "Are you sure you're not hurting too much?"

"I need you." Jude wrapped her legs around the back of Sax's thighs, lifting into her, pressing as tightly as she could. "Inside me. It's all I've been able to think about since I left there."

Sax *wanted* to be inside her—inside her body, inside her

heart, inside her soul. She wanted to bleed into her, until their very cells were indistinguishable. She wanted her so badly she was afraid. Tenderly, carefully, she spread her fingers through Jude's tangle of still strangely short hair, and kissed her eyelids, her temples, the corners of her mouth. Jude smelled fresh and clean from the shower, her skin faintly roughened from the wind and sun. Sax traced the edge of Jude's jaw with the tip of her tongue, then trailed kisses down her neck. The stress of holding back the flash fire burning through her, coupled with her anxiety over going too fast, sent her already on-the-edge nervous system into overdrive. She struggled for breath as her body quivered uncontrollably.

"Oh, baby," Jude murmured, caressing Sax's back and ass with long, urgent strokes. "Oh, baby, don't hold back. You need me. And god, I love that you do." She knew just how to break Sax's control, and as she gripped Sax tighter with her legs, she bit down hard on the thick muscle that slanted from Sax's neck to her shoulder.

"God!" Sax roared, rearing her head back and trying to pull away. "You don't know what I'll do. I'll hurt you!"

"No, you won't," Jude said fiercely. "You can't. Please, please, help me!"

Jude's tears did what nothing else could. They penetrated the shroud of desperation and fear that had clouded Sax's mind and heart for weeks. She saw her lover clearly, saw her need, saw her vulnerability. And reflected in her lover's eyes, she saw herself—slowly dying for want of this woman. Rocking back on her knees, Sax placed her palm between Jude's breasts and spread her fingers, bracing herself as she brought her other arm between Jude's legs and entered her. She knew this woman, this body, this flesh that welcomed her, and she buried herself there. Jude bucked off the bed, her voice a strangled scream, and Sax held her down as she thrust into her.

"You feel me?" Sax rasped, the muscles in her chest and arms straining as she held herself in check even as she pushed deeper. She rolled her thumb over Jude's clitoris until it hardened. "Can you?"

"Yes," Jude cried, her heels digging into Sax's legs as she forced herself harder against Sax's hand. "Deeper, please, deeper. Oh god."

Sweat dripped from Sax's face onto Jude's, mixing with her lover's tears, as she filled her again and again. Jude strained and writhed beneath her, struggling to climax. Her head whipped from side to side, her breath torn from her in strangled moans.

Jude's eyes opened wide, her face a mask of agonized need. "I can't. Oh god, I can't feel...I can't..."

Instantly, Sax stilled, panting to pull air into lungs that burned. Her arms trembled, her stomach was rigid with her own need for release, but she forced her voice to be quiet and calm. "It's okay. Just breathe for a second. Breathe, baby."

Tears leaked from Jude's eyes as she gasped for breath, and Sax stretched out beside her, cradling her face against her chest. She stroked her sweat-soaked hair. "It's okay, baby."

"I need...Oh god, I feel numb. I can't and I need..."

Jude's heart pounded against Sax's breast, erratic and urgent. Sax cupped Jude's face and brushed her thumb over Jude's mouth. "Look at me. Look at me, baby."

When Jude focused on her, Sax whispered, "Stay with me. Stay right here with me." Then she reached down and began to stroke her. When Jude whimpered and thrust against her hand, Sax kissed her and whispered again, "Look at me. Just look at me and know I love you more than life."

"I need you to make me come," Jude moaned, clinging to Sax's shoulders, her back arching with the growing pressure. "Need you. Need you so much."

"I'm here." Sax felt the rapid pulsations in the swollen flesh beneath her fingers that signaled Jude's gathering climax. She bore down on Jude's clitoris, giving her the short, firm strokes she knew she needed to push her over the edge.

Jude closed her eyes, crying out her pleasure, and then Sax filled her again. She turned Jude on her back, riding Jude's leg as she pushed into her, stroke after deep stroke. Sax came swiftly with her clitoris crushed to Jude's hard thigh, and Jude came a second time and then a third. Sax didn't stop until her strength gave out and she collapsed into Jude's arms.

"You okay?" Sax gasped, unable to raise her head from Jude's shoulder. She felt Jude weakly caress her neck.

"I will be," Jude murmured. "I'm here with you. I'm home."

PAYOUT

···················

Karin Kallmaker

o how does it feel in the light of morning?" Alison spooned behind Carolyn, massaging her shoulders gently as the sun slowly illuminated their room.

"I'm still not sure." Carolyn rolled onto her stomach. "Your hands are wonderful, as always."

Alison shifted her position, continuing the soft touches with one lazy hand. "I know you're young for this sort of thing, but then you started out young as a published writer, too."

"True. I just…" Carolyn stretched out an arm to touch the Lucite statue of an old-fashioned oil lamp that rested on the bedside table. "It's an award, and it's been a long time since I've seen one."

There was the tiniest edge of bitterness in Carolyn's voice, and it pained Alison. "You wouldn't do it any other way, would you?"

"Of course not." She snuggled around in Alison's arms. "I'm glad I came out. I'm glad I've been living free. I just feel a little bit young to get the Lamplight Award."

"You did light the way, and it was very cool that Amelia Wainwright was the one who presented it to you, and I swear, Barrett Lancey had tears in her butch little eyes. They wouldn't get to be who they are if Carly Vincent, hot new best seller, sweetheart of the twenty-four to thirty-two demographic, hadn't taken one for the Sappho team all those years ago. There are other people who could have come out, no doubt, but you're the one that did it."

"I was waiting on the world to change and it did, I guess. I didn't lose all my readers."

"Just the narrow-minded ones, and you weren't writing for them anyway. I'm glad you don't regret it."

"I don't." The eyes that gazed up at Alison were the clear blue she'd lost her heart to at least two decades ago. "I might whine a little sometimes, but I don't regret it."

"God, you feel good this morning." Alison breathed in the cologne, the shampoo, the wonderful blend of scents that equaled Carolyn to her. "I loved dancing with you last night."

"Me too you." Carolyn burrowed into Alison's shoulder. "It was a fun evening, even if Farrah Fotheringay was hitting on you."

"Was not. She's straight. She probably just wants a new agent."

"No, she was after the hottest woman in the room." Carolyn twisted a lock of Alison's hair around her finger. "I love the way your hair is changing color, silver and platinum threads all woven in."

Alison smoothed her love's short curls and turned the adorable face up so she could see it. All these years and it was still like waking up to sunshine. Sleepy eyes blinked at her.

"I love you."

"You're just saying that." Carolyn stretched.

"Why would I just make it up after all this time?"

"Because you want to have your way with me."

Alison cupped one alluring breast under the covers. It firmed at her touch. "I don't know what you're talking about."

"It was late last night, and I recall being promised something if I wore those thigh-high stockings that get you all hot and bothered. But alas, all I remember were some vague mumbles about wine and the hour." Carolyn's light tone was at odds with the small arch of her back in response to the tip of Alison's finger lightly stroking under her nipple.

"Then I need to make it up to you, don't I?"

"I would think so."

"Okay." Alison threw back the covers and hopped out of bed. "How about a nice breakfast?"

"Get back in this bed this instant." Carolyn gave her a wry look.

"Oh, so you want breakfast in bed."

Carolyn dissolved into laughter. "Honey, I want to *be* breakfast in bed."

"My thought exactly."

She began with slow kisses along Carolyn's calves, eliciting a soft, encouraging sigh. She would never get enough of the taste of Carolyn's skin, and lazily worked her way up the welcoming, curvaceous body. It made sense to get out of her nightshirt then, and use her breasts to massage Carolyn's thighs.

A long, rising moan rewarded her efforts and Alison stretched out so their bodies could meet in the full delight of skin-on-skin.

"Ally," Carolyn breathed. "You've got some kind of magic hands."

"Tell that to my teammates. I drop any more fly balls and—"

Carolyn pressed her fingertips to Alison's mouth. "Why on earth are you talking about softball at this moment?"

"Cause mostly…I'm an idiot."

The little laugh they shared was intimate and ended with the kind of kiss that reminded Alison of the backseat of Carolyn's old Mustang convertible. Now was not the time to admit she was having a fast food craving. Other cravings took precedence.

"Close your eyes," Alison whispered. "Think about Melissa and the concert tonight and the backstage passes your fabulous agent got you."

Carolyn laughed again. "I thought they were a birthday gift from my girlfriend."

Alison kissed away the laughter—she loved doing that. Making her Carrie laugh and then moan ever so slightly. Every time they shared this dance it had all the fever and fireworks of their first time, combined with layers of familiarity. There was still plenty of mystery, but no terror of doing something wrong or too hard or too soft. Make her laugh, and kiss the smiles. She could do this all morning.

She did do it all morning, as it turned out. No doubt Carolyn would have the right metaphor for the way her body was melting over the bed, spreading like warm honey, only not so sticky and leaving a less romantic soul to wonder who was going to clean all that up.

"More, Ally, please…"

Those were Alison's favorite words.

Her second favorite set of words were said shortly thereafter.

"Your turn." Carolyn gave her a searing look, no longer melted honey or melted anything, she was firm and soft all at once, just a little commanding and more than a little eager.

Alison moaned when Carolyn's tongue swept through her, then she couldn't help but laugh.

Carolyn immediately stopped what she was doing. "Am I distracting you?"

"Sorry, honey. I was just—I realized how good it was to moan really loudly and not have one of the puppies come to investigate what we're doing."

Carolyn grinned and kissed Alison's inner thigh. "Okay, yes, that is nice. But no more laughing." Her tongue pressed into the soft place where thigh met really sensitive areas.

"Hell, no, oh..."

She scrabbled among the rumpled sheets for Carolyn's hand, clasping their fingers as her legs fell open and she lost herself in the exquisite attentions of that wonderful, thorough mouth. She felt the love all through her bones, and she did want to smile at her happiness. Another laugh threatened— maybe it was watching her beloved Carrie, who had suffered in classy silence all these years after the onslaught of hate mail and plummeting sales, publicly recognized by her peers as the brave woman she was. It had been a risk, and there had been a price, but now—

Carolyn's sensitive fingers moved inside her and the laughter transformed to passion. Her memories of last night, dancing, her daily ecstasy of waking up with Carolyn, they went away and the only focus she had was for the pressure building behind her eyes, along her shoulders, down her arms to where her hand clasped Carolyn's. She rose, Carolyn held on, their bodies frozen until a white, hazy afterglow gently surrounded her.

❖

"Did I go to sleep?"

Carolyn leaned against the bathroom door, drying her hair. "Yes. And you missed the chance to shower with me."

"Damn." Alison stretched, not wanting to get out of the bed.

"Honey, there are two floors of casinos, five swimming pools, three hundred fountains, and an art gallery waiting for us, now that the convention is over."

"Um-hmm." Carolyn's mouth had felt wonderful, she mused.

The bed jolted from Carolyn's swift kick. "So get up!"

Alison reluctantly swung her legs over the side of the bed. "If only your fans knew what Carly Vincent is really like." Her gaze fell on the award and she touched it with one fingertip.

Crossing the warm carpet to the bathroom, she turned Carolyn from the mirror to take her into her arms. "You know, right? That I'm proud of you, that you're the world to me? That I love you?"

"I know," Carolyn said. "I was feeling sorry for myself last night, for a while. But this morning, today—I know why I made those choices, and I've gotten everything that ever had value to me. I got you."

"Let's go back to bed."

"You just want to sleep more."

"We can play breakfast in bed again, first." She blinked innocently.

Carolyn laughed and Alison kissed the smile.

SOLITAIRE

....

Karin Kallmaker

ell, that was a total cock-up." DJ unknotted the short scarf from the collar of her white shirt. How was she supposed to sell emergency room supplies if the company sent the wrong samples for the exhibit hall booth? The convention had been a total bust for her, a complete waste of time.

A hot shower, fresh clothes, and then she was going to lose herself at the poker tables—any table where Texas Hold 'Em wasn't the game. What was wrong with a good round of seven-card stud?

What she really wanted was for Lyn to walk through the door right now. That would be heaven. She'd been on the road too long, and their phone calls were too unsatisfying. It wasn't like her to leave her clothes all over the floor, but right now, she couldn't care less. Tomorrow morning she packed up the booth and then caught a plane home.

The aroma of Lyn's shampoo was soothing. She traveled with a little bottle of it to remind her of the things she really loved in this world, and one of them was the way Lyn smelled. She scrubbed her short hair free of gel and washed the sweat of the day from her body, then stood just a little longer under the hot spray, inhaling steam to soothe her dry sinuses.

Maybe she was too tired for the tables tonight. That would be awful, though, to be in Las Vegas and too bleedin' tired to do the one thing she could do with her girl so far away. Lord knows every other temptation was available, and she'd said no to a few in the hospitality suite earlier.

Maybe a trip to the fitness room? Even as she thought it, she dismissed the idea. It would be overrun with men, and American men were second only to Aussies in their unwavering belief in their universal sex appeal. She was too tired to deal with them.

The Palace towels were thick and thirsty, and normally she'd have delighted in the little luxuries of the heated towel rack, the warming lamp—someone else was paying for it, too. She had a major case of the post-convention blahs, though. Her hand reached for an old, comfortable T-shirt. She hesitated, knowing if she put it on she wouldn't go out. If she put on the tight black tank then she would hit the tables. She looked back and forth between both garments, then opted for the hotel robe before she got chilled. Decision deferred.

She flipped open her cell phone and tried not to be disappointed that Lyn wasn't home. Of course she wasn't. DJ had known that all day. Lyn's eldest was finally performing live and DJ was sorry to miss it. She was sorry she couldn't hear more than Lyn's voice telling her to leave a message.

Drifting to the window in hope of some form of distraction, she watched the lights change in the famous fountains she could just glimpse through an opening between buildings. Her room faced inward over the hotel grounds and her view was of two of the swimming pools, ringed in lights. One had a floating bar in the middle. Maybe that was the way to go. Lounge in warm water, kick back with a good drink, and daydream. That might be okay if the temperature had dropped enough. There was nothing more dismal than sweating while sitting in a swimming pool.

She unlatched her sliding glass door and stepped out onto the balcony. It had cooled off quite a bit from midday. The pool with the bar was appealing more and more. She turned to go back inside when she heard a voice from the adjacent balcony—a woman's voice possibly—say plainly, "Are you sure it's okay, baby?"

"Yes." Laughter, definitely a woman this time, then, "What happens in Vegas, right?"

"Let me get it out of the package and clean it, then. You stay right there."

The lights that bathed the hotel exterior didn't quite reach this floor, but DJ still tried to discreetly peek through the separating barrier. It was dark, though, that is until the first person came back and a glow from inside their hotel room dimly illuminated the small confines of the balcony.

Definitely both women. Lounging in the chaise was a lovely creature whose slender charms were quite noticeable, given that she was naked. There was something comfortable about her beauty, quiet even. Maybe it was just the contrast with the glitter, spandex, and artifice of Las Vegas in general. Her hands briefly brushed over her natural, yielding breasts as she relaxed in the chair.

DJ told herself to stop looking. But when the other woman, a no-apologies butch, shucked her tank top and briefs and joined her lover on the chaise, it was more than DJ could do to look away.

"You're sure?" The butch kissed her girlfriend with a melting tenderness. "Do you want to hold it? Just to get used to it?"

DJ lost the reply, but there was no mistaking the object in the woman's hand. If she remembered correctly, that was the Mighty Aphrodite. One like it was at home.

The butch had stretched out alongside the other woman, stroking her breasts and shoulders. "It's up to you, Marcie."

"I want to. How many times do I have to say it?"

"I'm sorry, baby, it's just that I don't want to hurt you, and I don't want you to regret it tomorrow."

"Did you bring the lube?"

The butch's voice got more gravelly. "Yes. Please, let me."

For a moment, DJ's view was obstructed, then the butch stopped moving around and settled on her knees between Marcie's legs.

DJ swallowed hard. She missed Lyn fiercely at that moment, because she knew how trickling lube over her fingers felt, and she knew why the butch moaned when she pushed those slippery fingers into her eager, receptive lover. Her own hand twitched, and her cunt did as well. If she were closer she would be able to smell them both, smell sex and the unmistakable blend of lube and silicone and woman.

The butch bent to lavish attention on Marcie's clit. Marcie let out a long coo, a single note of pleasure that finally broke as she hooked one leg over the butch's shoulder and lifted her hips to offer more. Their words were lost for several seconds, then Marcie said, her voice taut with desire, "Please, Keri, fuck me with it."

Now DJ could hear everything. The slippery, wet noises and the mutual quiet grunts they shared were enough to send her own fires leaping.

"Fuck me…"

"I am…"

"More…"

DJ put her hands over her ears and stumbled back into her hotel room, collapsing on the bed.

The women in the hospitality suite had all loved the accent, and while so many men never figured her for a lesbian, the same number of women did. She could have been with someone tonight instead of peering like a pathetic Peeping Tom at her neighbors. What happened in Vegas stayed in Vegas, or so they said. Trouble was, none of the women offering had short hair, piercing eyes, and a sense of humor sharper even than her own. None of them were Lyn.

"Oh, yes! Yes, baby, don't stop…"

DJ quietly closed the balcony door, but she fancied she could still hear those pleas.

She'd be home tomorrow night and Lyn would meet her plane, and they might even take care of some of their itches on the way home from the airport. Maybe she'd surprise Lyn with a night in a motel. Just the two of them and lots of sex.

The wall behind her bed began to thump. Bloody hell, they'd moved inside. Now she wasn't eavesdropping or peeping, she couldn't help but hear it.

If there had been any trepidation about whether Marcie would like the toy, it sounded like they were over it. Marcie not only liked the toy, she liked getting fucked hard with it, hard and deep and for a very, very long time.

DJ called Lyn again and listened to, "I can't come to the phone right now, but if you'll leave your name and number, I'll get back to you." She listened to it three times before snapping her phone shut.

Marcie was getting well and truly fucked, and from the sound of it, she was going to scream in five, four, three, two—

"Oooh, fuck, baby! Fuck me!"

DJ knew how sheepish she had felt the first night with Lyn, when her vocabulary had abruptly become that limited, too. That had been such a good night. All the nights together had been that good.

Tonight was not a good night. Now her body ached and she was turned on and wet, with no recourse but to get on her own bed and touch…touch…

Fingers always knew what to do, they knew every circle to make, when to glide over the nerves, when to pinch and lift. It was her mind that wandered, sifting through memories and fantasies for the one that would catch like kindling.

Tomorrow she would get into the passenger seat of their car and she would let Lyn drive, but when they got as far as the scattered office buildings, she would tell Lyn to pull into a deserted parking lot. She'd pull her across the seat, put Lyn's hand down her slacks and beg, beg for Lyn's touch, beg to come, right there in the car. She'd strip off her pants, spread her legs, and pull Lyn's fingers inside her, and Lyn would know, like she always knew, how much, how hard, how fast, like that.

"God, yes, baby, do me again, I can't believe how good it feels when you do that…"

How good she feels, DJ thought, how good Lyn always feels. She moaned, feeling the dance of electricity start in her clit, then spread upward, outward until the sizzle escaped from the top of her head. She would lie back in the seat, sated, drifting, while Lyn drove them home.

She smiled lazily, feeling much better, but the fantasy in her head continued. Too soon to stop, she thought, as she envisioned herself in her own bed. Lyn's shoulder would be against her cheek, their knees bumping and shifting until arms and legs got just right.

And she was falling asleep in Lyn's arms, surrounded with the scent of her. It was the best fantasy of all.

LUCK ON THE RIVER

Radclyffe

I leaned over the brass railing to get a better look at the feature table. The glaring television camera spots lit up the playing surface like high noon in the desert, while the rest of the room faded into gloomy darkness. I doubted Evie could see me, but I knew she knew where I was. Every now and then she glanced in my direction, and I could feel her gaze find mine. Surrounded by big men with big personalities and even bigger egos, she glimmered like a jewel in the midst of drab stones. She'd been playing twelve hours a day for six days, and she was tired. Her normally pale skin was nearly translucent now, stretched thin over arched cheekbones. The luster in her green eyes had faded, and even her red-gold hair had darkened to heavy copper. On an ordinary day, when she walked through a room, she turned heads. For the last forty-eight hours, she couldn't step out of the elevator without being mobbed. Everyone wanted something from her—a comment, an autograph, or, under the guise of offering friendly advice, to prove they weren't afraid of her.

They should be afraid. Eight players left out of a field of forty-three hundred, and she was the only woman to make it to the final table. I knew what it took for her to get there, because I held her through the nights, or what was left of them, when she jerked awake an hour or two after finally unwinding enough to fall asleep. Keyed up, exhausted beyond the point where real sleep was possible, she struggled to find the calm place inside where she needed to be to win. She was a pro; she'd earned her stripes in cash games up and down the West Coast, but she'd never played in the big tournament before. That was a strike against her. And she was young. Even though there were college boys younger than her who had qualified by whiling away their college tuition money playing poker on the Internet in their dorm rooms night after night. Another strike against her. And she was beautiful, which some took to mean she couldn't also be smart, and she was a girl—*my* girl, which she made sure everyone knew. Strikes three, four, and five. More than enough to put her out of the game, but she was still in the running.

Only right this minute, her tournament life was on the line. She'd come in short-stacked at the beginning of play ten hours ago, and she'd managed to stay alive by betting smart and playing smarter, but she didn't stand a chance of winning without a bigger chip count. She had to double up soon while she still had chips to bet with, and that's exactly what she did. Because she played to win. She pushed the rest of her chips into the middle of the table and said coolly, "I'm all in."

The room fell silent. One player folded immediately, leaving just her and the favorite. She looked poised and confident, when I knew acid had to be eating a hole through her stomach.

I tried not to be nervous. I trusted her. Hell, I loved her. But I knew how much she wanted this, how hard she'd worked, and how fucking tired she was. I grabbed the rail with both hands, willing her to feel my support across the twenty feet that separated us. I wished I could be standing behind her, rubbing her shoulders, whispering encouragement.

"I call," her opponent said, and matched her bet.

Evie turned over an ace and a king, suited. It was a strong hand to go all in on, and I wanted to shout, *Way to go, baby!* Some people in the audience did.

Her opponent studied her cards, then her, and slowly turned over pocket aces. Fuck. The best draw in poker. Evie didn't blink. I stopped breathing.

The dealer buried a card, counted out three, and turned the flop. A deuce, a jack, a king. Evie paired her king, but a pair of kings looked pathetically small against those two aces. Evie seemed composed, but she stood up, and her hands were clenched. The dealer buried another card and turned fourth street. Another king.

"Oh yeah," I murmured. Evie's three of a kind beat her opponent's two pair. Only one card in the deck could beat her now, and that's if the dealer turned an ace on the last card. The river card. And there was only one ace left in the deck.

"Good luck," the favorite said to her, sounding as if he meant it.

"You too," Evie said.

The dealer buried a card and slowly dealt the river card. A sigh passed through the room. An ace, giving Evie's opponent a full house, aces full of kings, to her full house, kings over aces. Evie smiled wearily and held out her hand.

"Nice playing," he said.

"Yeah, thanks." Evie nodded to the others at the table as she walked away.

As soon as she stepped past the rail and into the crowd, reporters descended upon her, asking her how it felt to lose after coming so far. How did it feel to be the only woman still playing? Stupid questions that made me want to get between Evie and all of them. Couldn't they see she was beat? I managed to shoulder my way up to her and put my arm around her waist.

"You did great, babe," I said.

"I did the best I could." She rested her cheek against my shoulder for a second, and I heard cameras click. "I've always had lousy luck on the river."

Then she straightened, smiled, and gamely answered questions as we walked slowly toward the elevator, people crowding around us. Thankfully, we didn't have to wait long and the car going up was empty. Everyone was coming down to hit the casinos or to watch more of the finals. As soon as the doors closed behind us, Evie sagged against me and buried her face in my chest.

I rubbed her back and stroked her hair. I couldn't tell if she was crying, but if she was, she'd earned a few tears for all the blood and sweat she'd shed in the last six days. When the elevator slowed and pinged at our floor, Evie didn't even move. I wondered if she'd fallen asleep standing up in my arms.

"Babe? Honey. We're here. Time to get you to bed."

Evie mumbled and burrowed a little closer into my chest. I wrapped my arm around her shoulders and kept her close against my side as I led her down the hall to our suite. I keyed the lock, got her inside, and turned the lights on low. She appeared a little dazed as she glanced around the room, then she gave me a sad smile. "I can't believe it's over."

"It isn't. There's always next year. And plenty of tournaments before this one rolls around again." I cupped her face and kissed her. "Come on, let's get you undressed."

I led her unresisting into the bathroom, turned on the shower, and undressed her—then myself. I guided her under the spray, turning her gently as I washed her hair. When I started to soap her breasts and belly, she closed her eyes and swayed a little bit, so I held her with her back against my chest with one arm around her middle. She rested her head against my shoulder and gently clasped both hands around my wrist as I lathered her breasts.

"Feels good," she murmured drowsily.

"I know." I kissed her damp cheek. Fact was, it felt great. We'd had a kid right after New Year's, and Evie's breasts were still as full as they had been when she was breast-feeding. Every time I hold her breasts, I think about how beautiful she looked with the baby in her arms, nuzzling her nipple. Watching them together like that, my heart used to ache at the same time as my body went crazy, and sometimes I had to leave the room just to get a grip. Sometimes I'd be so damn excited I'd have to go somewhere and just get off. My clit was jumping now just from rubbing soap over her breasts, and I knew my timing was off again. What she needed right now was sleep, not sex.

"Honey," Evie whispered, "are you thinking what I think you're thinking?"

"No," I said quickly.

She pivoted in my arms and wrapped hers around my neck. "Liar."

I massaged her ass and rubbed her back as I turned us under the hot water and sluiced the soap from our bodies. "Okay. I *was* thinking what you think I was thinking. But it'll keep until morning."

"You know what I'd like?" Evie said when we stepped out of the shower.

"What?" I wrapped one of the big fluffy hotel towels around her shoulders. There was plenty left over for me to dry her breasts and belly, and as I rubbed the soft white cotton over her, I felt myself grow firm again. I wasn't going to keep until morning, but I'd deal with that after I took care of her.

"I'd like it if you put me to sleep." She took the towel from around her own shoulders and blotted the water from my body. Then she pressed against me and put her lips close to my ear. "Make me come with your mouth."

I kissed her and she melted into me. With an invitation like that, if I hadn't known how close to falling apart she had to be, I would've boosted her up onto the granite-topped vanity and made her come right then and there. With my mouth. Just the way she likes it. But what she needed was to come hard, close her eyes, and finally get some sleep, so I took her hand and pulled her from the warm, steamy bathroom and over to the bed. I tossed a few pillows on top of one another and guided her down onto them so she was half sitting. She liked to watch me make her come. Then I dove under the covers and pulled them over both of us, leaving a tunnel around her belly so she could see me. Then I licked her.

Evie smiled and played with my hair. "I'm glad you were there tonight. I needed you."

Her clitoris was a small, hard beating heart, and I kissed it. "I'm really proud of you, babe. You did great."

"I wish I could have won for you."

"You've won for me a million times. And not just at poker." I brushed my hand up her stomach and felt her ribs too close to the surface. She hadn't been eating right. I cradled her breast and used my mouth and teeth and tongue to suck and toy with her until she writhed against my face.

Her breath came fast and hard now, and her legs trembled against the outside of my shoulders. I played with her nipple, sucked on her clit, and slid three fingers inside her. She gasped in surprise and pressed hard against my mouth. That was her signal she wanted to come, and I knew she would if I kept doing what I was doing. If we'd been at home, on a Saturday night with the baby asleep and a lazy day ahead of us, I might have held her off. I could do that if I wanted, but not tonight. She needed this now, and trusted me to give it to her. I pushed a little deeper with my hand and set my teeth gently against the shaft of her clitoris. It was my signal I was about to make her come, and her fingers clenched in my hair.

"Oh, yes," she whispered, and she came in sharp, wrenching spasms against my mouth that finally tapered off to slow contractions under my tongue.

When I was sure she was finished, I grabbed the covers and pulled them up with me as I stretched out by her side. She curled against my body, her head on my chest and one leg partially over my thigh. Sighing softly, she cupped my crotch and rested her thumb against my clitoris. That was usually her signal that she was going to make me come in her hand. My clitoris recognized the sign and got harder, even though my head knew it wasn't happening. Not tonight. She'd be asleep in seconds, in fact from the sounds of her slow, even breathing, I thought she might be already. I held still because I didn't want to wake her, even though every muscle in my body clamored for me to lift and thrust and rub against her hand.

Evie murmured something I didn't understand and her fingers twitched on my clit. The pressure was almost enough to get me off and I held my breath, waiting for the next stroke. Nothing. Just my poor helpless aching hard-on held in the grip of the love of my life as she slumbered. I shifted my hips, trying to ease away from her hand because even the weight of her motionless fingers was more than I could take. The muscles on the insides of my legs were starting to cramp from the relentless tension, and the pounding in the pit of my stomach was all I could think about. That, and getting some relief.

I moved another inch and Evie jerked the way people do who are asleep but verging on waking up.

"It's okay, baby," I whispered. "Go back to sleep."

"I didn't get you off, did I?" she mumbled.

"It's okay. I'm okay." I stroked her hair and gently moved her hand from between my legs.

"You do it." Evie's warm breath tickled my neck. "Like it when you do it."

I didn't need a gilded invitation. I need to come so bad. I slid my hand where Evie's had just been and groaned at how good it felt to drag all that thick, hot wetness over and around my clit. A few good strokes was all I was going to need, so I tightened my grip around Evie's shoulders and closed my eyes. Evie must have felt me stiffen, or maybe I moaned, because she twitched awake again.

"Coming, honey?"

"Uh-huh. In a second."

She surprised me by reaching down below my hand and sliding her fingers inside me.

"Wanna feel."

I had my clit worked up to the point where nothing could stop me from coming, but when she amped up the pressure inside, I just shot off. I grabbed onto Evie and yelled so loud they probably heard me out in the hall, but it felt so good, and when I started coming she started fucking me and then it was more than good. It was great and I was thrashing and crying and begging her to just keep *please* keep fucking me. And she did until I was boneless and completely fucked out.

"You know," Evie sighed, her hand still inside me and her thumb hooked around my clit, "I might have lousy luck on the river, but coming home to you means I always end up a winner."

"I'll be there after the last hand is played, baby, no matter what," I whispered.

Evie was already asleep, but I knew she heard me.

WINNING HAND

Karin Kallmaker

*B*etter luck next time."

I turned to stare at the woman who had just passed me in the hall. "Were you at the seven-card finals?"

She didn't pause, but said over her shoulder, her chin brushing the mink casually draped there, "I was watching on closed-circuit."

She was fifteen feet away from me, and farther away by the second. "Do you watch me often?"

That made her turn around. The hotel's opulence was compromised by the housekeeping carts that dotted the hallway. I needed to check out before the cut off. Needless to say, after my losses at the tables, I couldn't really afford another night's charge.

She fiddled with her Gucci bag. "I watch you every chance I get."

I was aware of my suitcase in my hand, my leather jacket

tucked under my arm. I was getting out of town and she obviously wasn't going anywhere.

She was staring. Given her chic dress and air of someone with places to go and things to do, it seemed out of character. However, since hitting the big time on the poker circuit, I'd attracted a few fans, some of whom offered more than their admiration.

In that long glance we shared, I thought about a couple of different things. I'd counted on winning more than I had, and private stakes games had also gone badly for me. I was going home with far less than I'd come with, and for the first time in my life, I'd been playing with money I couldn't afford to lose. It ached, the losing, when it hadn't before.

And I was thinking about home, and I knew I had to go back. I wasn't seriously debating that. Every day my mother stayed at the hospice was a larger bill I was going to have trouble paying. My kid brother couldn't be trusted not to slip a paper in front of Mom to sign, giving him more of her money and some of mine to feed his meth habit. I had a day job waiting for me, unlike most high stakes players, because poker didn't give a steady enough stream for insurance and taxes and Mom's medical bills.

Sometimes I wanted to run away from home, and certainly heading out to these tournaments was an escape. Coming home with cash made it a legit way to spend my time. I was fully intending to go back home, back to my responsibilities. So okay, I wasn't exactly Skipping-to-My-Lou to do so.

And I was thinking that this woman thought I was the Big Time. Thought I must fuck as good as I played cards. I wasn't a quickie kind of gal, though, never had been. I wasn't crazy about the players who'd take a break, pick one of the dewy-eyed girls out of the crowd, and disappear for fifteen minutes.

I looked at her, and I could tell what she was promising, and I didn't want to be one of those guys.

But she wanted me to be one of those guys. Part of me wanted to tell her that I was a little insulted by her presuming I'd fuck and walk. The rest of me was thinking this could be the best thing I got out of this trip to Vegas, that I could smell her on my fingers during the flight back to San Antonio.

If we both got what we wanted out of fifteen minutes, did it matter if it was different things?

A housekeeper emerged from a room in between where we stood staring at each other. She moved on to the next room, swiping the lock with a card key and disappearing inside.

She hadn't made sure the door of the room she'd just left had closed completely…it was slightly ajar. Before a puff of recirculating air blew it fully closed, I quickly pushed it open.

After a glance back at her, I walked into the room. I didn't have to look to know that she'd followed me.

I made sure the door closed.

My first thought was that she was a little younger than she looked from a distance, not exactly a compliment to her makeup and hair designer. But the difference between forty and fifty didn't matter to me. I pushed her against the wall. The mink slid to the floor along with her handbag, and she yielded completely to me.

When all the players sit down at the table, it's a swirl of motion and chatter, posturing and positioning, everyone planting their early bluff. When the cards were dealt, the players quieted. TV cameras became invisible, the drone of announcers was silenced, the cacophony of bells, alarms, wheels clacking, and a thousand voices talking all at once faded into the background.

For me, everything went away except the eyes and hands

of my opponents and, of course, the cards. Her hands were warm and pliable on my back. Her eyes were gray and her pupils slightly over-dilated. Lust, I thought, and I kissed her. She wasn't an opponent and I was going to pay attention to all of her.

"So you watch me every chance you get, huh?" I grazed my teeth over her jaw and down her throat.

"Especially your hands," she said. "I'm obsessed with them. Lesbians should have to wear gloves."

"I think right now you're happy I'm not wearing gloves." There was no point in being subtle. I squeezed her breasts through the thin fabric of her wrap dress before quickly unfastening the tie that pulled it so alluringly around her body.

"Your hands are as amazing as I thought they'd be. It's the way you hold the cards. The way your fingers curl and you hold them like you can will them to whatever you want them to be."

She shivered when I peeled opened the dress. Victoria's Secret's finest shaped and molded her breasts and hips, setting off her honey-tanned skin with satiny pink. I pulled the bra straps off her shoulders, then yanked her bra down to her waist.

She gasped.

"I have a plane to catch, so we're gonna make this quick."

"Yes, baby, that's what I want." She ground against me, her eyes closed. I didn't know what I was to her. Maybe she did this with all the female players. A raw fire lit in me. She was obsessed with my hands?

I cupped her ass as I bit down on her inviting nipple. A winning hand was what I wanted, and I thought I could get us both there. Her skin was tightening along with her muscles. She was on her tiptoes, head arched back, offering her breast to me.

There was no time to spend on foreplay. We were in somebody's room and had to get out fast. I needed to get out of town. She didn't want a relationship, she wanted to get fucked. I shoved my hand between her legs, pulled her panties aside, and cupped the luscious beauty of her.

She thrust down on my hand with a little cry. "Take me, baby. Any way you want."

I knew what I wanted, but she was moving all over the place. I let her go long enough to pull her into the bathroom, then I pushed her up on the counter and spread her legs.

"My purse," she gasped. "In my purse there's lube."

"You really want this, don't you? Take your dress the rest of the way off." I was gone only long enough to find the small bottle, but the dress was on the bathroom floor when I got back. I hooked my thumbs in her panties and yanked them down until I could drop them on top of the dress.

She watched me lube my hand, watched me smear lube up to my wrist, watched me sink into her, two fingers.

There was room, there was plenty of room. She pulled my mouth to hers, kissing me frantically as one hand closed around my forearm.

She showed me how hard she liked it. She showed me how deep, and she wanted more. I grinned against her mouth because I wanted more too, I wanted all of her, and that was exactly what she was giving.

She braced herself when I tucked my thumb and I slipped in with hardly a push. The little incoherent cries were all encouraging as I pressed deeper and rubbed my knuckles all along the ridge of her inner muscles.

"I knew, I knew," she repeated.

I knocked away her grip on my forearm, curled my fingers inside her and pulled halfway out.

"No," she moaned. "Stay inside me—"

I pushed in hard. "Is that what you want?"

"Yes." Her eyes flew open. "Fuck!"

"Okay," I said. "Let's do that."

Wet and wild, she arched into every thrust. There was no restraint in her at all, and I wasn't finding any either. My hand was clasped inside her where she so badly wanted me, gripping her against me as I pushed inside her, again, and again, and again.

I gave it to her quick, hot, and hard.

She came for me exactly the same way.

❖

A few minutes later, she shrugged her bra back into place and pulled on her dress.

I gave her the bottle of lube. "The next tournament is in—"

"Atlantic City." She tucked the bottle into her handbag, and slung the mink around her shoulders.

Opening the door just a little, I saw no one in the hallway. I stepped back to let her out of the room first. She turned right. I turned left.

In the elevator I surreptitiously examined my still wet hand, then raised it casually to scratch my nose. The scent of sex overwhelmed all my other senses. Home was still a long way away. For just a little while, I had a winning hand.

...Doesn't Stay In Vegas

Karin Kallmaker

ho are you?" Debbie didn't mean to bark, but her throat was incredibly dry. She swallowed, which caused a tight pain behind her eyes, and she recognized the signs of a champagne hangover.

The red hair spread out on the pillow jerked out of reach as the woman abruptly sat up. "Fuck you, too."

"Sorry." Debbie wasn't even going to try to sit up. "Is this my room or yours?"

"Yours. I'll leave if you want me to."

The full, rounded breasts were enough to make Debbie sincerely regret her hangover. "No, it's okay. Did we...?"

Eyes that were jade, and jaded, gave her a narrow look. "Yes, as a matter of fact. You seemed pretty happy about it."

"Were you pretty happy about it?" Something in the women's bad temper was actually grounding and refreshing, as if they'd already moved past all the show and pretense and it was Get Real or Get Out Time. Sort of like her last two relationships without the months of wasted courtship.

She turned her head, eyes slicing. "Are you paying me to be happy about it?"

With a jolt, Debbie remembered meeting the woman in the bar. God, she'd been a total ass. "Oh, man, I'm sorry. I could have gotten us both arrested."

"Which is why I hustled you up here. You stuffing twenties down my shirt and announcing you'd double it if I'd—how did you put it? Eat you on the back of your Yamaha at eighty miles an hour? Yeah, that was going to get us arrested, and I didn't need that."

"I'm sorry, honey. Really. I don't drink much, but last night…"

Another jolt and Debbie remembered why she'd hit the hotel bar. A slow, hangover-banishing grin spread over her face. A twelve thousand dollar pot was truly a beautiful thing. She thought she'd drink some champagne, pick up some companionship. "Cara."

"What?"

Relieved she remembered the woman's name, Debbie managed to sit up. "I'm really sorry. Do you want some breakfast?"

"Maybe I'll just go."

"No, please stay." Hazy details were slowly coming into focus. Cara had half-carried her upstairs and dumped her on the bed. They'd been playful, shucking clothes, shinnying under the covers, kissing…

Trouble was, the memories stopped there. She wasn't sure what had happened after that.

"Are you sure that we, um, you know?"

Cara rested her arms on her knees. "Maybe we didn't."

"I promised and passed out."

She shrugged. "I'm not on the clock, so it's irrelevant what did and didn't happen. I should go." She swung her legs over the edge of the bed.

"No, really." Debbie put a hand to her head, rubbing a little to ease the persistent throb between her eyes. "Stay."

"I'm having a bad convention—okay, a bad year. I'm not much good as company."

"At least you can have some breakfast." She pulled the phone onto her lap and punched the speed dial for room service. "What would you like?"

Cara tossed her long hair over her shoulders with a heavy sigh. "Eggs and toast."

She disappeared into the bathroom while Debbie conveyed their order. Eggs and toast sounded good to her, too, as long as it came with bacon and fried potatoes. Within a minute or two she'd also visited the bathroom, downing a couple of aspirin and quickly brushing her teeth.

The hotel must have had her room tagged as a high roller, because room service had never arrived so quickly before. Cara had pulled on one of Debbie's button up shirts, and now looked better than anything on the room service menu as she perched on a chair, legs crossed, and plate balanced on her knee.

"So what's with the bad year?" Debbie chowed down the potatoes as she watched Cara fork up her eggs far more sedately.

"Got dumped. My car was stolen the day after I paid for a new engine. That sort of thing. I came to the convention thinking I'd figure a way to change my life, somehow just get out of the place I was in. I agreed to be eye candy for some writer, and then she dumped me for someone else. Then this attractive dyke picked me out of the crowd to flirt with, but it turned out she was drunk and I didn't get any action." Cara gave her a resentful look.

"That's a crime. That dyke sounds like she owes you."

"What's she got besides breakfast?" Cara nibbled toast.

"A red vintage Yamaha and the open road?"

"So you weren't joking about what you wanted last night, were you?"

Debbie laughed. "Of course I was. I'm a safe biker, and sex on a moving bike is asking for death. Foreplay, on the other hand—"

"I thought the *bike* was foreplay."

"It can be." She was feeling much better for having some food in her stomach. Champagne—it always gave her a headache. Twelve grand in her pocket and she didn't think to get a good Scotch? "Sex on a stationary bike, say one parked in the hotel garage, now that's foreplay."

"Sex is foreplay?"

With a crooked smile, Debbie said, "Because after that we get on the bike and go for a long ride in the wind and the sun."

Cara had a little frown creased between her eyebrows. "Are you telling me that riding your bike is better than sex?"

"Depends on the woman and the sex, don't you think?"

"And the bike."

Debbie laughed again. In spite of her bitter overtones, Cara was diverting. She squinted at the clock. "If we hurry, I can prove it before the day gets too hot to ride."

"Believe it or not, that's the best offer I've had in months." Cara finished her eggs in two mouthfuls. "Is there time to shower?"

"Sure." She'd no sooner said that than Cara was in the bathroom turning on the water. The mirror gave her a multi-reflected look at the tumble of deep red hair down the lean, curving back. She did her best to finish her breakfast in time to join Cara—her stomach was demanding that she finish every bite—but the shower was turned off before she was done.

She had her own quick shower and came out of the bathroom to find Cara in the tight black jeans and sapphire blue top of the previous night. She took a deep breath, remembering perfectly well now why she'd picked Cara out of the crowd of women. She was beautiful. It was that simple.

A quick call to fellow traveler Rose scored her a jacket and second helmet, and in no time at all they were down in the parking garage and Debbie was eagerly showing off her pride and joy. Cara didn't say much as Debbie rambled on about the restoration, the year, and model, but she didn't act bored either.

When Debbie finally paused for breath, Cara threw a leg over the back, easily straddling the bike. Her red hair and that blue shirt looked glorious against the bike's custom paint job. Her black boots were perfect against the chrome, and her legs were long enough to flat-foot it, well, with the help of those spiked heels. With a grin of pleasure, Debbie helped her strap on her helmet, then secured her own. The jackets were unpleasantly warm. Cara didn't argue about their necessity. They had them on and half-zipped before she joined Cara on the bike. Cara had the pegs down all by herself—no novice— before she leaned into Debbie's back.

The club had been out for a ride yesterday morning, so Debbie followed the route, hoping Cara would enjoy it, even if the desert was at its least interesting in August. She started with the famous Strip, which truthfully didn't look very glamorous at this hour as the neon blinked dully against exteriors that baked daily in the sun.

Heat rose off the pavement as they headed west out of the city. The dry dust of the desert slowly yielded to hints of green in the ground cover, then the formations of the Red Rock Canyon rose into view. The road rolled out silver and white in front of her. The loop drive was a delight to navigate, and the warmth of Cara behind her was very welcome, even as the day grew hotter and hotter. She had a beautiful woman hugging her back and more money in the bank than she'd seen in years. It was a gorgeous, new day.

By the time they were back in the parking garage, it seemed blissfully cool by comparison. They both immediately took off the jackets, then she helped Cara out of her helmet, doffed her own, all the while grinning helplessly.

"So what did you think?"

"That was pretty fun." Cara grinned back at her, looking greatly refreshed. The jaded eyes had a new sparkle. "But I'm still not convinced."

"Of what?" The woman looked damned sexy, Debbie thought, her feet still on the pegs. Her top was soaked to her skin, which left only the really best parts to her imagination.

"That the ride is better than sex on the back of the bike."

Debbie's chest got tight, but in a good way. "Can I help you with your decision in some way?" She was already glancing around, aware that this corner was low traffic, which was why she and a number of other members in the club had chosen it.

Suddenly looking vulnerable, Cara said, "I think you know the answer."

"I'm sorry about last night."

"I said yes because I thought you were cute and I just

wanted...time with someone, no obligations but what we might decide we wanted to do."

"That's pretty much what I was after, too, and I passed out on you." Debbie urged her forward so she could straddle the bike behind her. "We can only get started here, though, at least in broad daylight. Remember that part about not getting arrested?"

"Yes." Cara leaned forward to grip the handlebars.

"If you weren't wearing pants, I could really make you feel good." Debbie ran her hands under Cara's ass, then between her legs. Cara's responsive shiver was inviting.

"I guess you have a challenge, then."

With a low laugh, Debbie leaned into her. "I do like challenges. You didn't meet the real me last night."

There was no law against public massage if her hands stayed off the parts of Cara that made her lusciously female. And maybe that wasn't a bad strategy, because every time her hand caressed Cara's ribs and shoulder blades, Cara arched forward in a pose that made Debbie want to fill her hands with those wonderful breasts. She hoped Cara was aching for it, that her nipples were hard and firm. She would find out upstairs.

For a few minutes, she abandoned Cara's upper body, and focused on thighs and hips. Cara lifted slightly as if to give Debbie access to her ass.

"Do you dance?" Debbie traced the defined muscles that had tensed to hold the pose.

"No, but I work out."

"You feel fantastic."

"You're feeling me pretty fantastically, too." Cara's little laugh turned to a half-moan as Debbie smoothed her hands up Cara's ribs again, then pulled hard enough to break her grip on the handlebars. She draped Cara over her, secure in her arms, and moved her crotch suggestively against Cara's ass.

"Oh, now if we were in my garage at home, I'd have something for you to really ride, honey."

Cara didn't miss the added purr in Debbie's voice. "Is that something you've given a lot of thought to?"

"Oh yeah." Risking arrest for just a few seconds, Debbie squeezed Cara's crotch with one hand and her breast with the other. "A really long, hot ride."

"Oh…And you still think the ride is better than the sex?"

She buried her face in the luxurious red hair and nipped at Cara's neck. "Maybe not if you're the woman. Let's go upstairs, honey."

The elevator ride was blissfully short and it was good to find the room had been tidied in their absence. At Debbie's insistence, they both drained a water bottle from the minibar. She was just about to suggest a piece of chocolate when the unmistakable sound of clothes falling to the floor whipped her head around.

Cara was wearing no pants and one long hand was gliding lightly between her legs. "I think you said something about making me feel good if I didn't have pants on."

Debbie rose to her feet, unable to hold back a reflexive licking of her lips. "Take everything off."

Cara lifted one eyebrow. "And is this the—"

The phone rang and Debbie snatched it up and growled hello.

The background noise in Rose's room was a jumble of television and Rose's girl singing in the shower. "Jeez, what bit your butt? I just wanted to see if I could get my jacket and helmet back."

"If you're here in thirty seconds or less." Debbie gave Cara a searing look as she put down the phone. "You do as you're told, now."

Cara's laugh did not convince Debbie that her attempt at

being in charge had been successful. She opened the door just enough to hold the jacket and helmet outside and waited for Rose to appear from down the long hallway.

Without warning, a fully naked, voluptuous female body pressed into her from behind. Rose appeared from around the corner, closing in fast as Cara rubbed her entire body the length of Debbie's.

"What's the hurry?" Rose gave her a puzzled look as she took the jacket and helmet from Debbie's outstretched hand.

Cara found one of Debbie's nipples and squeezed. Debbie's answer was strangled.

Rose started to ask again, but the sight of a very feminine hand with pink-tipped nails over Debbie's shoulder shut her up. The hand waved a definite buh-bye. Rose grinned and backed off, mouthing, "Call me later."

Debbie managed to get her arm back on the same side of the door with her body. The door slammed and Cara yanked up her T-shirt.

They headed right for the floor, in a flurry of clothes and kisses. Cara was determined to keep her grip on Debbie's nipples, and Debbie didn't mind, but it wasn't going to stop her from pinning Cara's legs open with her hips for a hot, steady grind. They ached, and it was a good ache, she decided. She kept that ache on the edge for a long time, watching Cara's eyes shimmer and flare.

When her nipples started to pulse from Cara's rough attentions, and her own cunt was sodden and hungry for more, she half dragged Cara to the bed, rolled over her, and shoved two fingers inside.

"Oh, yeah." Cara spread her legs and arched up. "I was starting to think you didn't care."

"I care, honey, and I'm gonna show you how much." She really wanted to wipe that still half-amused look off Cara's face. She didn't care what it took. She shoved in hard again and Cara's legs went limp. Oh, now she was getting somewhere.

"Finally." Cara's voice was significantly weaker.

Debbie got into her groove. Her hips behind her hand, she fucked Cara thoroughly, watched the flush climb her shoulders, sweep up her neck, felt Cara's arms drop away, saw her eyes glaze. She panted for breath with little moans and all the while Debbie could feel her tightening around her fingers. It was as if all the other muscles in her body had no strength left while her cunt tensed further and further.

She'd not felt anything quite like it before. Cara was abruptly sopping wet and the power of her climax surged back into the rest of her body. For a moment Debbie swore they levitated, like the bike catching air as it crested a rise.

And Cara screamed, not a wimpy, pampered girl scream, but one from deep down. There was no way anyone who heard it wouldn't know that a woman had just come, and had loved it.

"Fuck, honey," Debbie breathed, then she kissed her firmly, more gently, and gentler still, until they slowed and Cara let out a noise that was laughter and tears combined.

She held her for a minute, listening to her heartbeat steady. "Well, I loved that."

"So did I."

Cara closed her eyes and Debbie decided to let her doze. It wasn't long until she stirred, though, and they shifted on the bed, Cara snuggled into the circle of Debbie's arms.

"So—sex or the ride?"

Debbie didn't think twice. "I want both."

"Greedy, aren't you?"

"Yeah. And I want both."

Cara said softly, "All I really have to do with my life is get out of Las Vegas."

"Same here. After a few days, I always feel as if the choice is leave or become a lifer. And I have a life I like already."

"Where?"

"San Francisco."

"Never been there."

Debbie wanted to ask, but her throat closed up.

"What you said about your garage and really giving me a ride?"

She nodded.

Cara smooched Debbie's shoulder, then looked up, bathing her in warmth. "That sounded to me a lot like a promise, and you wouldn't want to let me down again, would you?"

Debbie gave a mock groan of surrender. "I think you have me. I made a legally binding offer, didn't I?"

"And I accept it, so you're stuck with me, for now."

She gathered Cara close. The road rolled out in silver and white in her mind's eye. Sharing the trip home, and maybe a longer journey, seemed like a very fine adventure.

About Radclyffe

Radclyffe is an award-winning author-publisher with over twenty-five lesbian novels and anthologies in print, including the Lambda Literary winners *Erotic Interludes 2: Stolen Moments* ed. with Stacia Seaman and *Distant Shores, Silent Thunder.* She has selections in multiple anthologies including *Wild Nights, Fantasy, Best Lesbian Erotica 2006, 2007,* and *2008, After Midnight, Caught Looking: Erotic Tales of Voyeurs and Exhibitionists, First-Timers, Ultimate Undies: Erotic Stories About Lingerie and Underwear, A is for Amour, H is for Hardcore,* and *L is for Leather.* She is the recipient of the 2003 and 2004 Alice B. Readers' award for her body of work and is also the president of Bold Strokes Books, one of the world's largest independent LGBT publishing companies.

Her forthcoming works include, *Word of Honor* (June 2008), and *Night Call* (October 2008). Read more about her novels at:

http://www.radfic.com

Story Attributions

"Full House" features characters from the novel, *The Lonely Hearts Club* by Radclyffe (Bold Strokes Books, 2008).

"All In" features characters from the novel, *Passion's Bright Fury* by Radclyffe (Bold Strokes Books, 2005).

"On the House" features characters from the novel *Night Call,* by Radclyffe (Bold Strokes Books, 2008).

About Karin Kallmaker

Karin Kallmaker's novels include the Goldie and Lammy award-winning *18th & Castro*, *Just Like That*, *Maybe Next Time*, and *Sugar*. Many have been translated into Spanish, French, German, and Czech. More than five dozen short stories have appeared in anthologies from publishers like Alyson, Circlet, Bold Strokes Books, Naiad, and Haworth, as well as her own collections from Bella Books.

She and her partner are the mothers of two and live in the San Francisco Bay Area. She is descended from Lady Godiva, a fact which she'll share with anyone who will listen. She likes her Internet fast, her iPod loud, and her chocolate real.

All of Karin's work can now be found at Bella Books. Details and background about her novels can be found at:

http://www.kallmaker.com

Books Available From Bold Strokes Books

Hotel Liaison by JLee Meyer. Sparks and wood chips fly as contractor Jocelyn Reynolds and hotel owner Stefanie Beresford struggle not to kill each other—or fall in love. Romance. (978-1-60282-017-3)

Love on Location by Lisa Girolami. Hollywood film producer Kate Nyland and artist Dawn Brock discover that love doesn't always follow the script. Romance. (978-1-60282-016-6)

Edge of Darkness by Jove Belle. Investigator Diana Collins charges at life with an irreverent comment and a right hook, but even those may not protect her heart from a charming villain. Romantic Intrigue. (978-1-60282-015-9)

Thirteen Hours by Meghan O'Brien. Workaholic Dana Watts's life takes a sudden turn when an unexpected interruption arrives in the form of the most beautiful breasts she has ever seen—stripper Laurel Stanley's. Erotic Romance. (978-1-60282-014-2)

In Deep Waters 2 by Radclyffe and Karin Kallmaker. All bets are off when two award winning authors deal the cards of love and passion... and every hand is a winner. Lesbian erotica. (978-1-60282-013-5)

Pink by Jennifer Harris. An irrepressible heroine frolics, frets, and navigates through the "what if's" of her life: all the unexpected turns of fortune, fame, and karma. General Fiction. (978-1-60282-043-2)

Deal with the Devil by Ali Vali. New Orleans crime boss Cain Casey brings her fury down on the men who threatened her family, and blood and bullets fly. (978-1-60282-012-8)

Naked Heart by Jennifer Fulton. When a sexy ex-CIA agent sets out to seduce and entrap a powerful CEO, there's more to this plan than meets the eye...or the flogger. (978-1-60282-011-1)

Heart of the Matter by KI Thompson. TV newscaster Kate Foster is Professor Ellen Webster's dream girl, but Kate doesn't know Ellen exists...until an accident changes everything. (978-1-60282-010-4)

Heartland by Julie Cannon. When political strategist Rachel Stanton and dude ranch owner Shivley McCoy collide on an empty country road, fate intervenes. (978-1-60282-009-8)

Shadow of the Knife by Jane Fletcher. Militia Rookie Ellen Mittal has no idea of just how complex and dangerous her life is about to become. A Celaeno series adventure romance. (978-1-60282-008-1)

To Protect and Serve by VK Powell. Lieutenant Alex Troy is caught in the paradox of her life—to hold steadfast to her professional oath or to protect the woman she loves. (978-1-60282-007-4)

Deeper by Ronica Black. Former homicide detective Erin McKenzie and her fiancée Elizabeth Adams couldn't be any happier—until the not so distant past comes knocking at the door. (978-1-60282-006-7)

The Lonely Hearts Club by Radclyffe. Take three friends, add two ex-lovers and several new ones, and the result is a recipe for explosive rivalries and incendiary romance. (978-1-60282-005-0)

Venus Besieged by Andrews & Austin. Teague Richfield heads for Sedona and the sensual arms of psychic astrologer Callie Rivers for a much needed romantic reunion. (978-1-60282-004-3)

Branded Ann by Merry Shannon. Pirate Branded Ann raids a merchant vessel to obtain a treasure map and gets more than she bargained for with the widow Violet. (978-1-60282-003-6)

American Goth by JD Glass. Trapped by an unsuspected inheritance and guided only by the guardian who holds the secret to her future, Samantha Cray fights to fulfill her destiny. (978-1-60282-002-9)

Learning Curve by Rachel Spangler. Ashton Clarke is perfectly content with her life until she meets the intriguing Professor Carrie Fletcher, who isn't looking for a relationship with anyone. (978-1-60282-001-2)

Place of Exile by Rose Beecham. Sheriff's detective Jude Devine struggles with ghosts of her past and an ex-lover who still haunts her dreams. (978-1-933110-98-1)

Fully Involved by Erin Dutton. A love that has smoldered for years ignites when two women and one little boy come together in the aftermath of tragedy. (978-1-933110-99-8)

Heart 2 Heart by Julie Cannon. Suffering from a devastating personal loss, Kyle Bain meets Lane Connor, and the chance for happiness suddenly seems possible. (978-1-60282-000-5)

Queens of Tristaine: Tristaine Book Four by Cate Culpepper. When a deadly plague stalks the Amazons of Tristaine, two warrior lovers must return to the place of their nightmares to find a cure. (978-1-933110-97-4)

The Crown of Valencia by Catherine Friend. Ex-lovers can really mess up your life…even, as Kate discovers, if they've traveled back to the 11th century! (978-1-933110-96-7)

Mine by Georgia Beers. What happens when you've already given your heart and love finds you again? Courtney McAllister is about to find out. (978-1-933110-95-0)

House of Clouds by KI Thompson. A sweeping saga of an impassioned romance between a Northern spy and a Southern sympathizer, set amidst the upheaval of a nation under siege. (978-1-933110-94-3)

Winds of Fortune by Radclyffe. Provincetown local Deo Camara agrees to rehab Dr. Nita Burgoyne's historic home, but she never said anything about mending her heart. (978-1-933110-93-6)

Focus of Desire by Kim Baldwin. Isabel Sterling is surprised when she wins a photography contest, but no more than photographer Natasha Kashnikova. Their promo tour becomes a ticket to romance. (978-1-933110-92-9)

Blind Leap by Diane and Jacob Anderson-Minshall. A Golden Gate Bridge suicide becomes suspect when a filmmaker's camera shows a different story. Yoshi Yakamota and the Blind Eye Detective Agency uncover evidence that could be worth killing for. (978-1-933110-91-2)

Wall of Silence, 2nd ed. by Gabrielle Goldsby. Life takes a dangerous turn when jaded police detective Foster Everett meets Riley Medeiros, a woman who isn't afraid to discover the truth no matter the cost. (978-1-933110-90-5)

Mistress of the Runes by Andrews & Austin. Passion ignites between two women with ties to ancient secrets, contemporary mysteries, and a shared quest for the meaning of life. (978-1-933110-89-9)

Sheridan's Fate by Gun Brooke. A dynamic, erotic romance between physical therapist Lark Mitchell and businesswoman Sheridan Ward set in the scorching hot days and humid, steamy nights of San Antonio. (978-1-933110-88-2)

Vulture's Kiss by Justine Saracen. Archeologist Valerie Foret, heir to a terrifying task, returns in a powerful desert adventure set in Egypt and Jerusalem. (978-1-933110-87-5)

Rising Storm by JLee Meyer. The sequel to First Instinct takes our heroines on a dangerous journey instead of the honeymoon they'd planned. (978-1-933110-86-8)

Not Single Enough by Grace Lennox. A funny, sexy modern romance about two lonely women who bond over the unexpected and fall in love along the way. (978-1-933110-85-1)

Second Season by Ali Vali. A romance set in New Orleans amidst betrayal, Hurricane Katrina, and the new beginnings hardship and heartbreak sometimes make possible. (978-1-933110-83-7)

Such a Pretty Face by Gabrielle Goldsby. A sexy, sometimes humorous, sometimes biting contemporary romance that gently exposes the damage to heart and soul when we fail to look beneath the surface for what truly matters. (978-1-933110-84-4)

Hearts Aflame by Ronica Black. A poignant, erotic romance between a hard-driving businesswoman and a solitary vet. Packed with adventure and set in the harsh beauty of the Arizona countryside. (978-1-933110-82-0)

Red Light by JD Glass. Tori forges her path as an EMT in the New York City 911 system while discovering what matters most to herself and the woman she loves. (978-1-933110-81-3)

Honor Under Siege by Radclyffe. Secret Service agent Cameron Roberts struggles to protect her lover while searching for a traitor who just may be another woman with a claim on her heart. (978-1-933110-80-6)

Dark Valentine by Jennifer Fulton. Danger and desire fuel a high stakes cat-and-mouse game when an attorney and an endangered witness team up to thwart a killer. (978-1-933110-79-0)

Sequestered Hearts by Erin Dutton. A popular artist suddenly goes into seclusion; a reluctant reporter wants to know why; and a heart locked away yearns to be set free. (978-1-933110-78-3)

Erotic Interludes 5: *Road Games* eds. Radclyffe and Stacia Seaman. Adventure, "sport," and sex on the road—hot stories of travel adventures and games of seduction. (978-1-933110-77-6)

The Spanish Pearl by Catherine Friend. On a trip to Spain, Kate Vincent is accidentally transported back in time...an epic saga spiced with humor, lust, and danger. (978-1-933110-76-9)

Lady Knight by L-J Baker. Loyalty and honour clash with love and ambition in a medieval world of magic when female knight Riannon meets Lady Eleanor. (978-1-933110-75-2)

Dark Dreamer by Jennifer Fulton. Best-selling horror author, Rowe Devlin falls under the spell of psychic Phoebe Temple. A Dark Vista romance. (978-1-933110-74-5)

Come and Get Me by Julie Cannon. Elliott Foster isn't used to pursuing women, but alluring attorney Lauren Collier makes her change her mind. (978-1-933110-73-8)

Blind Curves by Diane and Jacob Anderson-Minshall. Private eye Yoshi Yakamota comes to the aid of her ex-lover Velvet Erickson in the first Blind Eye mystery. (978-1-933110-72-1)

Dynasty of Rogues by Jane Fletcher. It's hate at first sight for Ranger Riki Sadiq and her new patrol corporal, Tanya Coppelli—except for their undeniable attraction. (978-1-933110-71-4)

Running With the Wind by Nell Stark. Sailing instructor Corrie Marsten has signed off on love until she meets Quinn Davies—one woman she can't ignore. (978-1-933110-70-7)

More than Paradise by Jennifer Fulton. Two women battle danger, risk all, and find in one another an unexpected ally and an unforgettable love. (978-1-933110-69-1)

Flight Risk by Kim Baldwin. For Blayne Keller, being in the wrong place at the wrong time just might turn out to be the best thing that ever happened to her. (978-1-933110-68-4)

Rebel's Quest, Supreme Constellations Book Two by Gun Brooke. On a world torn by war, two women discover a love that defies all boundaries. (978-1-933110-67-7)

Punk and Zen by JD Glass. Angst, sex, love, rock. Trace, Candace, Francesca...Samantha. Losing control—and finding the truth within. BSB Victory Editions. (1-933110-66-X)

Stellium in Scorpio by Andrews & Austin. The passionate reuniting of two powerful women on the glitzy Las Vegas Strip where everything is an illusion and love is a gamble. (1-933110-65-1)

When Dreams Tremble by Radclyffe. Two women whose lives turned out far differently than they'd once imagined discover that sometimes the shape of the future can only be found in the past. (1-933110-64-3)

The Devil Unleashed by Ali Vali. As the heat of violence rises, so does the passion. A Casey Family crime saga. (1-933110-61-9)

Burning Dreams by Susan Smith. The chronicle of the challenges faced by a young drag king and an older woman who share a love "outside the bounds." (1-933110-62-7)

Fresh Tracks by Georgia Beers. Seven women, seven days. A lot can happen when old friends, lovers, and a new girl in town get together in the mountains. (1-933110-63-5)

The Empress and the Acolyte by Jane Fletcher. Jemeryl and Tevi fight to protect the very fabric of their world: time. Lyremouth Chronicles Book Three. (1-933110-60-0)

First Instinct by JLee Meyer. When high-stakes security fraud leads to murder, one woman flees for her life while another risks her heart to protect her. (1-933110-59-7)

Erotic Interludes 4: Extreme Passions. Thirty of today's hottest erotica writers set the pages aflame with love, lust, and steamy liaisons. (1-933110-58-9)

Storms of Change by Radclyffe. In the continuing saga of the Provincetown Tales, duty and love are at odds as Reese and Tory face their greatest challenge. (1-933110-57-0)

Unexpected Ties by Gina L. Dartt. With death before dessert, Kate Shannon and Nikki Harris are swept up in another tale of danger and romance. (1-933110-56-2)

Sleep of Reason by Rose Beecham. While Detective Jude Devine searches for a lost boy, her rocky relationship with Dr. Mercy Westmoreland gets a lot harder. (1-933110-53-8)

Passion's Bright Fury by Radclyffe. Passion strikes without warning when a trauma surgeon and a filmmaker become reluctant allies. (1-933110-54-6)

Broken Wings by L-J Baker. When Rye Woods meets beautiful dryad Flora Withe, her libido, as hidden as her wings, reawakens along with her heart. (1-933110-55-4)

Combust the Sun by Andrews & Austin. A Richfield and Rivers mystery set in L.A. Murder among the stars. (1-933110-52-X)

Of Drag Kings and the Wheel of Fate by Susan Smith. A blind date in a drag club leads to an unlikely romance. (1-933110-51-1)

Tristaine Rises by Cate Culpepper. Brenna, Jesstin, and the Amazons of Tristaine face their greatest challenge for survival. (1-933110-50-3)

Too Close to Touch by Georgia Beers. Kylie O'Brien believes in true love and is willing to wait for it, even though Gretchen, her new boss, is off-limits. (1-933110-47-3)

100ᵗʰ Generation by Justine Saracen. Ancient curses, modern-day villains, and an intriguing woman lead archeologist Valerie Foret on the adventure of her life. (1-933110-48-1)

Battle for Tristaine by Cate Culpepper. While Brenna struggles to find her place in the clan, Tristaine is threatened with destruction. Second in the Tristaine series. (1-933110-49-X)

The Traitor and the Chalice by Jane Fletcher. Tevi and Jemeryl risk all in the race to uncover a traitor. The Lyremouth Chronicles Book Two. (1-933110-43-0)

Promising Hearts by Radclyffe. Dr. Vance Phelps arrives in New Hope, Montana, with no hope of happiness—until she meets Mae. (1-933110-44-9)

Carly's Sound by Ali Vali. Poppy Valente and Julia Johnson form a bond of friendship that becomes something far more. A poignant romance about love and renewal. (1-933110-45-7)

Unexpected Sparks by Gina L. Dartt. Kate Shannon's attraction to much younger Nikki Harris is complication enough without a fatal fire that Kate can't ignore. (1-933110-46-5)

Whitewater Rendezvous by Kim Baldwin. Two women on a wilderness kayak adventure discover that true love may be nothing at all like they imagined. (1-933110-38-4)

Erotic Interludes 3: Lessons in Love ed. by Radclyffe and Stacia Seaman. Sign on for a class in love…the best lesbian erotica writers take us to "school." (1-9331100-39-2)

Punk Like Me by JD Glass. Twenty-one-year-old Nina has a way with the girls, and she doesn't always play by the rules. (1-933110-40-6)

Coffee Sonata by Gun Brooke. Four women whose lives unexpectedly intersect in a small town by the sea share one thing in common—they all have secrets. (1-933110-41-4)

The Clinic: Tristaine Book One by Cate Culpepper. Brenna, a prison medic, finds herself drawn to Jesstin, a warrior reputed to be descended from ancient Amazons. (1-933110-42-2)

Forever Found by JLee Meyer. Can time, tragedy, and shattered trust destroy a love that seemed destined? Chance reunites childhood friends separated by tragedy. (1-933110-37-6)

Sword of the Guardian by Merry Shannon. Princess Shasta's bold new bodyguard has a secret that could change both of their lives: *He* is actually a *she*. (1-933110-36-8)

Wild Abandon by Ronica Black. Dr. Chandler Brogan and Officer Sarah Monroe are drawn together by their common obsessions—sex, speed, and danger. (1-933110-35-X)

Turn Back Time by Radclyffe. Pearce Rifkin and Wynter Thompson have nothing in common but a shared passion for surgery—and unexpected attraction. (1-933110-34-1)

Chance by Grace Lennox. A sexy, funny, touching story of two women who, in finding themselves, also find one another. (1-933110-31-7)

The Exile and the Sorcerer by Jane Fletcher. First in the Lyremouth Chronicles. Tevi and a shy young sorcerer face monsters, magic, and the challenge of loving. (1-933110-32-5)